Praise for Christy® Award finalist
Susan May Warren and her novels

"Susie writes a delightful story...
A few hours of reading doesn't get better."
—Dee Henderson, CBA bestselling author of the O'Malley series

"Susan Warren is definitely a writer to watch!"
—Deborah Raney, award-winning author of
A Vow to Cherish and *Over the Waters*

"Warren's characters are well developed and she knows
how to create a first-rate contemporary romance."
—*Library Journal* on *Tying the Knot*

"Susan May Warren is an exciting new writer whose
delightful stories weave the joy of romantic devotion
together with the truth of God's love."
—Catherine Palmer, bestselling author of *Leaves of Hope*

"Susan's characters deliver love and laughter and a
solid story with every book...a great read!"
—Lori Copeland, bestselling author of the
Brides of the West series, on *The Perfect Match*

"...authentic detail...plunked me into Russian life.
The result was a dynamic read!"
—Colleen Coble, bestselling author of *Dangerous Depths*,
on *Nadia*

"...a nail-biting, fast-paced chase through the wilds of
Russia. A deft combination of action and romance provides
superb balance. Spectacular descriptions place the
reader in the center of the intriguing setting."
—*Romantic Times BOOKclub* on *In Sheep's Clothing*

SUSAN MAY WARREN

Everything's Coming Up Josey

Steeple
Hill
Café™

Published by Steeple Hill Books™

STEEPLE HILL BOOKS

ISBN 0-373-78561-5

EVERYTHING'S COMING UP JOSEY

www.SteepleHill.com

Printed in U.S.A.

For Your Glory, Lord

Acknowledgments

"Why don't you write your life story?" During my eight years as a missionary in Russia, friends from all over the world, in response to my letters, would pose that question. I'd shrug, saying, "I'm not sure how to do it."

Fast forward three years. Chick lit is beginning to hit the shelves. An insightful editor at Steeple Hill challenged me to try my hand at this new genre. I thought, What would I have to write about—missionary stories?

Thankfully, she had vision, and when I proposed an idea about a single missionary headed to Moscow for a year, she embraced it. Finally I'd found a venue for my story, although fictionalized...mostly.

I laugh that, finally, I got to write about all the fallacies, all the frustrations and all the foolishness of being a freshman missionary. Mostly, I got to write about the one thing that God taught me—that He'd been at work in my life to bring me to this place, and the places beyond, all my life. And that I didn't have to be perfect. I just had to surrender and trust.

Thank you to the following people who walked this journey with me:

Christine Lynxwiler, my faithful "critter"—thank you for your commitment and encouraging words!

Tracey Bateman, for your prayers and encouragement to press on, and for your insightful suggestions.

The Twinklings—Jane, Sharron, Michele, who prayed me through and gave me a reason to leave my house.

All my missionary friends—I hope you also feel as I do, richer for the experience.

My high school pals, for the moments and friendships that molded me.

Joan Marlow Golan—for your insight and wisdom.

Krista Stroever—for your excellent editing and ability to see the final product.

My sweet children—for living the lit with me.

And, my very own hero, who crossed the ocean with me. Andrew, I love you.

Chapter One:
Poppies and Eternal Purpose

It's important to acknowledge that Chase was right and if it weren't for him I might have never found my answers. He likes being right. And, for the most part, he's consistent in his predictions—has been for all of the twenty-four years I've known him. Like the time we raced down Bloomquist mountain on our Radio Flyers. He sat in his wagon, hands white from gripping the handle, and grinned against the sun, a dark shadow of superiority and wisdom. "I'm going to win, and you're gonna get hurt," he said.

At seven, and full of tomboyish bravado, I tucked my feet into my red wagon, grabbed the handle and pushed off. The world whooshed by my ears as we careened down dirt and gravel. My next clear memory is staring into the glaring sunshine from a sprawled position in the ditch. The wagon lay on its side, wheels still spinning. And pain. I remember pain. Blinding, screaming, burning down one side of my leg where I'd left way too much skin on the road.

And then Chase. He stood broad and tall, blocking the sun, blue eyes full of concern. What came next ignited my love/hate feelings for him for the next decade or two. He picked me up, one hand around my waist and said, "Josey, you just don't know when to quit."

I took it as a compliment.

I should have paid attention to the gleam in his eyes—the one that said, "Told you so!" It was the first sign that he would break my heart, and a smart girl would have gathered up her battered wagon and headed for cookies and milk. But what does a seven-year-old know of the shades of love? All I knew is that he ran faster and could eat more than me, and his Tarzan whoop, with that little inflection in his voice, sounded right out of the jungle and left me with tingles.

Most of all, he had the best backyard sandbox on the street. That fact alone made him downright irresistible.

Fast-forward seventeen years. Chase sits down at the linen-clothed table, a scant breeze pushing around that burnished blond hair, that same knowing gleam in his eyes and he says, "You didn't want him anyway."

Unfortunately he's referring to the groom, who is presently dancing with his new bride center stage behind me—a man who has soft gray eyes and a smile that can turn the right girl to oatmeal. My ex-boyfriend, Milton Snodbrecher.

And oh, the bride—wearing lily-of-the-valley in her blond hair, and a Vera Wang dress off a rack in Minneapolis—is my sister, Jasmine. My younger sister.

Isn't it written somewhere, "Nay shall thine youngest sibling marrieth before thine oldest?" Perhaps, the *Bible?* I'm suddenly feeling a kinship with Leah the morning after, when Jacob realized he'd been hoodwinked.

How could I have believed that Milton might work seven years, let alone seven months, for my love?

Who knew that getting my college boyfriend/jerk a job at our restaurant/lodge in central Minnesota doing the books would slaughter my matrimonial prospects? I thought it sounded like a pretty good idea. Especially since I was just down the road dotting *i*'s and crossing *t*'s at the *Gull Lake Gazette*.

I do get my own attic office facing the lake with the oh-so-picturesque view of the seagulls squatting on the roof and ogling the goodies piled near the back entry to Lou's smoked fish shack. It's breathtaking, to say the least.

It boils down to this—while I was rewriting news blurbs from the AP wire and trying to make sense of eighty-three-year-old Tipsy McKeever's scrawled recipes, Milton was getting familiar with more than the books at the old Berglund resort. "Bring Milton home and we'll give him a job at the family business," (five acres of shore front, general store and five small cabins) said Dad. My summer-after-graduation, wedding-saturated brain thought, *Yes*. Embraced by the pine and birch, swept fresh by the breeze of Gull Lake, Milton would finally drop to his then-bony knees and declare his love. And we'd all live happily ever after.

Naive me.

I should interject here that I wasn't even supposed to be in Gull Lake. My grand life plan included a stint at a New York newspaper, maybe even a tour as an overseas journalist for the Associated Press. Inside this five-foot-four-inch, slightly over-endowed (I did *not* say fat) body lives a hard-muscled, brave and adventurous, tomb-raiding Lara Croft/Mother Teresa blend, itching to toss the seeds of faith as she cracks open diabolical plots to enslave humanity.

In short, I had hoped to make an etching on the spiritual landscape of the world. To follow the Matthew 28 Great Commission (and look good doing it).

Sadly, there isn't a plethora of enslaving despots in Gull Lake, MN. Except, perhaps, my mother, who somehow talked me into working as head of housekeeping (read: the only maid on staff) on Saturdays. Note to self: don't believe it when your mother suggests you come home for a little while until you get your bills paid off and figure out where you want to go next. It's a ploy. Before you know it you'll have an account at the local Java Cup, a library card and a standing order for Jerry's Friday night pizza special, while every available bachelor slinks out of town for greener pastures.

Not that there were many eligibles to begin with. Chase, perhaps, only he doesn't count.

But I digress. Milton and Jasmine—how did it happen?

While I was bent over the hieroglyphics of the local Dear Ruth column, Jasmine used her formerly unbeknownst charms to wheedle down the road to my man's heart. No, not that road. His stomach. Out of all the pastries in the Norwegian's arsenal—*lefse, krumkaga, roll kuchen*—I especially blame the *kringle,* that flaky, almond-frosted pastry that calls to a good Norseman's (or woman's) heart early Saturday mornings. Good old Jasmine, our junior baker, had the boy eating out of her hands. Literally. I should have seen the writing on the wall—or on his face, rather—when I found him, face flaky and dripping sugar within two days of his arrival.

In Jasmine's defense, she can't help it if she can bake like heaven, or that Milton is a true Scandinavian.

He gained thirty pounds in seven months. One hundred and thirty the next year by adding my sister to his list of assets. Remember, he's a bookkeeper. I guess he thought the skinny one with the eager smile and associate degree in Home Economic Arts was the Berglund who offered the greatest long-term benefits.

The sad thing is that I thought Milton and I made a good couple. We loved reading, and…well, reading. He played a cutthroat game of Boggle, and could occasionally smoke me in Scrabble. Mostly, we studied together at college, which I suppose doesn't produce the elements of a good spouse, but rather an excellent quizzer—"How many lines are in a sonnet?"

On a saner day I might recognize the peril of bringing such a trait into a marriage. "Name for me the leading ways to unclog a drain. Give me the three causes of apathy in a relationship."

And he had the uncanny ability to spoil every romantic climax in a chick flick, e.g., knuckle-cracking during the toll-booth proposal in *While You Were Sleeping*. I had to fight the gut urge to rip out his eyebrows one hair at a time—a response that surprised me and should have forewarned of darkness yet to come. And what was with his need to circle the parking lot eighteen times before finding the perfect place? I called it Vulture Parking.

He called me uptight.

The breakup wasn't pretty. And made even uglier by his nearly immediate pursuit of Jasmine. Can anyone say Vulture Parking?

Which brings me to the present, when I'm banging my head on the linen-covered tables, arranged expertly by Susie's Catering on the front yard of the Berglund Acres, thinking, "This is a joke, *right?*" A cool, end-of-May twilight breeze rustles the linen tablecloths and the lily-and-lilac center-pieces. I'm purposely not watching the happy couple circle the dance floor, and wishing that I weren't wearing a dress that makes me look like a poppy.

Oh, yes, marshmallow-me agreed to be the maid of honor. Like my mother said, "Wouldn't the wedding pictures look nice with our whole family in them?" Hello, did anyone else—Grandma Netta, my brother Buddy, Jasmine the groom-stealer or either of my beaming parents—notice that the groom used to belong to me? That this moment in my life might be slightly painful?

Not. I've never been able to outflank my mother. She could teach an online course in practicality. So here I sit, my cleavage pushing out of the princess top (hey, I like *kringle,* too!), wanting to melt into a poppy puddle, or maybe just make a run for the border, when over to my side of misery slides Chase. I didn't exactly expect him to show up at the wedding, but when I spied him an hour ago weaving his way through the receiving line, I suddenly felt as if God might care, just a little. Despite the poppy dress. And, although I've spent most of the last hour hiding in the kitchen, I'm not sad Chase has found me.

That's his specialty, actually. Chase-Me, I called him (not to his face…*please!*) in high school. Most of the time I meant it in a good way.

"What?" I say in greeting, not able to look at Chase full in the face.

"I saw Jerry."

Oh, thanks, Chase. Could you please bring up every small-town mistake I've ever made? I shrug, as if this is news but I don't care, although, yes, I know my senior prom date/successful lawyer is back in town. I still track his movements like a panther, lifting my ears with every mention of his name, my nose to the wind, hoping to catch his scent. He's arrived for the wedding, good friend of the family that he is. Good thing I don't have another sister.

Suddenly I feel a little sick.

"You're looking…what color is that exactly?" I hear him chuckle.

"Get away from me." I lower my head onto my arm. It's a beautiful day out, waves from the lake lapping the shore, the smell of summer in the breeze. The sun, of course, is totally on Jasmine's side. Okay, I admit it! Evil me did walk in the smallest of circles this morning saying, under my breath of course, "Tut tut, it looks like rain." But Jasmine must be much holier than I, because God heard and answered her prayers.

Okay, I'm not that mean to really want it to rain. But a little ripple of thunder might have been nice. Just to shake things up.

"You look good," I say, to lessen my bark. I don't actually look at Chase, but he always looks good, so I'm being honest. Thankfully, Chase alone understands the knife-in-the-gut affair this is. He, too, is a last fish in the sea. I figure that in our geriatric years, we'll be hobbling to the local library from North Shore Acres, still trying to race each other down the hill.

I'm thankful for some consistencies in my life. He told me, sophomore year, as he hid out at Berglund Acres during one of his parents' many skirmishes, that he'd pull out his fingernails one by one before he even thought about trudging down the aisle.

Yet, here he is, at the scene of the crime to help me through this moment of need. I find a smile.

"It's not really all that bad, is it?" He puts his hand on my shoulder. "I mean, c'mon, G.I., the guy has three chins."

"He didn't when I was dating him."

I'm moved by both Chase's touch, his warm, strong hands, and the use of his nickname for me. He couldn't bear to think of me as a girl when we were seven, so he called me G.I. Joe. Not that I minded, but I didn't so much love his later embellishments, Gastro-Intestinal, The Great I, and my least favorite, Gone Insane. But his tone is sweet, and the G.I. term makes me warm in a way that has nothing to do with the sunny May day.

"And aren't you glad you know now the price you may have paid?" Chase tucks his finger under my chin (thankfully I still have only one, despite my *kringle* weakness), lifts my gaze off my arm and onto him. Hidey ho, what happened to the boy next door? Where are the braces? And I distinctly remember acne. Lots of it. He looks, I might add, totally not the anthropologist he says he is—smart and even sexy in his wire-rims, black suit pants and pressed silk shirt… And those eyes—still blue, still friendly, still gleaming…

Sorta makes a girl wanna run for her Radio Flyer and have another go. What do I get if I win?

"You didn't want him anyway," he says.

Who? Oh, yeah, Milton.

"I didn't?" I say. Who exactly did I want?

"No," he says, chuckling. "You're better than that."

"I am?" I moan, not wanting to sound pathetic, but after all, this is the same guy who saw me necking with a boy— not my date—at senior prom and covered for me. He knows a few secrets. "I don't feel better."

"Well, you are." The music changes. Now, the crooning of Roberta Flack. Is this necessary? Movement toward the dance floor, laughter. Oh, everybody's happy. But Chase is staring at me, an odd look in his eyes, and I see our past flash in them.

I'm glimpsing a moment, a rip in the fabric of this horrific day, exposing hope. In fact, my life has suddenly changed tempo. Old promises play in my mind. Chase and I, nine years old, ensconced high in the trees, the sun kissing late autumn leaves. A crisp wind rustles the canopy around me as Chase turns around, hammer in hand. His curls are long, poking out of his homemade knit cap. "Will you marry me?"

"Of course," I say and glare at him. Slacker. We have a fort to build.

But now, nearly fifteen years later, I realize he's returned to ask me to dance. To twirl me around the floor in front of my sister and her husband, saying, Thank you, Bozo, for not realizing what you had and saving her for *me*. Then he'll sweep me in his arms and kiss me and…time to cash in the promises.

Wait! This is Chase. My last resort. Didn't I use those very words two days before graduation under a starlit sky? My friend. My tormentor. My neighbor. The guy who bailed me out of the clink the night I got arrested for skinny-dipping and didn't laugh.

The last line of defense before I'm a lone gal out in the world of singleness.

Kissing Chase would be like kissing the cousin you always had a crush on—daring but just way too creepy. He knows too much. Besides, ever since I got serious with God, there's been a gulf between Chase and me. The more I try and share God's grace with him, and the richness of life with a Savior watching my back and setting my course, Chase pulls away and turns me off.

It makes me ache, and pushes me to prayer. Most of all, it puts a stop sign between us. Not only emotionally but spiritually. I groan to think of Chase not with me in heaven. The thought burns a hole in the center of my chest, and if I could have one thing, it wouldn't be Chase's embrace around me. It would be his embrace around Christ.

I smile anyway, touched that Chase is still "Chase-Me," my next-door-neighbor hero.

Then, as I'm grinning at our past, our friendship, his smile fades and he glances away at…a girl. She's glaring at us with a possessive look that comes straight from the Isle of Amazon. And, in her strapless dress and buff arms, well, she just might be able to take me.

Especially with me stuffed inside the poppy affair, barely able to take a full breath. I sit back in my chair, and something inside my heart has snapped. Of course, Chase and Buffy the Amazon Queen, the perfect match. Why would I ever think that Mr. Anthropology, I-Travel-The-World, might return home for me?

Shyster. We had a deal.

Then he opens his mouth, and if this day could get worse, he shatters every last Cinderella dream in the ashes of my dustbin existence.

"C'mere, Josey. I have a surprise for you. I'd like you to meet my fiancée, Elizabeth."

Did anyone else hear that howl?

I blame my sneaking out halfway through the reception, right after the maid of honor speech, completely on my renegade high-school pal H. She is on hand to share the weddings joys because she's in town helping her now-widowed mother downsize the family home. I fall back into blaming H without blinking. After all, I spent three years of my high-school life perfecting that move.

H epitomizes the wild thread in me that just couldn't rip

free from the conservative churchgoer I was raised to be. She dropped her full name, Hyacinth, which her former hippie mother shortened to Heidi, then Cinthia, then Cindy, before H took control in ninth grade. She took a letter for her name—like Prince—and became her own icon. She was my alternative mind, the part of me that delved into the deeper meanings of life that only high-schoolers and art students have the ability to do, at least while sober.

After high school, H hitchhiked off on the road less traveled. While I attended the University of Minnesota and earned a perfectly respectable English degree, she went into art—as in body art. She has multiple piercings and a tattoo—a cross with barbed wire around it. I asked her what it meant once, and she said she didn't know. But we conjured up some interesting scenarios, and I was hoping that it might lead to one of those evangelism moments our pastor keeps nudging us toward. It's not that I don't want to share my faith with her. It's just…well, you know how people get when you mention Jesus in your life. They stare at you and something turns dry and sluggish in the conversation and you're wondering who turned on the carbon monoxide. I wonder, sometimes, if I have the courage it takes to share what I believe without flinching.

Still, my faith, and especially an excursion through the Bible, has been the only thing keeping me sane lately, let alone a smile on my face. I really dug the "heaping burning coals on their head" verses. Especially when Jasmine showed me a sample of the maid of honor dress she'd purchased. Burning coals. Burning coals. Smile. Smile. But, I have to admit, all this time on my knees, begging for Jasmine and Milton to elope has done wonders for my relationship with God.

I've needed Him more than ever.

In fact, I've wondered, without letting the concept tunnel too deep lest it carve me out from the inside, if it was supposed to happen this way.

Ouch. See?

Nevertheless, losing the love of my life led me to a relationship that feels somehow cleaner. Richer.

Did I say love of my life? Maybe that was overstated.

The Calgon feeling stirred up by time in the Word vanished at the altar, however, watching the bride and groom coo into each other's eyes.

I resorted to plan B. Escape with H.

H: It's not you, you know.

She says this while leaning back in her jeep, her boots on the dash, my bare feet hanging out the window. We're parked on the Bloomquist overlook just up county road 58. She's smoking and I'm trying not to inhale. Usually cigarette smoke makes my head spin, a reaction that probably saved my lungs during my impressionable high school years. But if I got upset every time she pulled out a pack, what kind of Jesus example would I be? Certainly Jesus experienced a few unsavory moments while He hung around all those tax collectors and prostitutes, right? Besides, the top is off the jeep and all I smell is pine, larkspur and a fresh breeze off the lake. Thank You, God, for small favors.

Me: It feels like me. I mean, why? Okay, I, too, can see the benefits of Buffy (oops! Elizabeth. Oh, forget it. She'll always be Buffy to me) from a merely physical point of view. But doesn't history count?

H: I thought we were talking about Milton.

Me: Right. Yes. Milton. And there again, some sort of nod should be given here for brains. Jasmine has a two-year degree in home management. And I am an investigative reporter for the local paper.

H: Your sister has brains. She just uses them differently than you. Besides—let's be honest—you correct grammar.

Me: (Pointing a finger in the air because it suddenly feels right and good) Which takes a college degree. Without grammar we'd have literary chaos.

H: (inhaling) Your problem is that you haven't figured out that life is chaos. You can't make it perfect with correct grammar. You still think someone is going to gift-wrap your future and hand it to you just because you decided to live life inside the lines.

Me: I don't think life owes me anything. I just want my own piece of cake instead of feeling like I'm picking at somebody's stale crumbs.

Well, okay, and I *should* get some credit for doing the right thing. Doesn't the fact that I have saved myself for twenty-four years, waiting for the right man, kept my body pure of drugs and haven't done anything more wild than skinny-dip in Gull Lake on the Fourth of July count for anything in God's tally book? I'm thinking yes.

H: I gotta say it. Milton is definitely cake crumbs. Not the gooey chocolate piece you deserve. You don't want him.

Is there an echo in the air?

Me: Thanks, H. I needed that.

H: And by the way, she's a geologist. They probably met off the map in some third-world country.

Me: Who?

H shakes her head and of course I know who. Honey-toned Buffy. The Amazon.

Me: I don't care. (Liar, liar, but then again, if I tell my-self this often enough, it will sink in, right?) What I re-ally want to know is, what's wrong with me that every guy I meet looks right through me. I mean, am I invis-ible? Or just so insignificant that I don't register on the radar screen of true love? (I lean back, prop my legs on the dash and stare hard into the stars.)
H: You just need a change. A new life. One that doesn't include Milton. (She takes her boots off the dash and leans forward.) Or Chase.

Okay, I flinch. Inside, I don't really want a world without Chase. Perhaps that's the problem. Perhaps I set myself up for disaster, somehow, unconsciously knowing that Milton and Jasmine would find true love, thus leaving me free for Chase. Good try, Josey.

Me: If by a change, you're thinking tattoo, the answer is no. Don't go there.

She quirks an eyebrow and all three hoops jump.

H: Still afraid of needles?
Me: Diseases.
H: Dreams. You're afraid to live outside the lines. To find your cosmic purpose.

She looks at me, and for some reason her black-rimmed eyes hold a hint of anger.

H: See, this isn't all about you, Jose. It's about Jasmine and Milton finding the perfect match and Chase hooking up with the queen of Buff and you feeling like you got left behind.

Okay, it freaks me out more than slightly that a woman I haven't seen for nearly six years can peg me in less than thirty minutes.

Me: I did get left behind. Or hadn't you noticed that I'm the one wearing the poppy dress.
H: That's hard to miss.
Me: (I glare at her.) You know what I dream of? I want to matter. To make a difference. I want someone to love me so much, they would cross the world just to spend one hour with me. I want to leave a trail of wow behind me. I don't believe in cosmic purpose, but I do wonder if God has a plan, or if He's still waiting to see if I'm worth the trouble.

That was way too vulnerable. I know, because H looks at me, suddenly silent, blinking. I shrug, feeling painfully close to tears.

Me: I want to be more than a bridesmaid in a poppy dress.

I attempt a smile intended to disguise the fact that I feel like I'm sitting here in my underwear.

H: You want the gold ring.
Me: (intelligently) Huh?

H: You know, that ring on the old-fashioned carousel
that won the riders a prize if they caught it? You want
that thing that makes the journey bearable. The one
thing that will make your life significant.
Me: I think that was a brass ring.

But my words fall into the breeze and I realize how much
she knows me, knows my greatest fears. Maybe there is more
of my mother in me than I want to concede. Maybe, deep
inside, I returned to Gull Lake toting Milton like a souve-
nir because I was actually terrified of reaching for something
brighter and falling flat on my derriere. Maybe I didn't want
Milton after all, but wanted failure even less.

I do want the gold ring. The happily ever after. The eternal purpose. I want to be that girl who takes her faith and
her Christian calling seriously. And, while I might have zippo
idea as to how a gal might do this, I do know that it isn't
within my reach from Gull Lake, Minnesota.

I glance at H. Her blond hair is in spikes, dyed black at the
tips. The moonlight glints off her nose ring. It seems as if H
has always been searching for something, trying to find it in
her appearance choices. But then, a gal can be dressed in
Lands' End and crunchy-granola Birks and still wonder at the
meaning of life. I guess I shouldn't be too hard on H, especially since I'm sitting here in poppy flounce, pretty sure I
have "pathetically lost" written all over me. I might have
found the eternal answer, but I still have earthly questions.

Me: Maybe I need to do something different. Outside
the lines.

I say this while little voices explode in my head like cluster bombs. What if I follow my gut and discover that on the

other side of sanity isn't freedom or purpose but even more chaos? What if breaking loose simply…breaks me?

H: (who is not inside my brain to read my panic) Like move to Colorado and become a ski bum?

Yes, that was another phase. But no, I'm not going to run off to Vail. Hopefully I've matured since then. Although, her words stir old longings…hot tubs, muscles, après-ski mochas…

Me: No. Something that makes a difference in the eternal fabric. Makes my life significant. I'll go after the gold ring. (Did I really say that out loud? With that much conviction?)
H: (chuckling). Let start with burning that dress.

I make it home well after midnight, creep into the house/office and up to my bedroom. Which, until tonight, I shared with Jasmine.

That feels weird. Aside from the fact that she married my former boyfriend, we capped off each night with low murmured gossip and verbal spars. She alone knows that I have a half-done tattoo just above my right hip, a product of my wild, pre-Christian college days, waning courage and not enough vodka. Tonight, I would have enjoyed Jas's company if only to squeal on Chase. Jas is good, real good, at indignation.

And, no, I didn't burn the dress. Which gives credence to H's accusation that I'm afraid to live outside the lines. Or maybe it was due to the shiver conjured up by the thought of driving home in her jeep, top down (in more ways than one) and sneaking past a houseful of relatives. My wild move is sneaking up the stairs without saying hello, leaving the dress in a heap and crawling into bed in my underwear. I still feel slightly rebellious. As the night sounds fill the room, and the moonlight reaches out to me, H's words ping in my heart.

Do something crazy. Go after the gold ring.

Only, what and where exactly is that?

Eternal purpose? Yeah, sure. I'd settle for a reason to get up in the morning.

The sun is way too bright this morning as I drag my body out of bed, wrestle a comb through my shellacked hair and somehow stumble out to the family sedan to go to church. Does my dad have to honk, alerting the entire neighborhood to my plight?

I spend much of the pre-service warm-up—the organ music and chatter—reading the bulletin. I take note that there is a guest speaker today—Message: Building Tomorrows by Professor Monty Beecher from Moscow Bible College, Russia.

I check him out. Because, well, I'm still single. Way single.

He's dressed like a missionary. Brown suede suit coat, dark brown suit pants and a nondescript tie, but he's got thick blond hair and a tan, which means potential—

Oh, good grief! He's a missionary!

Perhaps it's the fact that I'm still feeling freshly flogged by the wedding, Chase's defection and H's accusations of cowardice, but when the Preacher Beecher says, "For we are God's workmanship, created in Christ Jesus to do good works, which God prepared in advance for us to do," it gives me another good jolt. His words feel like a custard-filled Bismarck, gooey and soft on my soul. I'm even willing to call it divine providence.

So, I sit up in the pew, suddenly awake as I listen to Mr. Missionary outline his English program. "We need teachers," he says to the audience, and looks at me.

I can teach. I taught Chase how to sneak into the back entrance of our bakery, right? I taught my sister the books of the Bible song. Once I even taught a kid I barely knew how to tie a bowline knot.

Hey, he thought it was cool.

I leave, but I feel butterflies in my stomach. I decide it is courage....

Not hunger.

"A missionary?"

There is way too much panic in my mother's voice.

"Yes. Didn't you hear the speaker this morning?" I'm scraping gravy into an empty orange juice can, feeling like I have eaten a buffalo instead of a roast, mashed potatoes, rolls, gravy, salad, Jell-O *and* apple pie. Okay, I admit it—I over-committed! First benefit to moving to Russia? Starvation.

"Honey, you have a job." My mother squeezes in beside me to throw a wadded handful of napkins away. She, of course, inherited all the thin genes from her Scandinavian father. "Why would you want to throw that all away?"

It is probably a moot point that the best part of my job is that I get free coffee from the Java Cup. Mom, who still runs Berglund Acres as head cook, who bakes her way to a blue ribbon at the state fair every year, who has published three recipes in the *Minneapolis Star Tribune,* can't possibly understand what it means to feel...insignificant.

I retreat to my room with a piece of wedding cake. I cut it big, too. No need for pleasantries now that the crowd is gone.

★ ★ ★

Dear God:

Just wondering if this is it. A missionary? Yes, I admit it hit me hard. But that was before lunch and now I'm just thinking that maybe it was just orange juice on an empty stomach. A sugar high.

Still, the tall, good-looking missionary with rich green eyes said, "I need you." Okay, he said it to the audience, but I heard it. I can teach English, right? I mean, I know it. I've spoken it for nearly twenty-four years. How hard can it be?

And, while we're chatting, what's with the Chase engagement? I know I never voiced it, but I'm saying it now. He's mine. He asked me first. So, what's with Buffy? I am not finding this funny.

It hasn't escaped me that I'm finding it easier to get over Milton than Chase. How sad it that?

Maybe Moscow, the other side of the world, is exactly where I should be right now.

I lay down my pen and tuck my nose into the journal, feeling the smooth pages cool my forehead. Russia? Okay, maybe it was indigestion, initially, but as I roll the word around in my brain, it fills the nooks and crannies and suddenly my heart feels warm and full. Russia. A missionary. Couldn't I do that for a year?

Eternal purpose.

I envision small children following me home, my name like a song on their lips. They smile, grab my legs to give me a hug. I've taught them to read. I've sung them Bible songs. I am Josey Berglund, missionary, teacher. Mother Josey?

Okay, definitely not. But, at least Josey—friend to the lost.

And maybe, in the end, I might find myself, also.

For we are God's workmanship, created in Christ Jesus to do good works, which God prepared in advance for us to do. That feels pretty good right about now. I'd even call the feeling that makes me gasp, peace.

Here I am, Lord, send me.

A bread maker!

Yowza, Grandma Netta went all out. I sit at the edge of the room, cradling a soggy paper cup of orange punch, watching the froth dissolve along with my verve. The late afternoon has brought the newlyweds back to the big house for a little personal torture: opening wedding gifts. Who, really, is thrilled by this event except the bride and groom? By the way, they've spent their honeymoon night in one of the Berglund cabins. How original is that? I'll never clean that cabin again, believe you me.

The redolence of jealousy simmers in the room along with the lunch in my stomach. Like we aren't all just forcing our smiles just a little, wishing that the cappuccino maker from Uncle Milt and Aunt Florence was going to sit on our kitchen counter. Or the painting by Monet was going to hang in our bedroom.

I'll let the happy couple keep the potholders shaped like aprons. Some gifts are too endearing to part with.

My brother Buddy has joined us for the celebration, and he sits on Mom's brand-new green sofa, cradling his own wilting punch cup. The plastic isn't even off the sofa yet, and if the past is any indication, that step won't happen until well into the next decade. We were the only family in town allowed to drink soda in the living room on Sunday afternoons. A privilege I found less than wonderful when I realized that sofas were actually supposed to be comfortable and not make noise when one sat on them.

This one looks nice, however, and matches the rest of the décor—straight out of Mother's decorator home parties. I especially love the flock of mallards springing from the wall, surrounded by the plastic flowers. I am hoping to inherit them when/if she ever dies.

I suppose I need a slap.

It doesn't help my outlook on life that Chase has arrived, sans Buffy thankfully, and is leaning near the door, arms crossed, giving me a Doberman look. I've avoided him like leprosy since he arrived an hour ago and plan to play hide-and-don't-seek all night. I smile at him, however. Never let it be said that Josey Berglund can't be gracious.

The two-timing chiseler.

I squeeze past Buddy and don't make eye contact with Milton's mother, a woman twice my size (which makes Milton's double chins inevitable, something I should have remembered and, today, assuages my pain just slightly). She's probably remembering the game of Scrabble I walloped her in the weekend I went home with Milton to meet the parents.

Come to think of it, my relationship with Milton took a quick nosedive after that incident. I am tempted to spill my punch on her bright red, poppy floral dress.

It's a diabolical plot. I know it.

Get a hold of yourself, Josey. I pick up a croissant sandwich and fill my punch cup. No need to go hungry while I watch the newlyweds rake in all my gifts.

"Oh, a hand-stitched dove quilt!" Jasmine holds up the wall hanging and Aunt Bonnie beams. Jas can obviously pull this off way better than I ever could. She even holds it to her breast and sighs deeply, while gazing into Milton's eyes.

Oh, brother.

Maybe now is the time for my announcement. The family is here, my mother distracted. I can just drop the bomb and run.

Except, why would I give all this up?

Jas unwraps another gift and holds up a bib. A bib? As a wedding gift? Talk about a hint. It says "Daddy's girl."

Okay, I just found my reason.

"I'm going to Moscow," I hear myself say. In one move, they turn, all ten heads, as if on a pulley.

The sudden entrance of Elvis would have produced fewer gasps.

Now that I've tried that on for size, time to get brave. It is now or never. Two years of post-college hiking on the treadmill to nowhere has left me with nothing but a single bed in the upstairs room of my parents' house, a beat-up Subaru and enough romance novels to paper an American Legion hall.

"I'm going to Moscow to be a missionary," I elaborate, with gusto.

My mother clutches her head in her hands, Buddy checks his punch as if it might be spiked and Dad frowns, turning up his hearing aid.

Chase stares at me, mouth slightly open, wearing an expression of horror that looks painfully reminiscent of the skin-scraping gravel-road encounter.

Certainly he didn't expect me to stick around to be his best woman, did he? *Drat!* Tears glaze my eyes and I look away, down to the green shag, where I know vermin reside. This is not about escaping. *Lord, please, wasn't that peace I felt earlier?*

Grandma Netta to the rescue. "That's in Idaho," she announces. "I learned that on *Jeopardy.*"

The heads swivel to her. All except Jasmine's. She's got tears in her eyes and the newlywed glow has vanished.

Suddenly, I wonder exactly what I might be sacrificing.

Chapter Two:
$17.23

My father sings. My earliest memory of him is in church, his wide hands gripping the podium, swaying to a rendition of "Fill my cup, Lord." He has a resonating tenor that wasn't too bad…until I became a teenager. Then I would slink out of the sanctuary and hide in the library, where I'd bury myself in a book. The only books our church library stocked were commentaries, Old Testaments of the Bible in various translations and missionary stories. Hoping for entertainment, I chose the missionaries.

Between the chapters on the Maasai tribes in Africa and the starving Ethiopians, I found my refuge. The Iron Curtain. The Siberian wasteland. The persecuted saints of the Soviet Union. They called to me from the pages with their cries for mercy, for justice, for running water. I saw them behind my eyes, wrapped in rags, clutching Bibles to their chests with chapped hands, and thought, now *those* are the real Christians.

I say all this to the man with green eyes as I sit nursing a cup of breakfast blend in the Java Cup. I've tracked him (I'm an investigative reporter, right?) through my pastor, intercepted his escape from Gull Lake and invited him out for lunch.

My entire future teeters on his expression. He's spent most of the meal devouring a Reuben on rye from the deli next door, while I, too nervous to eat (how about that for a divine sign?), convince him that I should go to Russia.

Something that I'm trying hard to talk myself into at the moment. After Jasmine's ashen look yesterday, the room resumed the hubbub and—aside from Chase's less-than-clandestine frown and obvious attempts to get me alone and nail my intentions to the wall—nothing more was mentioned about Russia, Moscow or even Idaho.

I am Lara Croft, Tomb Raider, adventurer, investigator. I've smiled, dodged Chase and tracked down Monty Beecher, missionary and gatekeeper to my future. And now I will woo him with my wit and educational prowess.

"I know that I would be a great asset to your team," I say, my confidence ringing through the tiny coffee shop.

"It sounds to me like God has been preparing your heart for years to serve in Russia," Monty says, wiping his mouth with his napkin. "Have you ever taught English?"

"I have an English degree."

"Teaching ESL takes more than a degree. You need training."

Training? To speak my own language? "Well, I um, sorta thought…well, you made it sound like you just needed willing bodies."

He frowns at me, one eyebrow squished tight, the other high, and I squirm. Maybe I've overestimated my abilities here.

"I can get training."

He relaxes, smiles. "We offer excellent classes, and I am sure the first year we could team you with an experienced partner."

The first year?

I take a long sip of my coffee.

"I'll leave you an application. Fill it out, send it in with your picture and we'll be in touch."

He reaches into his briefcase and pulls out folder. I'm thinking he'll take out one of those sheets. He hands me the entire folder. "I know it looks big, but we just like to get to know our applicants."

Now I do the one-eyebrow-up move. Get to know me? I flip through the wad of papers. Biography. Spiritual history. Psychological profile. Medical form. Theology quiz. Dental exam. Waiver. *Waiver?*

I scan it and every hair stands on end.

RELEASE AND WAIVER OF LIABILITY

The undersigned is an adult 18 years of age or older who desires to volunteer his/her services for a mission trip to Russia. The undersigned understands and acknowledges that there may be risks of bodily injury, illness or security (including death) inherent in travel to Russia, and that he/she voluntarily assumes all such risks and releases Moscow Bible College, or any of its directors from all liability for these and any other risks in connection with his/her activities.

The undersigned acknowledges and affirms that he/she has carefully read this release and has asked for and obtained a satisfactory explanation to any questions he/she has and has signed it voluntarily.

Signature of Volunteer

Date

★ ★ ★

My mouth is full of cotton as I mumble goodbye. He lets me buy lunch and drives off in a 1988 Ford Escort.

I stand on the street, feeling the cool air brush off the lake, smelling freshly cut grass and tasting my future sour in my mouth.

Including death?

Killing Off The Gypsy Moth by Josey Berglund

They ravage our birch trees; strip the heart from our aspen. In large droves, the gypsy moths are one of the most destructive insect tree defoliators in North America.

Gull Lake, do not despair. Mother Nature is on our side.

The gypsy moth life cycle is short, desperate and focused. After emerging from the pupal stage, the male moth has ten days to find a female moth to begin the reproduction cycle. It isn't too difficult—the female gypsy moths don't fly. They stay by their cocoon and wait for their man.

However, a gypsy moth male can only complete the instinctual life cycle under warm conditions, and only during late August and early September.

Be thankful for the cold north. Because of our cooler climate, the male moth develops more slowly. His prime reproductive activity occurs during the fall. The cold snaps of last August and September have rendered the Gull Lake gypsy male ineffective.

Maybe Mother Nature has a sense of humor.

Finally, a woman getting even.

★ ★ ★

"Feeling testy this morning?" My editor Myrtle's breath streams over my shoulder. I smell garlic—her egg-salad secret ingredient. Ew.

I stare at her blankly. She smiles and points to the screen. "Opinion, not fact. No editorializing." She pats my shoulder and winks, like, oh, honey, someday you'll get it.

Excuse me, but last time I looked this wasn't the *New York Times* or the *Washington Post*. We are not breaking open a conspiracy or unearthing CIA files, and frankly the gypsy moth article needs a little spice.

And I did not, *did not,* compare the gypsy moth to Chase, wondering if his engagement to Buffy was a rash swoop-and-mate decision made during a warm spell. Nor did I wish upon him a cold front.

Shake it off, Josey.

I delete the last two lines.

The Minnesota Department of Natural Resources is tracking the population of the male gypsy moth using pheromone traps, green triangles set into trees, designed to lure the little suckers—*Delete, delete*—to lure the insects to their demise and calculate their decline or increase in numbers. Their findings will be reported to The Natural Resources Research Institute at the University of MN-Duluth.

I spell-check it and hit Send before I'm tempted to add any more "editorial." Like why their numbers should be counted, why all measures should be made to exterminate—

I sigh and lean back in my leather desk chair. I purchased it myself after the old one, a 1952 squeaker that used to belong to the school, dropped me onto my backside. I stare out my window. The sun is low, and turns the lake to cobalt-blue as a slight wind bullies a scattering of cirrus. It's a warm day, but I keep the window shut, and let the fan propped on the file cabinet behind me dry the sweat off my neck. Gull droppings aren't my favorite scent, and at the moment I'm trying to avoid further inducements to fleeing.

Not fleeing. *Finding new opportunities.* Chase has gone back to Montana, where he's been studying the Kootenai people in a village somewhere in Glacier National Park. He took Elizabeth with him, grr.

I wonder how the gypsy moth population is doing in the mountains.

Behind me, in the one-room *Gazette* office, Myrtle is tapping on her keyboard. She's laid the Dear Ruth column and a new recipe on my desk. I glance at the recipe.

Edible Modeling Clay

1/2 cup creamy peanut butter
1/4 cup honey or syrup
1/2 cup instant dry milk powder
2 tbs powdered sugar
Mix and knead into a pliable dough, adding more powdered sugar to taste.

Okay, how pitiful am I that that actually sounds good?

"I'm going down for a cup of coffee." I push away from my desk and don't look at Myrtle. It's okay, she doesn't hear me anyway. I pick up my satchel, bulky application folder stuffed inside and stroll down the back stairs.

There are two good things about my job—Number One, Java Cup is located below our office, and they let me drink unlimited cups for a free block of advertising in our weekly. My favorite is their house breakfast blend, but sometimes I take a stroll on the wild side and go with the flavor of the week.

Today it is a vanilla chai. That sounds exotic. I order one and find a perch next to the window. It overlooks our main street—three cafés surrounded by an antique store, a quilting shop and a dime store. Obviously we take food very seriously in Gull Lake.

Number Two, Myrtle Shold is my father's aunt, his mother's sister. Thus, I'm allowed excursions to Java Cup, the Right Moose Café and an occasional walk down the Gull Lake pier.

She's okay, Myrtle. She's been the editor of the newspaper for nearly thirty-five years, and to her credit, knows what Gull Lakers like—the fishing report, weather forecast, recipes, school news, obituaries and an occasional editorial by a pastor. There are five from the stock Gull Lake churches—First Baptist, Our Savior's Lutheran, Gull Lake Congregational, First Methodist and Holy Rosary Catholic. It's a good mix. Not a lot of fighting, except when there's a new baby born to a mixed family. Then we'll get a slew of infant baptism op-eds. Myrtle edits those, to keep everyone happy, being that she is an agnostic.

Myrtle lives just up the road, on land owned by the Berglunds, in a two-room cabin. I remember as a child being enthralled by her lawn art—a display of Bambi and all the forest animals that looked so real I always found myself sitting in the middle of the crowd, chatting.

Maybe that's why she hired me. My active imagination.

I'm going to need it if I hope to fill out this application.

I slap the folder onto the table and a little thrill of fear and hope rushes through me. Russia. I want to imagine European bistros and excursions to ancient sites, but suddenly all I see is ice.

Snow.

Siberia.

Gulag.

Maybe I should do some checking first. Thankfully the Java Cup has their pinky on the pulse of the needs of the local tourist and offers free Internet service with a cup of java.

I log on and Google: Bible church, Moscow.

My first choice nets me a congregation in Moscow, Idaho. So Grams was right. Interesting stuff, but I click the next link.

Did you know that there is also a Moscow, Pennsylvania? I can't wait to trump Gramma on that one.

Third time's a charm—www.moscowbiblechurch.com.

I wait while my browser finds it, tapping my fingers on the wooden table. I sip my chai—it's not bad—and watch the pictures load.

Children reading Bibles. A man being baptized. Men and women sitting at desks. They look eager, clean. There are no bedraggled rags or barbed wire fences. Or snow.

I search Moscow, Russia, and the screen lists over 1,000 pages. Top of the list is the embassy. I like that word. It sounds so espionage, even dangerous. "Hey, let's check in at the embassy," or "Is the embassy having a ball tonight?" Yes, I like embassy.

I scroll down to *Weather Underground*.

Twenty-one degrees? In June? My heart just went into hiding. No wait. That's Celsius. Okay, this is better. 70 degrees with a low of 62. That I can deal with.

Just for fun, I enter average temperatures for January. Ew. Eighteen below. That's painful. But again, Celsius. A comparison in reality lists that as 0 degrees. Still not a heat wave, but then again, I'm currently living in Gull Lake, the ice fishing capital of Minnesota.

Things are looking up.

I skip over the *Moscow Times* and go right to *Moscow Insiders Guide*.

Jackpot!

The welcome page tells me that I am not only lucky, but should feel happy and confident about my trip to Moscow. I like upbeat webmasters. The page loads and the choices look promising—culture, entertainment, *shopping…*

Click.

Art galleries. I guess I wasn't expecting a shopping trip to Fifth Avenue, but a Saks would be nice.

How about culture?

Now this is more like it.

Museums, underground palaces of the Metro, the *Golden Ring* tour.

Okay, anyone else have chills? I click on the tour. It's a listing of cities, *ancient* cities. "Museums under the open sky" with 12th century Russian architecture. They have exotic names like *Yaroslav, Rostov, Suzdal* and *Palekh*. I say the last one out loud and it sounds like I'm spitting. I kind of like it and say it again.

Benny over at the cappuccino machine glances at me and I click on *Palekh*.

It has, among other relics, a monastery with white towers and gold cupolas, and a prince buried in a convent. (Kinda makes me wonder what he's doing there—what kind of prince was he, exactly?)

I go back to the home page and click on entertainment.

Tour of Moscow. Okay, I'm game.

I tour the Arbat, where the poet Pushkin lived, check out the grandeur of the Bolshoi theater, and linger long in Red Square, enraptured with St. Basil's cathedral.

What about…food?

Restaurants, click.

Score! Chose by type of establishment or cuisine. Cafés, pubs (I've never been in one of those, but don't they sound cute?), night eateries and delivery. On the other scroll bar are cuisines from India, China, Taiwan, Thailand, Greece, Italy, America and something called Caucasian. That trips me up and I click on it. It takes me more than a few seconds to realize that this is specialty food from the Caucasus mountains. Not some sort of pre-civil-rights-era club. Phew.

Mutton pie sounds…well, maybe I'll stick to American for the first couple weeks/months/centuries.

I go back and click on cafés. Oooh, I like this picture. Umbrella tables, plants, people laughing.

I could be laughing. Letting the sun soak my arms, nursing a…slushy? Or maybe something more exotic?

There would be music playing, something hip and upbeat, maybe a Duke Ellington remixed jazz tune, and around me birds chirping, the smell of summer, the sounds of unfamiliar speech—

Wait, I have to speak another language?

Don't interrupt!

The sounds of unfamiliar speech. Perhaps I'm picking at a Greek salad. I'm looking svelte in a sleeveless silk blouse and black capris. My hair is long, sun-bleached, straight and a hint of pink dots my nose. I'm chewing, noiselessly of course, when a shadow cascades over me. I look up.

"Hi, Jose."

I expected him and I push out the wicker chair with my foot. "Sit down, Chase."

He's looking tan because he's been spending all that time in the mountains. His blond hair is long, slightly tangled and he's a little rumpled in an oxford and chinos, as if he's been in a hurry to get to me.

Of course.

"Are you in town long?" I ask as he sits.

He shakes his head, and there is definite disappointment on his face. "Just for an hour. But I had to see you."

Elizabeth, eat your heart out.

"What do you want?" I'm buying. After all, the guy crossed an ocean for me. But he leans across the table, takes my hand. It is warm and strong, and for a second the touch sweeps the breath right out of my chest. Then he smiles, his blue eyes gleaming.

"Just you."

"Josey, I'm going over to Red Rooster to pick up their grocery ad for the week. Can you man the office for me?" Myrtle hollers from the Java Cup doorway.

I blink out of the moment. Chase's hand dissolves in mine, leaving it cold. I'm staring at my screen, which has gone into saver mode. The Microsoft icon twirls around the page. "Man the shop. Yes, right." I sigh, straighten my shirt and quickly exit the browser.

Yeah, I can man the office. But not for long.

I'm going to Russia.

H gave me two things when she exited Gull Lake.
1. The name of her hairdresser in Minneapolis.
2. Her AOL IM identity for future counseling purposes.
I'm not quite ready to coordinate my hair color with my

clothes, but I need a friend tonight at 2:00 a.m., as the moon slants across Jasmine's empty single bed and crawls toward me. I'm in my jammies—an old T-shirt with the Tasmanian devil plastered on the front. I've had it since I was sixteen and my future mate will have to pry it off my cold, dead body before I'll part with it. If he doesn't like cotton, an oversized beast and a little rip in the sleeve, then I'm not his girl. He might actually like the rip.

I've got my laptop on my legs, and a glass of water with lemon sweating on the bedside table.

One good thing about having a friend who makes her living mixing margaritas and fuzzy navels is that 2:00 a.m. is her prime time. Besides, Jasmine is still on her honeymoon. H answers my IM query.

<Wildflower> Hello, Jose! What's up?

<GI> Remind me why I'm doing this.

I've spent the last two weeks tracking down references, talking to my pastor, fielding objections from my mother, answering questions like, "What do you believe about Baptism?" (I don't let Myrtle see my answer), taking a mug shot and getting a physical. (And I didn't appreciate the doctor mentioning that I'd gained fifteen pounds since my last one. Good grief, I was twelve! Give me a break!) The finished envelope is sealed and sitting on my dresser. Like a bomb.

Tick tick, I can nearly hear it waiting to explode and change my life.

<Wildflower> You want more from your life.

<GI> But I have a pretty good life. I like Myrtle. And I have a view.

<Wildflower> Do you want to be Myrtle? I'm asking because if you don't do this you'll end up inheriting her cabin.

<GI> And the lawn art, I hope.

<Wildflower> I'm not laughing at that. If you don't go, you'll regret it for the rest of your life.

<GI> Just tell me how you feel, will you? This isn't the only opportunity to travel I'll have.

<Wildflower> Yeah, you're right. When you sign up for AARP, they'll send you an entire catalogue of cruises.

<GI> Now that wasn't funny. Mine was.

<Wildflower> Or you could stay in Gull Lake and marry Fuzzy. I hear he's single again.

Fuzzy Zoman was the quarterback for our high school team until he knocked up Patty Lowe, had to quit and took a job running maintenance down at the local municipal pool. He's blond, big and brazen and Patty kicked him out like a mangy dog when she walked in on him and Kerry Fitger doing water aerobics after closing. He's moved on, a couple times I think, since Kerry.

<GI> Don't get nasty now. I'm not looking to get married.

I want to add "ever" but I think that's a little drastic. I'd probably say "I do" to the right guy, someone with blue eyes, a kind smile, enough muscles to prop me up when I'm feeling down and the wisdom to know when to keep his mouth shut unless I get in over my head. Notice those qualities do not define Chase. Well, mostly not.

<Wildflower> I know. But I'm making a point. Leap now or forever hold your peace.

<GI> What if I flop? What if I get over there, find I can't speak a lick of Russian, my students hate me, I alienate everyone, and—

<Wildflower> If you don't try, you'll never know. Besides, you'll alienate *me* if you don't do it.

<GI> Thank you for that unconditional love.

<Wildflower> My pleasure. You need a change. It's either this or a nose ring. Take your pick.

Two days before high school graduation, Chase and I sat on the beach, tossing in stones and talking about our futures. The moon parted the waves as they lapped the shore, and the smell of freedom taunted, still just out of our reach. Shania Twain played on the stereo of his Kawasaki 350, which we'd just driven from graduation rehearsal.

"I can't believe you're not going with me. I thought we had a deal," he said as he skimmed another rock across the waves. I hated how he could always out throw me. I snaked one across the water and only got three skips.

Those were the days when his curly hair took possession of his entire body. Cut short on top, it snaked down his back, where the wind brushed it against his leather bomber jacket. I was looking pretty hot myself in a pair of stonewashed jeans and a cotton cami. The nights were losing their chilly edge, but sometimes, when it was cold, he offered me his jacket. I liked it because it smelled like Chase.

I dodged his question (as you know, I'm very good at dodging). No, I wasn't trekking out to North Dakota State, thank you very much. They may have had an excellent journalism program, but I just couldn't—I mean, what is in North Dakota anyway?

And I just knew that if Chase hadn't nailed that scholarship, he wouldn't have gone there, either. But I didn't say that.

"You'll write to me, right?" I suddenly felt a gash across my chest. Chase wouldn't be there for me to track down after my dates and lament on the shortage of decent non-groping boys in Gull Lake. Or be the hero-friend to rescue me on those lonely Saturday nights when groping boys just might be appreciated. Who would follow me around school, hang out by my locker, run me down to Jerry's for a pizza lunch?

Who would haul me home when H talked me into trying some locally made hooch? Who would lecture me on the perils of hanging out with the one girl who might just make it all the way to the state penitentiary in Stillwater?

My throat was thick as he stared at me. His blue eyes were so powerful, they snatched me up and reached down to my heart. Sometimes, I can still feel it.

"I'm going to miss you, G.I.," he said and ran his fingers down my cheek. He smelled good, and the moon was touching his face, turning it to gold. He leaned forward, his gaze on my lips.

And then I blew it. It is precisely at this moment, in all my reminiscence, that I want to grab the Josey of the past by the throat and smack her good.

"I suppose if I don't find the right guy in college, I could come back for you," I said with a smile. "Sort of my last resort…"

At the time, I thought I paid him a compliment. He flinched, and leaned away.

"Yeah, right." His voice was clogged, and I thought it was due to his emotions, being so touched that I'd consider him.

The breeze came up, rippled the lake. I shivered as it lifted the hair off my neck.

He didn't offer me the jacket.

It was then I began to suspect I'd ground to dust something precious in our friendship.

I awaken, that memory outlining my dreams. Until the sun clears the horizon I stare at the ceiling, adding up the profits and losses of sending the envelope. At 8:03 a.m. I throw my shorts and a sweatshirt over my Taz jammies, slip on my Birks and race down to the post office. Overnight FedEx costs $17.23.

$17.23 to change my life. Or regret it forever.

Chapter Three:
Finding Full Boil

July 3, 2004
Moscow Bible Church/Mission to the World
1237 Righteous Boulevard
Waukee, IA 55302

Dear Ms. Berglund,

It is with warm congratulations that we inform you that your application for a short-term ESL teacher for our Moscow Bible Church outreach has been reviewed and accepted. Your eagerness and background in English are outstanding qualifications for this position and we look forward to seeing how God will enhance them to benefit His work in Russia. We were especially taken in by your comment that "although I've never seen myself as a missionary, I am willing to explore new avenues and take on new challenges. Even if it means having no running water." Willingness is an admirable trait, and Russia certainly has its opportunities for growth. With and without running water.

We would like to invite you to our headquarters to interview with our selection board the weekend of July 16-18. If you are approved, you will be invited to our one week orientation and training event, held July 19-23, at Lake Okiwaya camp. You will be responsible for your own transportation, but housing and meals will be provided.

Thank you for your interest in the ministry with Moscow Bible Church. We look forward to your response and getting to know you further.
In His Service,
Dwight Wills
Director of Personnel
Mission to the World
Cc: Frank Bemouth

"Where exactly is Waukee?"
Jasmine is sitting on her bed, cross-legged, leaning back on her palms, and critiquing every item I fold, put in my suitcase, take out, toss into a pile, then grab, refold and add again. It's been a week of packing and still I can't decide the look I'm going for here.
"It's in Des Moines."
Conservative or liberated? My short, very cute low-rise Gap capris that make me look carefree and smart, or my J.G. Hook nautical dress, the one down to my ankles? Or do I wear a suit?
"That would be Iowa, right?" Jasmine shakes her head no to the nautical dress.
I guess I'll also say no to the cute little black leather skirt

I picked up two years ago at a Saks sale. I'm envisioning having to drop to my knees to make sure my hemline touches the floor. Do they wear leather in Des Moines in July?

Fine, I admit it, the tag is still on the little black skirt. And the matching stiletto sandals I found at Macy's to go with it. But a girl can dream, right?

"Hey, how about the dress I gave you last summer?" Jas gets off the bed and pulls a floral shell from the back of my dusty closet, where I've hidden it behind two bridesmaid's dresses.

What is it with Jasmine and poppies? I can already feel my lungs bunching up.

"It's too small," I say, trying to deflect the truth and pretty sure I'm right.

She shakes her head. "No, it's a size bigger than I wear. I know it will fit you."

Oh, thanks, sis. I force a smile. "Right. Thanks."

"Besides, you look great in sleeveless."

She's the one who looks great. Tanned, blond hair down her back and a glow in her eyes that hasn't dimmed once since the honeymoon two weeks ago. Even when I told her that yes, I was for sure going to Des Moines. And Russia. She blinked a couple times, but the glow stayed.

I don't want to know why. Please, I'm not even going to wonder.

Okay, yes, it bothers me more than just a little that I am the last remaining virgin over the age of eighteen in a sixty-mile radius. Not that I want the goodies without marriage, but the fact that my younger sister can sit over there and glow—well, see, I knew I was better off not pondering all this.

I throw the dress on the bed, unsure what sisterly urge to pursue at the moment.

"How long will you be there?" she asks as I survey my shoe selection.

"Ten days." I'm adding in the training session because I know they'll accept me. But ten days is my limit because, being practical as well as confident, I only asked Myrtle for time off instead of quitting altogether.

I return to my closet. I really like my black, high-heeled sandals, but I'm not sure I can afford a pedicure before I leave and well, my toes aren't my best feature. I grab my old faithful leather closed-toe mules. (I'm sorry, but when in doubt, go with comfort.) Which then commits me to the capris, a few cotton sweaters and tanks. And I add in the floral shell (Jas is looking, and I'm past the petty moment) and a black shirt-waist dress that sheds a few pounds. Especially if people squint a little. You know, I've found that if we all just squinted more often, the world would be a much easier place to live. Blurry is nice.

Reality hurts.

Like the fact that I haven't heard from Chase since he left, not a huge issue, but still the guy has my e-mail address. And I happen to know he has a cell phone. I helped him pick it out last summer when he was home for vacation.

He hadn't mentioned Buffy then. Hmm. Not even when I drove him back down to the Twin Cities for his flight out. Nor do I remember him looking as good as he did at the wedding. I do recall, however, grimy jeans, a torn flannel shirt and a battered Twins hat.

I don't want to know who his personal groomer has been.

We listened to country music—his choice—and he crooned a few songs and told me about the assignment he just finished in Tuk, Alaska. He specializes in studying people. Which seems like a pretty strange profession for a guy who couldn't figure out that half the Gull Lake senior class was in love with him. I mean, couldn't he see the girls trailing after him like groupies, hanging out at the Dairy Queen (he did look kinda cute in that paper hat) and showing up at his baseball games? I practically had to fight the crowds as I brought him his chilled bottle of Gatorade!

But now the guy contemplates humanity. He writes studies and reports on people groups, on behaviors, on marriage rituals. I wonder what kind of marriage ritual he's preparing for him and Buffy.

Do. Not. Go. There.

I should have kissed him goodbye instead of the one-armed hug at the curb.

There are a lot of things I should have done.

"Are you flying?" Jas asks, reminding me that I have a future for which to prepare.

"No. It's only seven hours. I can manage."

"But can your Subaru?" She laughs. *Oh, hardy har har.*

"I'll be fine. Lots of Diet Coke." I close my suitcase—wait, I thought this bag was bigger. Ten minutes of zipping and grunting and it is finally shut. The suitcase looks like a…Teletubby. Round and fat. I jerk it off my bed and nearly rip my arm out of its socket.

Jas gets off the bed and grabs the handle. "Good *night,* Josey! What do you have in here?"

"A few books?" All right! Yes, I did bring along four new romances—all inspirational. I might have some free time, and I get four a month in the mail. I don't want to fall behind. And my study Bible, of course. And a notebook.

And a picture of Chase and me in high school, the one we took just before we went backpacking with the 4-H club. He's bunny-earing my head and I am looking trim,

toned and tan. I should have grabbed him and hiked into the
hills, never to return.

Jas and I double-team the suitcase and wrestle it down to
the car. Popping the hatch, we muscle it in and the car actually groans as it settles on its haunches.

"You're going to come back, right?"

"Yeah, sure." Maybe. I suddenly have a knot in my stomach. The July sun has already started to cook the morning.
My mother is over at the restaurant, Dad is fixing something,
the AC perhaps. Maybe I should say goodbye.

Or maybe I'm just asking for another round of questions.
I've decided that if my mother ever wanted to change ca-
reers, get out of baking award-winning Norwegian special-
ties, she'd have a stellar career as a CIA interrogator. She
knows how to put a person to the screws.

"I guess this is it," I say. I hug Jasmine. She holds on just a
little longer than I expected and when I pull away, I have to
squint, just a little, through the tears.

There are exactly five rest areas between Gull Lake and Des
Moines. I know because I also discovered that I have a bladder the size of an acorn.

I pull into Mission to the World HQ just as the sun is dip-
ping into the corn fields. Des Moines turns out to be flat-
ter—and hotter—than expected, and poor Stevie Subaru
(yes, I name my cars, but that is another story) has drunk
enough gas to put him in lock up to dry out for two weeks.
I leave him woozy and panting in the parking lot and go in
search of the office.

I have to say, I expected more. After all, the letter was written on linen stationary with a gold embossed return address

on the envelope and a multicolored return address stripe on the bottom of the letter in navy blue and gold.

But maybe they spent all their money on letterhead. Mission to the World is headquartered in a 28-by-40-foot aluminum-sided…shed? My uncle Bert has an identical building for his tractors. I trudge up a cement walk, surrounded on each side by semiwilting shrubbery and a bed of thirsty pansies. They nearly beg me for sustenance as I stumble forward.

I push open the door and a gust of glacial air hits me in the face. My nose reacts and pain makes my eyes water.

Correct above assumption. They spent all their money on letterhead and Sahara-strength air-conditioning. Gooseflesh rises on my bare arms as I turn toward the receptionist sitting at the front desk. I notice she's wearing a pink crocheted cardigan and her long white-blond hair is tied into a low bun. She looks about thirty-five and when she smiles, lines of what I hope is good humor appear around her eyes.

"May I help you?"

"I'm Josey Berglund, and I'm here to meet with…with…" My eyes widen and I'm digging in my pockets for the letter, which I've folded and tucked, oh, please, somewhere accessible. "Dwight Wills."

"Just a moment." She picks up the telephone and five minutes later I'm sitting in Dwight's cubicle. Everyone in the building has cubicles. Dwight leads me down a maze of turns and twists and back alleys to the very bowels of the building where I am offered a metal folding chair. Shouldn't they have blindfolded me first? Is this a good or bad sign?

On his sixties-era desk sits a family picture. A tall, lanky boy and a little girl in ringlets. His wife is thin, and her smile seems tired. Dwight sits down and I realize he's aged, a lot, since the picture. Rail-thin, his hairline is defecting from his forehead leaving behind a smattering of age spots. He's wearing a dark green cardigan—I guess that's the uniform around here. I'm wishing I had a cardigan as the fine hairs on my arms stand on end. I think I've lost feeling in my (still unpolished) toes.

"So, Ms. Berglund. You made it okay. Thank you for taking the time to travel down to Iowa. We have quite a weekend planned and I hope you will enjoy it as we get to know one another." He folds his hands on his desk blotter. I notice it is neat. No doodles. To his left on a tiny table, a black Corona typewriter indicates a nod toward the twentieth century. This, I think, is good, but I'm giving myself kudos for not bringing the black skirt. See, I can be a missionary. I can be conservative.

I cross one leg over the other (mostly in an attempt to stay warm, but it also looks relaxed) and begin to field his questions.

Why do I want to be a missionary? "I want to change the world, of course. I want to follow the Matthew 28 Great Commission."

Why Russia? "Because I've always been fascinated with the Soviet Union, and I want to help them in this new era."

How do I respond under pressure? I blink at this, just a second before I smile and say, "Well, I try and look for the positives. And of course I read my Bible." Which is true, but also sounds really, really good, don't you think?

Can I work on a team? "Sure, as long as I am the leader." Ha ha.

He's not laughing. Whoops. I stop laughing. "Of course," I say. "I think teams are essential to good ministry. Everyone has something to add."

Hey, that sounded pretty good. Where did I come up with that?

Tell me your testimony. Aha, I was prepared for this one. I had to write it all out on my application, but long after I sent it in, I pondered this.

I admit my testimony isn't very flashy. Born into a church-going family, baptized at age twelve, went on a short-term mission trip once to inner-city Minneapolis. Mostly I remember learning to play the guitar, spending a lot of time braiding hair and friendship bracelets, and sleeping on a church pew. "I'm hoping I get a real bed in Russia," I say. Again, no laughter. What's the deal? I'm really funny, doesn't he know that?

I fold my hands in my lap and I'm wondering if they turned the temperature up because my hands are sweating. Dwight has dark inscrutable eyes.

This is where my testimony really picks up speed, and for a second I wonder if I should gloss over the two years where I chucked religion into the street, opting for the party life. But, this may be important, so I sum up. "After high school, I spent about two years wondering if my parents' faith belonged to me. I admit, I did a few things I wasn't proud of." Wow, I got a hint of a smile with that confession. I lean into my story. "In fact, I'm pretty sure I wouldn't be alive right now if God hadn't intervened."

He nods, and his expression gentles. Maybe Skin-and-Bones has a past of his own.

"I guess it was in my junior year that I hit the wall. I got depressed and wondered why we were all here. What is the meaning of life?" Good grief, I sound like Forrest Gump. Life is like a box of chocolates....

"I guess God used that emptiness to remind me that when

I was following Him, I didn't feel so empty. I felt useful and whole. And by this time I was keenly aware of my sins—"

He chuckled! It was small and guttural, but I definitely heard it. I smile, wipe my palms on my pant legs and lean back.

"So I asked God to refresh my life. Forgive me of my sins and help me be His girl." There. Done. That wasn't so painful. Not quite as eloquent as the application, but it did have inflection, and angst. And I made him laugh.

So, did you find the meaning of life?

Arrgh! Blindsided! Dwight and my mother—partners in the CIA! I'm suddenly feeling tired, desperately hungry and fat. "Um…well…"

He smiles, as if he didn't really expect an answer and rises from his desk. I hear his knees crack. "I think that is enough for today. Why don't you head over to the barracks and settle in."

The word "barracks" hits me like a two-by-four and I barely make it to my feet.

He puts his bony hand on my shoulder and I'm suddenly wondering if he arrived here fat and full of humor ten years ago and they slowly sucked it from his unwitting soul. The receptionist is gone. As is everyone else. We go through the door into the heat and it nearly scoops the breath out of my chest. Please, God, let the barracks be air-conditioned. To my happy discovery I see that the pansies are wet and glistening. I have a feeling the receptionist cares.

I somehow wrestle my bag out of the car while Dwight watches. He doesn't offer to take it, but then again, I'm doubting he can carry it. Thankfully it has little wheels and I trolley it down the sidewalk, around the back and down a cement trail to another long shed. There is a teeter-totter and a rusty swing set out front, and a giant plastic turtle holding sand set off to the side. The lawn has been recently mowed, and the smell is fragrant and reminds me of home.

"We have two families staying here at the moment, going through the application process. The walls are thin, but I don't think they'll bother you."

Walls? Phew.

The barracks are air-conditioned and redolent with the smell of cleanser, which I take as a good sign. I tread down a brown, carpeted hallway, grateful there are no stairs, and he opens the door to a numbered room.

Inside is a twin bed covered in an orange bedspread, a small dresser, a chair and a darkened bathroom.

No television. So how am I going to keep up with the *Lost* gang?

"Get some sleep. We'll see you in the morning." Dwight smiles at me, not showing teeth, and closes the door behind him.

Dwight is not the warmest coat in the closet. I dig out a romance novel (see? handy), plug my earphones into my MP3 and listen to Point of Grace. I'm not real hungry, having eaten a bag of Cheetos—the crunchy kind—on the way down. But that was the only thing I consumed, so maybe I'll lose a pound by the morning. I flop onto the bed and the last thing I do before diving into my book is put Chase's picture on the bedside stand.

Just as a reminder.

The competition is wearing dresses. Oh, boy, am I in trouble. I know their names, even without meeting them because the walls aren't thin. They're rice paper. They're vapor. Thank you, but I didn't need to know how Ken's stomach was feeling this morning, nor did I need to hear Janice tell Junior to make sure he goes tee-tee before they leave.

Come to think of it, that was actually a good reminder.

And now I'm standing in the barracks lobby in my really cute capri jeans, a sleeveless pink tank and friendly mules, rubbing my arms as I realize I am way, way, *way* out of my depth.

I follow the crew as we hike over from the barracks to the office. It's always good to survey the contenders. Here's the rundown: Janice and Ken Moose and little Ken junior from Belleview, Nebraska. And Patty and Bruce Abramson and their three precious daughters (all right, I did mean that sarcastically, but truthfully, they are kind of cute, in their blond pigtails, flouncy dresses and white patent shoes) from Wyoming, Minnesota.

Mission HQ is serving us breakfast in the lounge, a plate of fresh fruit, granola bars and yogurt. I was kind of hoping for low carb, but I grab a banana and find a place at the U-shaped table. We spend the first hour in Bible study and, wouldn't you know it, I left my Bible in the barracks. Well, nobody told me we were going to use it. I know, I know, some missionary I'm going to make. I sneak out after the Bible study, race down to the barracks, grab it off the desk and return sweaty and hungry. The cheese and strawberries on the snack tray are gone. Figures.

We then spend about four hours on the history of Mission to the World. I find out they have missionaries all over the world, most of them teaching English, but many helping plant churches and some in medical missions. Would that, by any chance, include doctors? I raise my hand and ask if there are any in Russia.

None, of course.

We break for lunch and I take my milk, whole-wheat sandwich and chips over to the Moose table. After all, I already know about Ken's stomach problems. I figure I have insider information.

I find out that Janice is nurse, Ken has a Ph.D in missions and little Junior (age 4) can already say all the books of the Bible as well as a wide repertoire of verses. I'm feeling trumped—a heathen, basically—as we take our places for the afternoon sessions.

While we're learning strategy of missions, we're called, one by one, like patients in a dentist's office, out of the room. It's piqued my interest and I'm having trouble focusing, waiting to see how the victims return. My blood pressure rises just a bit (or maybe that is my sugar level dropping) when Patty returns with mascara treads down her face.

They call me next.

I follow the receptionist (whose name is Lisa, by the way) through the maze until we stop at yet another conference room. She smiles but reveals nothing about my fate as she opens the door.

I feel like a convict meeting the parole board. Before me, behind a long table, sit five souls who will decide my fate. I see Dwight at the far end, looking tall and pasty and he gives no flicker of recognition. A white-haired woman near the center, her wire rims on a chain and resting on a bosom that annihilates my visions of mission-induced starvation, is flipping through a folder. It is a fat manila folder containing nearly a ream of paper—no, that can't be my…it is! I recognize my picture paper-clipped to the top. Yikes. Everyone has a folder. They've been studying me. Like an insect. Like a gypsy moth. Learning my habits, delving into my past.

These people know more about me than my own mother does. (Actually, there is some relief in that thought.) Still, my breath is thick, rapid. Or maybe that is the air conditioner, which hums in the corner. Since there is a folding chair in the middle of the room I walk over, sit down, cross my legs. Force a smile.

Dwight stands, as if suddenly he's figured out that yes, he talked to me yesterday. In fact, we had a riveting conversation and I even made him laugh. He's smiling as he introduces me. "We're glad you could join us today," he says to me as if I had a choice.

"This is the review board," he continues. (See, I told you!) "Marilyn Chadder, our review chairman," (he points to the woman perusing my darkest secrets) "Todd Benedict," (short, wide—think: Danny Devito) "JoAnn Bush," (now, I could like her. She has long brown hair and black wire rims. I have the feeling that if I look under the table, she'll be wearing Birks.) "and Frank Bemouth. He's in charge of our psychological review."

Dwight sits down as my eyebrows go up. Yes, I remember filling out that psych test, but we're actually going to talk about it?

Frank clears his throat and I grip the seat of my chair. In my defense, I should speak up and tell them that a few of the questions on the test they gave me just didn't make sense. Like, "Do you feel like people are watching you?" If I answer yes, it makes me paranoid, but a no makes me naive. Or maybe, "Are you often afraid of touching doorknobs?" How often and what kind? A little elaboration would have been nice. I didn't even think when I answered yes on "Do you sometimes wish you were a person of the opposite gender?" I'm not going to explain why, it just felt right.

The one I pondered a long, long time was "Do you fear falling off cliffs that aren't there?" Well, if they weren't there, the question wouldn't come up, would it? But if the cliff felt like it was there, then it would be reasonable not to want to fall off it, right? At what point do I realize the cliff is delusional, and if I do, do I stop fearing falling off? And is just seeing the cliff a sign that I'm delusional? Or is the fear of falling delusional? That seems sane to me. I answered no, but it still haunts me.

"Josey, you seem like a well-put-together young lady with a lot of depth and maturity," Frank says.

I like this Frank fellow. He reminds me of Harrison Ford. Brown hair, soft eyes, sort of a tenderness wrapped up in uncertainty. I smile at him.

"But the one thing we see lacking in your application is a definite sense of calling."

Calling? Calling who?

He leans forward, his lips are pursed and he nods like this is a real problem. I don't recall making any calls since arriving, although I would have done so on my cell phone. They can't trace that, can they? Can they read my need to call in the cliff question? Maybe it was a metaphor for leaping out and waiting for someone to answer—

"We just don't see a passion to serve the Russian people." He's nodding again. "Josey, has God called you to serve Him in Russia?"

I love my cell phone. I got it on special in Minneapolis at a cell phone kiosk in the Mall of America and found a cover that has daisies in multicolors. I sometimes hang it from neck gear, but it also has a snap that I clip to my purse. I play games on it, change the ring tone every month and have my entire list of friends on it, in speed dial. H is #3. Chase is #2, although I very rarely call him, but the most important person, the big dog, my very best friend for life, is #1.

She might have married the guy I loved/thought I loved, but she's still my confidant, and the one person I turn to in times of serious trouble. And I definitely feel like I'm in it up to my ears right now.

"They asked you if you had a calling?" Jasmine asks.

Oh, good, she sounds as incredulous as I felt sitting there, gaping at the parole board. I stammered something about wanting to help the Russian people, but I felt scooped out and raw, and it took all my Minnesota nice not to run screaming from the room.

The afternoon dragged out in agonizing microseconds. I choked down lasagna for dinner (I've lost track of the carbs) and, at the moment, I'm missing comfort popcorn and a showing of *The Princess Bride*. Which attests to my need. Anybody want a peanut? Oh, I'm sorry, I can't help it. The words, "I mean it," out of my mother's mouth got me grounded more often than I truly deserved.

"So, don't you have a calling?" Jas asks, bringing me back to the inadequacies in my life.

"No, I mean, do you?"

"I'm not going to Russia."

I sit there in silence for a second, conjuring up a comeback. "Well, okay. But, do I have to have one? And what does it look like?"

"I dunno." I picture Jasmine sitting on the green floral sofa that used to take up space in my parents' living room. It is now in the apartment over the restaurant where she and Milton have set up housekeeping. Another place I will never again clean. "Have you ever seen *The Mosquito Coast?* About that guy who wants to bring refrigeration to the Indians in South America? Maybe it's like that."

Harrison Ford and River Phoenix. I always loved that movie. But I admit to thinking the Harrison character was downright nutso, even from the beginning. "No, I don't think that is it," I say quickly. Then I slow my words, roll the thought around in my brain. "I think it is something…more. It's deeper. In your gut. Or your soul. Something that you can't dodge. Something that you must do or you won't be able to breathe or look at yourself in the mirror. Something you'd regret forever if you ignore it. Maybe even something you've been thinking about all your life."

She's silent.

I have the weird sense I've answered my own question. Do I have this feeling? I close my eyes and feel around inside, checking every corner of my soul. No burning, but I do feel a simmer. Something alive.

"I'll call you back when I know," I say, all at once eager to explore this discovery.

"If you don't have one, will you be rejected?"

Rejected? Oh, ouch. They wouldn't, they couldn't…rejected? Who gets rejected as a missionary? "I gotta go, Jas. I'll call you later."

I lay there a long time, staring at the ceiling, testing out the feeling in my chest. Yes, definitely something. But is it a calling? A passion to serve?

I'm suddenly struck with the idea that this trip is about more than a change of pace. More than doing a cool and exotic thing for a year. It's not about architecture, or culture, or even cafés. It's not even about forgetting Chase.

It's about…eternal significance.

The feeling in my chest grows and I am suddenly on my

knees. I haven't spent a lot of time there since Jasmine's wedding, but maybe that's about to change. I bow my head, and in a voice that seems much smaller than I've ever heard it, I say, "Lord, I admit that I don't know what I'm getting myself into, but if You want me to go, I will." Wow, that feels freeing. And the warmth inside starts to sizzle. So, just to get a fix on exactly what this means…

"However, if You *do* want me to go, would You give me a calling? Something really loud and plain, too, because I'm not very good at listening." I take a deep breath, knowing there is more inside that needs to flush out if I want to do this missionary thing right. "And, while I'm down here, I might as well add that I'm sorry for being so angry at Chase. If he wants Buffy, well, just help me not to freak out. Help me to be happy for him. And most of all, Lord, do what it takes in his life to show him he needs You. Thanks and Amen."

I feel better. Lots better. I get off my knees and for the first time in over a month my chest doesn't ache. In fact, I feel good. Energetic. Thin!

I stroll down the hall to the unused bedroom where the gang is gathered watching *Bride*. Only, the movie is off and instead they're watching a documentary about Russia. I lower myself to the floor and am sucked into the story of believers suffering for the sake of the gospel, of new Christians finding hope and peace. Of families restored, communities changed.

My old-time missionary stories in rich Technicolor and Dolby sound.

The simmer inside me bursts to full boil. And with a gasp I realize that I do have a calling! I do! In fact, I've had it since childhood. Only now, I'm finally listening.

For we are God's workmanship, created in Christ Jesus to do good works, which God prepared in advance for us to do.

I can't wait to tell Dwight.

Chapter Four:
Going...going...

July 23rd

Dear Chase,
How's Montana? You're probably wondering why I'm writing. I mean, it's not like we've spent a lot of time in correspondence, but I can write, you know, since I'm a writer by trade, and well, I thought I owed you an apology. Or at least a congratulations.

So, congratulations on your upcoming wedding to Elizabeth. She seems nice.

I'm sorry we didn't get a chance to talk while you were in Gull Lake. I mean, about the Russia thing. The truth is, I was still trying on the idea for size, and didn't want anyone to talk me out of it. I know you were surprised, but after talking to H, I knew that I had to make a change in my life. Go after something...significant. I know that's hard to understand, but well, I thought long and hard about it, and to cut to the chase, I filled out the application. And, after a thorough (you have no idea) examination, I've been accepted by Mission to the World to serve at Moscow Bible Church.

I leave August 25th.

I know this is short notice. I haven't even told my mother yet, but I think probably this is for the best. Sorta like thinning eyebrows. Do it quickly and with a hard jerk and it hurts less. (Maybe you didn't need to know all that.) Anyway, I wanted you to know because, well, I might not make it back for your wedding (since I'm going for almost a year) and I wanted to tell you that I was very happy for you. And Elizabeth.

I'm at training camp right now. They presented us all with certificates and an invitation to go to "boot" camp, and I had visions of PT and weapons instruction. The only weapons-grade instruction I've gotten—in-between learning how to cut hair, how to recognize the symptoms of burn-out and a quickie course on beginning Russian—is learning the four spiritual laws in Russian and a book on "Russian culture for beginners."

Did you know that one of the staples is raw pork-fat soaked in garlic? It's called *Sala. That* will never touch my lips.

Anyway, because there is a shortage of Moscow Bible College teachers, they are fast-tracking my application and giving me a funding grant so I can leave quickly. I don't really know how to say this, except to just say it. Thanks for being my friend all those years. I wish you the best.

Josey

★ ★ ★

I sneak into town after midnight. Okay, so it isn't really sneaking. I guess I'd define sneaking as something attached to trouble. Like, for example, when I hid behind the wood-pile just a stone's throw from the Berglund house in tenth grade, waiting for Kip Minson's headlights to flash by on the service road that parallels our drive. The plan was for him to slide by, then circle around while I dashed out, Starsky-and-Hutch style, and dove for the car.

Who knew what would have happened after that? Kip wasn't only a senior, but a senior with a reputation embedded in his Metallica-shirt, black-boots, spiked-hair and chain-necklace persona. But he had a reputation for kissing well, and me, being the curious Berglund, had asked him for a ride to Lew Sulzbach's party.

I said curious, not smart.

The funny thing was, and I never really figured out how, Chase got the skinny from someone—maybe H—and guess who I found in the car when I flung open the door?

He could have knocked me over with a pine needle.

"Get in," he'd said, and something in Chase's voice told me that he wasn't afraid of Kip, nor impressed by my shiny black silk camisole and green camo pants. I quickly weighed my options…and decided Chase was a pretty good alterna-tive. Especially since he was just returning home from base-ball practice and wore his cute little smashed hat and grime on his face. Maybe, deep inside, I heard a tiny voice cheer-ing, but my curiosity meter was louder. Why would Chase care whom I tooled around town with? And, was there a free pizza in my near future?

As it turned out, the cops raided the party and I would have ended up in the clink. Two years too soon.

So, I guess I'm not really *sneaking,* but it feels that way as I roll past the dark library, the unlit Dairy Queen, the Red Rooster's dim night-lights on my way home from Iowa.

Maybe the sneaking part comes from the knowledge that I have a secret, one that I'm not quite ready to expose to Gull Lake. It felt weird enough telling Chase. On paper.

Or maybe I started with the hardest task first.

The Holiday station is open, and I debate cruising in, just for a current copy of *People,* but, since I'm going to have to learn to do without for the next year, I decide to bypass it. I'm fairly proud of my self-control. See, I can do this! I am a missionary!

There are going to be a plethora of changes over the next year. Evident from the fist-thick binder belted into the passenger seat. I step on the gas as I leave town and turn onto the gravel road that runs out to Berglund Acres. Rolling down the window, I let the air whip my hair. It smells of lake and pine and home.

The Conquering Hero(ine) returneth.

I have a certificate of acceptance in my bag in the trunk and about six more books, items of interest I picked up at the campus bookstore, all delving into the world of missions, from John Piper's *Let the Nations be Glad!* to *Bruchko* to *Operation World.* (Don't I sound prepared?) For some reason, receiving that eight-by-ten slip of paper felt better than when I got a callback for the senior play. As I shook Dwight's bony hand, then hugged all one hundred thirty pounds of him, I wanted to twirl in a circle like Julie Andrews and cry, "The hills are alive with the sound of music."

They liked me, they really, really liked me!

I even made friends with Janice and Ken and learned our fighter verse faster than little Kenny. (It helped that he couldn't read, but I didn't let that stop me from gloating. The kid needs competition, right?)

I am a *missionary*. I roll that word around a few times, and make myself three promises.

1. I will not, ever, dress in missionary barrel dregs nor tape my glasses in the center with duct tape.

2. I will not let the inflection of my mother's voice in any way make me feel like I've parted with my sanity.

3. I will not, even if I am stationed in Siberia, become so out of touch with relevant culture that I resort to singing songs by KC and the Sunshine Band or Styx. (But I am allowing myself cuts from Karen Carpenter now and then. She'll always be in fashion.)

I pull up to the Berglund Acres house, and sit there as the car ticks, reprimanding me for keeping him out so late. It's after 2:00 a.m., but I wanted to get home and begin packing for my new life.

The moon is full tonight and it turns the nearly still lake to sterling. I get out, let the cool summer air rake over my bare arms. I'm buzzing from the long drive and the hope inside me pushes me out to the lakeshore. I can feel change in the air, something fresh, something vibrant.

No, it's not the scent of fresh rolls from my mother's time-baked oven, it's my future. I can nearly taste it—full, sweet, quenching my hunger. It even slides into the empty crannies of my heart. I'm going to spend a year in Russia, teaching kids how to speak English, maybe even leading them to salvation.

Which means that my life matters, in the eternal scheme, right? I chew on that, let the flavors explode in my mouth. The wind rushes over me, a belated welcome that tangles my hair over my face and raises gooseflesh. Russia, it says.

I smile.

Oh, and the fighter verse that I slam dunked little Kenny on? Isaiah 43:18-19. *Forget the former things; do not dwell on the past. See, I am doing a new thing! Now it springs up, do you perceive it? I am making a way in the desert and streams in the wasteland.*

Is that a sign or what?

I don't even look at the darkened windows in the apartment above the restaurant, or ponder the look on Chase's face when he gets my letter.

Because I am a missionary.

Three killed and thirteen injured in Moscow blast
MOSCOW, (Reuters)

Three Muscovites were killed today when a gas line ruptured and ignited a four story apartment in central Moscow, officials said early this morning. Ludmilla Khakhaleva and Lena Rosivna were among the first victims, found still in their bedclothes, thirty meters from the blast site.

"The gas line was located just below their flats," said Gregory Borisovich, local firefighter. "It just blew them out of their home with the other debris."

Thirteen others from Kalenina 13 were treated for injuries as the building was evacuated. The three-alarm blaze took two hours to suppress.

The Stalin-era apartment had already been cited once for a leaky pipe, but Gasovaya officials claimed to have met the state requirements.

I find this news article, a printout from www.theMoscowTimes.com, on my bed as I return home from a grueling day of reporting on produce supplies at the local farmer's market. It's the third such article I've received in the last three weeks since returning home from Camp Make-Me-A-Missionary.

I might have mentioned earlier that my mother would make an outstanding CIA interrogator. I can even picture her, dressed in black leather, her blond hair greased back, leaning close and whispering into a victim's ear with her flat Midwestern accent, "Give in, we're only trying to help." I'm telling you, the woman has crafty down to a science. She's prowled through my past, found my Achilles heel and hauled out the heavy artillery.

The article is especially underhanded on account of Uncle Albert and his cat, Boots.

Uncle Albert, actually a great uncle, owns a farm outside Gull Lake. He's single, which is evident by the assorted farm machinery scattered around his property like lawn art (Myrtle would be so proud). Last fall he parked a manure spreader by the road. Sorta like a sign, just in case we're lost and need a pointer to the Berglund Farm. Just follow the John Deere.

Uncle Albert lives in a trailer awkwardly set up on four big blocks and shadowed by his 36-by-120-foot, four-story barn. I think he'd rather live in the barn, but since the trailer was a present from his parents (which makes it much older than me), he surrenders for the sake of good PR. He refuses, however, to give into the decorum of bathing.

But we won't go there. The important snippet in all this is Albert's mouser, Boots, a fluffy thing he found under his woodpile. Albert took a liking to Boots, maybe because it could live inside the trailer with him and still make him feel like he lived with the animals. I liked Boots, too, only for different reasons.

He had four white paws and lots and lots and lots of fur. And he looked adorable in my pink crocheted baby bonnet.

Okay, I'm getting sniffly. See? My mother's evil worked. CIA, CIA.

In the summertime, when Albert gave into the desire to live in the barn (due to the cool recesses of the hay loft versus the relative furnace of his trailer), Boots lived under the trailer. On July 23, 1988, the day I got my headgear (another topic I don't want to discuss), Boots was curled up beneath the step, when the propane tank, probably leaking due to a rusty fitting, exploded.

My mother and I happened to be driving to Uncle Albert's place to deliver a box of yesterday's Bismarcks. I was suffering under heavy gloom over my impending iron mask, when the entire trailer went *Boom!*

Fire shot into the sky, and Mom slammed on her brakes. My mother's arm caught me across the chest as I flew toward the windshield.

And then we saw it. A streak of fire, racing across the field.

Boots. I watched in throat-choking horror as the animal ran until it collapsed. And there it died. A black smudge of fur and flesh.

I hurled. Then, I wept for days. And to this day, the words gas and explosion in the same sentence bring hives.

See, my mother is diabolical.

Sighing, I crumple the news article and throw it into the corner, next to the other two—an article about the growing Russian hepatitis epidemic and one about the rise of the communist party under Zhirinovsky.

I'm ruing the day I taught my mother to use the Internet.

Okay, so honestly, I expected some resistance to my declaration of defection. I mean, my mother's feelings about

Russia are woven with McCarthy hearings, air-raid sirens and taking shelter under her desk at school. (I would have raised my hand and asked the obvious—just what good was a desk going to do in the face of plutonium?) To an entire generation of people, the Cold War is still brewing and they're not buying this "democratic and free" Russia business. According to my mother, Russia is just waiting for a weak moment in our defense when they can inundate us with vodka and pickled herring. I told her that we could fight back with some all-butter *kringle*. Clog their arteries, raise their cholesterol.

She went back to kneading. And that's when things got really ugly.

She served lasagna.

I know it is a weakness to be enticed by food. Still, the smell blindsided me and drew me into its clutches.

"I wonder what you'll eat in Russia?" was all Mom said.

I admit to crying myself to sleep to visions of pork fat and moldy potatoes.

Good thing I stocked up a bit at dinner.

The thing is, I thought she'd be happy. Scared, yes, but still, how many mothers can say their daughter is a missionary?

Or maybe, that word rolling off my mother's tongue during her weekly bridge club isn't quite so easy. I wonder if it is followed up with words like, *Nunnery. Celibacy. Poverty.*

Where was that article again?

I toe off my sandals and sprawl on my bed, listening to the fan whir. I've decided to use Jasmine's bed as Packing Central, and on it, the pages of a few dozen books flap, as if saying, *pick me, pick me.*

I fling my arm over my eyes—ew, that doesn't smell so good. I sit up and pull off my shirt and skirt, grab a towel and exit into the bathroom. While I sit on the edge of the tub, adding in bath beads and listening to it fill, I hear Myrtle's whine join my mother's predictions of gloom. *"Where will I get another staff writer?"*

Uh, hello? Try the local fourth-grade class? I'm sure my second-niece-twice-removed, Valerie, can figure out how to retype Tipsy McKeever's recipes into the computer. I swirl my hand in the water. It comes out soapy. Sweet.

So maybe I'm being too rough on Myrtle. It's kind of endearing that she is angry. Maybe I should read between the lines of, "How could you leave me?" and "You know, you won't have a job waiting for you when you return," to the truth. She'll miss me. And, deep down, she thought I'd be her replacement in life.

Whew! I barely escaped the lawn art.

That thought pushes the only smile I've had in days up my face. I strip and get in the tub and let the bubbles slick away the remains of another scorcher in Gull Lake.

I sink down to my chin, doubts suddenly tightening my stomach. So far, I'm three for three. My mother thinks I've turned to the dark side. Myrtle believes I've left her for greener pastures, and Jasmine...well, Jasmine looks like a deer caught in the headlights. Big eyes, frozen.

Good grief, I'm not moving to Pluto.

Still, as I run over the to-do list in my head, I'm starting to wonder.

1. Get passport. Say it with me. Passs-port. Not long ago, I ran that word through my brain a few dozen times and bought into the glitz of it, conjuring up embassy events and caviar. The ticket to a new life. The Passs-port to adventure. Here's the unadulterated truth: I got the pictures taken at Jack's Hardware, in between the lawn and

garden department and plumbing supplies, standing against a grimy wall that used to hold the display of lures. My father picked up the pictures on his way home from purchasing a new bathroom plunger. I look like a refugee from Macedonia in my sweaty white shirt and tousled (and I'm being nice) hair. So much for glitz. Note to self: when encountering the exotic, keep expectations fluid.

2. Hepatitis shots. Yes, *shots.* As in long needles inserted into…fleshly places. I found out that the clinic in town will suffice, with sufficient advance notice. And I have to go back not once, but twice. My…you know where still hurts and if Myrtle makes another comment about why I'm sitting on a heating pad, someone is going to get hurt.

3. Pack. This one I expected, but the list MBC gave me is a little…sparse? Clothing, Toiletries, Bible. That's it. Yes, I know, I was pretty surprised myself. I mean, a girl's gotta live. I thought, how about my I'm-not-sure-what-I-want-to-read-so-I-have-to-have-it-all book supply? What about my CDs (Thank goodness for my MP3 player!) and most importantly, no where on that list does it mention my insulated silver coffee mug, the first season of *Lost* on DVD or my cell phone.

That will work over there, right? *Right?*

Actually, the sparseness of the list isn't the most jaw-dropping aspect of the packing expectations. The thing that is most disturbing, is, well, I can hardly bear to say it…I can only bring one suitcase. *One.*

Yes. Now I know why Dwight is so thin. He wasn't allowed to bring with him a year's supply of chocolate chips, Werthers caramels and hot chocolate mix. I decided to lump them in with Toiletries, under "medicinal." But one suitcase? What about my shoes?

I swish the washcloth around through the bubbles, watching them catch and foam. The bath is alive with tiny hisses as the bubbles fold into themselves. Outside, I can hear sparrows calling out the twilight hour. And downstairs, my mother is probably making…oh, something particularly sneaky, like…chocolate-chip cookies. She'll probably even leave the bowl out for me to lick.

Doesn't the Bible talk about being on our guard for the attack of the evil one? I'm sure Paul didn't consider chocolate-chip cookie dough.

The thing is, I haven't found this leaving thing particularly difficult. I'm nearly buzzing with excitement, and it's only dimmed by the fact that Chase hasn't written back.

Not that I expected him to, but it would have been… Oh, who am I kidding? Chase and I are kaput. A guy can't be friends with the girl from the sandbox when he's marrying an Amazon. Besides, I wished them well.

And sort of meant it.

Funny how a girl can smell "liar, liar pants on fire," while immersed in fifty gallons of bubbly water.

I sink into the tub, wet my hair, scrub it good. When I emerge, there's knock at the door. My crazy heart leaps right out of my chest. So, not good to be thinking about Chase in the bath. "Yes?" I say. It's not like I'd let him in, but still, what if he's returned for me—

"It's me, Jas. Can I come in?"

Okay, I admit, I'm a modest person. And it has nothing to do with too many bagels hiding on my hips. Although I'm under bubbles, there's something about being naked that feels, well, naked.

I pull the curtain so only my eyes are showing. "Enter," I say causally.

Jasmine cracks open the door. "Hey ya," she says and scoots in to sit on the toilet. "I have an idea."

One that couldn't wait until I was dressed? "Yes?" I ask, however, because I hear the ticking clock. Seven days until I leave.

"I think we should throw you a goodbye party." She smiles, but it doesn't quite reach her eyes. Bless her, she's trying.

I grab the peace offering like a starving widow. "That sounds great! I'd love it." I begin mentally ticking off the people I'd like to invite, but only one name blazes through my mind.

I'm hoping once I cross the ocean, the waters of distance will extinguish this burning pain inside.

"I'll get right on it." Jasmine leans forward and braces her elbows on her knees. "Maybe Milton and I will come and visit you."

Oh, that would be swell. I duck behind the curtain. "Yeah."

"But, you know, we're trying and all, so I'm not sure."

Trying? Trying for what? A sick feeling in my chest replaces the Chase-induced inferno.

I peek back around the curtain. "Trying to—"

She reddens. "You know. Get pregnant."

Okay, over-sharing. Did. Not. Need. To. Know. That. Or, the accompanying mental picture.

"Right," I say. The bath is getting cold and I need to get out. "That's great." But it isn't great. So isn't great. Somehow, deep inside, I knew this time would come, and that I'd be the single, dumpy aunt saying, "Sure, I'll babysit," while I peruse issues of *Crochet Today* and *Lawn Art for the New Millennium.*

I'll be Myrtle.

Oh, joy.

"I gotta get out, Jas," I say, and I'm meaning more than the bath.

"Sure," she says and gets up, moves toward the door, her head down, smile gone. Suddenly I'm feeling petty and cheap. As well as chilled to the bone.

"Jas," I say, "I'm really happy for you and Milton. And, well, I'll be praying that everything goes well."

And, as I say the words, I mean it, too.

She smiles, and this time it comes from inside. "You're going to do great in Russia," she says as she leaves.

I run more hot water, linger longer, letting those words work into my wrinkled, softened skin.

You are cordially invited to:

A going away party!
Come and wish Josey Berglund luck as she traverses the ocean for a year in Russia.
When: 7:00 p.m., Friday August 24
Where: Berglund Acres
No R.S.V.P. needed.

Fourteen hours and thirty-seven minutes. I'm tying red balloons across the porch railing. Jasmine thinks it's a hoot that she picked red and white, the colors of Russia as the theme for this event. My mother doesn't. I'm ambivalent, my mind on more important things like, will customs notice that I have two suitcases, and if they do, which one will I send home?

C'mon, you didn't really think I'd leave for a year and not take all my foot attire options?

I did mange to whittle the books down to thirteen. Including my Bible. That's one book a month. Let it not be said that I can't sacrifice for the Lord. I also managed to squeeze in the new Kim Hill CD, and the latest from Avalon, Sara Groves and Point of Grace.

Of course, I'm keenly aware that Chase hasn't called, written or e-mailed. It's like the residue of ache after a long-healing wound. But I'm not thinking about it.

Not.

H, at least, is on my side. She's IMed me twice. I guess I've inspired her or something. In my wildest dreams.

"Josey, can you grab the streamers? I left them on the kitchen table."

Jasmine looks fabulous. She's not only charged like a rhino into this idea but embraced it. She's made a Red Velvet cake for the occasion, and eight dozen chocolate-chip butter cookies with red food coloring. I've already stuck a dozen into my carry-on. Just in case I get hungry between here and JFK Airport.

Milton has kept his distance (smart man), but today he's outside, setting up chairs, heating the charcoal. They're having shish kebabs, and from the looks of it, expecting a packed house. I think they're overestimating my popularity. Or rather, they're keenly aware of the lack of entertainment this close to Labor Day weekend in Gull Lake.

The sky is azure, with only a few clouds, and sunlight bedazzles the lake as it laps the shore. Ducks check out our shoreline and, farther out, a handful of fishing boats dip and bob in the water, their outlines suggesting tranquility.

I run into the house and grab the streamers. Jas tells me to wrap them around the banister while she hangs a sign. I watch it go up and a funny feeling curls through my heart. "Good Luck, Josey," the sign reads in big blood-red letters.

It brings me back to the closing ceremony of boot camp. The Moose family on one side of me, the Abramson family closing ranks behind me, we stood like knights before the king and were commissioned. I had gooseflesh as Marilyn Chadder, the Review Board chairman said, "Therefore go and make disciples of all nations, baptizing them in the name of the Father and of the Son and of the Holy spirit…and surely I am with you always, to the very end of the age."

Those words send another chill through me as I tie streamers around the banister. I have a feeling that any success I have in Russia will have nothing to do with luck.

And I do want to succeed. Yes, it's true, in my mind's eye, I see parades at my homecoming, a news article. Maybe a Josey Day. Okay, that might be going too far, but at the least, hushed, awed whispers…

"Did you hear what Josey did there? She led an entire school of youngsters to Christ. And not only that, but wiped out poverty and suffering."

Lara Croft meets Mother Teresa! But, in the snippets of reality, I can confess that I'm not hoping to change more than my allotted portion. Still, I've just sold Steve, quit my job, given my news chair to Karen, my eighteen-something replacement (I told you, Myrtle just had to troll the local high school. Which says what about my abilities? Arrgh!), and written my will. I am the poster child for Commitment.

Oh, rewind to the will thing. Yes, I was more than a little taken aback when Dwight called and told me that I had to have one. As if I had personal assets. Still, it gave resonance to this adventure, a sort of solemnity that made me walk the beach at least twice before entering Bill Dejong's law office.

I have a will. Oh, and I left everything to Jasmine. Just in case the trying works. (See, just give me a little time and

I can be magnanimous. It's not all about me. It's not all about me.)

Milton has fired up the grill. The smell tweaks my stomach, but I am determined not to eat before the guests arrive. Besides, that cinnamon roll I had an hour ago hasn't completely digested yet. I know I probably shouldn't have surrendered, but I keep reminding myself that I won't have a decent pastry for another year.

Okay, yes! I admit it. I've let the "last time" mantra man-handle my self-control. Doesn't mean it isn't true. Good-byes are cluster bombs on the waistline. Still, like I said, I plan on losing all this goodbye debris once I land on Russian soil.

I dash upstairs to peruse the remnants of my closet. On my bed, my overstuffed Teletubby suitcases (I found a reddish orange one in the bottom of my mother's closet, and it matches the poppy dress quite nicely) contain the smashed bulk of my wardrobe. I've even flung wild hope into the wind and purchased three sizes of straight-leg Gap jeans, anticipating the need for apparel during the "acclimation to Russia" process.

I fully intend to return svelte and a size six.

Okay, maybe a ten. Uh-oh, I'm hearing parades again.

Sadly, my leather skirt hangs limply in the back of the closet. Right next to the two bridesmaids dresses and the poppy floral dress. I hope Jas doesn't see it. I packed my jean skirt, my capris and my cardigan sweater sets, going for a conservative look.

Which leaves me with two options for tonight's barbecue. My khaki "oh-she-has-hips!" pants. Or…the fruit skirt.

Yes, I said fruit. Two days ago, my mother got desperate. As if defecting to my side (hello, like I wouldn't recognize

Bad Cop, Good Cop?), she went to the Goodwill and purchased nearly everything in my size.

Discolored blouses. Unraveled brown knit vests. A pair of khaki culottes that made the khaki pants look like a slenderizer.

And a fruit skirt. Prairie style, with three tiers of hemming and lots of flounce. The most, ah, *stunning* aspect is the pattern. Plums. Apples. Pears. Large ones decorating the skirt like bounty from heaven.

I think she's pushing the "poverty" part of the missionary definition. She doesn't know about the will and my many assets, however. Someone who stands to inherit (as the second beneficiary) $3,542 in cold hard cash should learn to kiss up a little.

The sad part about my mother's flanking move is that the fruit skirt is actually slimming. Maybe because of the sheer volume at the ankles. It sucks in my waistline and shows off everything north without me looking like I'm trying too hard. I wadded Mom's Goodwill bribe into a bag and dumped it off at its source.

But I kept the fruit skirt. Just for…naked moments when I need to feel thin.

I shouldn't…I mean…today isn't…

I reach for the skirt, a wild hair twining through my spirit. With a giddy smile, I pull it on. And like magic, there goes the cinnamon rolls, and Jas's oh-so-excellent *kringle*.

I pull on a short sleeve red shirt (hey, I'm trying to be thematic) and brush out my hair. I have short, totally defiant blond hair that I've managed to tame, on a good day, with a blunt cut and a wide paddle brush. Today it is as lifeless as a rummy in a Minneapolis alley. I try putting it up with clips. Uh, no.

Maybe pigtails? I part my hair, pull it back into two stubby tails.

Perhaps no one will show up. It's not like I was homecoming queen. In fact, I distinctly remember *not* being a cheerleader. It's a wound I still carry. I mean, wouldn't I have made a great cheerleader? Bouncy…in so many verbal and visual ways.

I make a face into the mirror, check my watch. 6:52 p.m. As usual, I've left the important details, like hair and makeup, until the last moment.

But this night is about the new Josey. The Josey not shackled to her past, or her appearance fears, or even her daydreams of men in Montana. Besides, I sorta look cute. In an Uma Thurman meets Laura Ingalls kind of way.

And, most importantly, I'm kicking the dust off this town tomorrow. I'm not trying to impress anyone. After all, I'm a missionary. We're above all that.

I shove my feet into a pair of open-toed red nubuck-leather slides I've had in my closet begging for use, and tromp down the stairs.

My mother raises one eyebrow, gives a tentative smile and disappears into the kitchen.

I go outside and am fairly shocked to see a growing multitude of admiring guests. Or maybe they're just hungry because they're gathered around Milton and the grill. Still, I attract some attention as I let the porch door bang shut behind me. I see Myrtle and Uncle Albert (who hasn't taken a shower, but changed overalls, an act I count as a real gift). And there is my pastor, Kevin Peterson, and his sweet wife, Mary, who wave. They're real proud of me. I know because every once in a while, he looks at me in the middle of a sermon and smiles. Or is that a grimace?

Tipsy McKeever is leaning over Milton's shoulder, perusing the marinade. Three of our Berglund Acres guests are also here (I'm assuming this because they don't look familiar). All seem focused on the smell of grilling meat.

And next to them…

I gasp because my heart has done a double flip with a half gainer and landed in the dirt at the bottom of the steps, taking my lungs along with it.

Chase.

Chapter Five:
Benny and Bagels

Chase Jordon Anderson, what are you thinking? Where have you been? Not a word, not one word from you all summer, even after I wrote you a heart-wrenching letter, at least from my perspective, and you show up twelve hours and thirteen minutes before I leave town? *Do you think I'm that easy?*

This is what I say to Chase *in my mind*. In reality, I'm still standing slack-jawed watching him saunter up to me with a half grin hello on his face. Oh, he looks good, too, back in that faded good-old boy attire and a Gull Lake Seagulls sweatshirt on, fraying threads where the arms once were. The boy still has his football muscles! He's got a two-day growth of reddish blond whiskers and his eyes, oh, his eyes. Am I breathing yet? I must be. But my heart has done a full stop.

"Hiya," he says.

Words? Words? I'm a *writer*. C'mon!

"So, you're really leaving me." He says it with a chuckle, touching his can of root beer to his chest, as if his heart is breaking. Oh, he smells good. Cologne with a hint of boy-who-played-football-recently. He's been in town at least three hours, evident by the grass stains on his jeans. I wonder...does Amazon girl know Chase that well?

Don't answer that.

"Uh," I finally manage. I sound like a caveman. Dressed in fruit. I want to swear, out loud, but I'm pretty sure a missionary doesn't do that. "Yeah."

"You look...cute. Is this your new Serving God attire?"

Honest, I'm really not a cursing girl, even without the Missionary label, but right now, I'd make Eminem tremble. Why, oh, why did I give in to the fruit skirt? I don't suppose God would just do me the favor of striking me dead. Right. Now. And, after the blue streak that just went through my head, I probably deserve it.

"Want a shish kebab?" Chase glances toward Milton and the grill. The smell wafting my direction makes my stomach clench, but if I eat anything I'm going to hurl.

I do, however, recognize an opportune moment, and search the crowd for the Amazon.

Nada.

Chase turns back. "You okay?"

Feeling better by the moment. "Yeah. I guess I'll get a soda." I sound casual, don't I? I swing over to the cooler, pick out a dripping Snapple and hold it away from me. Don't want to drip on the fruit skirt. "So, where's... um..." Oh great, now I really did forget her name, and I sound—

"We broke up."

My hand is on the Snapple top as he says it, and it not only gives, but spews brown liquid into the air, neatly spraying both Chase's sweatshirt and my skirt.

So I'm a bit shocked. And now he knows it. "What?" Oh phooey, I didn't mean for that to sound so…hopeful.

He shrugs as he wipes his sweatshirt. And I see the faintest hint of red. "Let's just say that after visiting Gull Lake, she wasn't all that impressed."

Ah, hence the discarded GQ attire. Oh, Chase, you weren't dressing to please, were you? Be like me! See, me, in a fruit skirt?

However, hurt flashes across his face. And somehow, it lands squarely in my heart. As if…he really cared about her.

I have this overpowering urge to hit someone. And now I know, without a blink of doubt, I could have taken her. One punch. Just one.

"I'm sorry, Chase. I thought you made a cute couple." Oh, gag. But, it's for Chase. And he rewards me with a sly smile.

"No, we didn't. She wasn't my type."

I quickly slurp down my Snapple before I launch myself onto that lead-in with a cry of, "Who is, who is?" Because, deep inside, I can hear danger bells. Two months ago, the idea of kissing Chase felt…well, sorta like sneaking into an R-rated show. Fun for the moment, but not sure if I should be there. Today the idea feels like dynamiting a beaver's dam. Light the fuse and look out for falling debris. The explosion could be awesome…and then what? Marriage? Little Chasies running around a Gull Lake double-wide, or worse, a third-world village while I wash their nappies in discarded rain barrel? I. Think. Not. Which makes me wonder…if this is what the Loving Chase package contains, did I only want Chase because Buffy had him? Where was the girl who an hour ago couldn't wait to climb on a plane and start a new life?

"When did you get back?" I ask. I'm willing to give Chase

a chance, however, because, well, for a fleeting second I see those arms around me, and that slightly curved smile has to taste good, doesn't it? Besides, little Chasies would have that smile, too, and maybe I'd simply hire out for nappie help.

Bad, bad Josey. Chase has just broken up with his true love.

Except, he's back here, in time to see me off.

To Russia.

Off. To. *Russia.*

Pay attention!

"A few hours ago," he answers. (See, I told you!) "Are you hungry?"

Ravenous. But again, if I get near food, it's not going to be pretty. "You go ahead. I'll save you a place near the lake."

I watch him stroll over to the shish kebab stand, grab a skewer and return. He doesn't take a plate, just a napkin, and we sit down near the water. The smell of late summer and drying leaves tinges the air, and the sun has begun to frost the lake in kaleidoscope colors.

"I can't believe you're doing this," says Chase, offering me a piece of meat. I decline. "It's so—"

"Wild? Crazy?"

"Brave."

Oh. "Thanks. I just…wanted to do something different with my life. And well, when I was at Missionary Camp, I realized that maybe God's been preparing me for this since I was a kid. In fact, I've never been more sure about anything in my life."

If I tell myself that often enough, it'll take root. Right?

"That's really cool. I mean, you know God and I aren't exactly in that same place." He gives a self-deprecating laugh. "I have to admit, though, Jose, you're the last person who I thought would get religious."

I guess all those years riding the fence didn't help my reputation, huh? What do they say about a prophet not being welcome in her hometown? Still, this is the longest paragraph we've ever sustained about My Salvation, so I'm shooting my gaze skyward, hoping for magic words. I shrug, oh so casual (not at all holding my breath). "Well, maybe that just makes me more sympathetic to the lost." Hmm, I wonder if that is true. I hope so.

His smile dims. "I got your letter. Thanks. You're a better friend than I've been lately."

Now what does that mean? Still, I can't bear to reply, fear clogging my throat. What if I accidentally give away my heart and he runs off with it to…oh, I dunno—Tibet? Besides, again…is this attraction real, or just a jealousy thing?

"How long are you in town?" I ask and I realize I can hear my heartbeat in my ears. It sounds like footsteps, heavy and on the run from (or toward?) something.

"All year. I just landed a job teaching social studies at the Gull Lake high school."

Wait. Did he say, *All year?*

"That's great." There is so much lying going on in this conversation, I'm sure I've lost all credibility with God.

"Yeah, I've always wanted to teach, and this will be a great break, in-between projects. I just wish…" His voice trails off and he looks at me.

I, of course, am staring at him, hearing those footsteps in my ears, and now I know where they're headed. Right into his arms. I swallow, and meet his eyes.

"I wish you were staying, Jose." He gives a sheepish smile, his blue eyes nearly translucent as he lets me see emotion. "Stay," he says softly.

What's a girl going to do?

★ ★ ★

I know that going for advice to someone who hasn't had a boyfriend longer than six months at a time, and who doesn't see the need for celibacy before marriage, probably isn't the wisest thing. And, frankly, I'm not buying everything she says. But H has two things going for her at the moment.

1. She alone knows how I sweated after Chase's engagement.

2. She is online as I prowl my dark bedroom, fighting the what-ifs.

<GI> What if this is my only chance with him and I'm ditching it, forever?

<Wildflower> It's one year. That's not forever.

<GI> What if he is the perfect one for me?

<Wildflower> Then he's perfect and he'll wait.

<GI> What if he finds another woman?

<Wildflower> Then he wasn't the perfect one, was he?

Okay, she's making too much sense right now. So I lay it all on the line, bare my guts to H. It's a lot easier over the Internet.

<GI> What if I never find someone?

Big Pause. Big, Big Pause. *H!*

<Wildflower> What if you never find *you*?

Ah. I wince, however, aware that she's nailed the biggest reason why I can't stay. Because this adventure is bigger than Chase. And it's bigger than H's gold/brass ring, although she doesn't know it. It's about finding my place in God's scheme of things. It's about eternal significance.

About Calling.

<GI> Thanks H. I'll see you at the airport. And bring bagels.

Saturday, August 25
7:27 a.m. Depart—Minneapolis, St. Paul (MSP)
11:10 a.m. Arrive—New York-Kennedy (JFK)
Flight time: 2 hrs, 43 min.
Connection time: 1 hour, 20 mins
12:40 p.m. Depart JFK
Sunday, August 26
6:26 a.m. Arrive, Moscow SVO, Russia (SVO)
Flight time: 9 hours, 45 min.
Total Travel Time: 13 hours, 48 min

H is late. I'm standing at the security gate, surrounded by Jas, my mother and Milton (excuse me, why did he come?). Noticeably absent is Chase, but then again, why rub salt into the wound? Besides, we had to leave at 4:00 a.m., and well, the days of my throwing rocks at his window to wake him are over.

Still, I suppose that's better than throwing myself at his feet. I check my watch again, excitement humming under my fatigue. Here I am, not only flying over the ocean, but going to Russia. The land of the czars, of exotic bistros and ancient architecture. The land of the persecuted saints.

I'm going to persecute H if she doesn't show up soon.

One of the glaring inadequacies of Gull Lake is that we have no bagel shop. And my mother, for some reason that baffles me, refuses to make them. Which leaves me no choice but to pick up six or seven dozen every time I'm in the Cities and haul them back north, precut them and fill my mother's freezer.

It's a small price to pay for daily sanity.

And, well, I'm thinking I'm going to need some sanity the first few days in Russia. I'm not afraid to admit I'm into comfort food. I also packed a ten-pound bag of popcorn.

I listed them under vitamins.

"Honey, I think you have to go," Mom says, worry in her brown eyes. She looks haggard this morning, and it touches a soft place inside. She may sound like General Patton, but underneath she's a mother, sending her eldest daughter off to battle.

Maybe I'm being overdramatic, but I like that thought so we'll go with it. I know she doesn't understand the bagel fortification, and I pat her on the arm. "She'll be here. Don't worry."

"I just don't want you to miss your plane."

I'm not even going to address this show of concern, this sudden surrender. "Here she comes." I wave my arm to catch H's attention as she runs through the sliding double doors. Her hair is lime-green and black rims her eyes, neatly matching her uni-color attire. But she smiles warmly, my one-person fan club. I embrace her and she holds tight. "Sorry I'm late."

She hands me a crumbled brown bag of bagels. "I didn't know what kind to get, so I got a dozen, one of every flavor." Now, isn't that sweet?

"Thanks, H." I notice the bag is warm. I'm feeling a little tense—maybe I should have one now. But I put the bag inside my three-hundred-pound carry-on that is slowly separating my arm from my shoulder. Well, what was I supposed to do—predetermine what book to read on my billion-hour flight? I mean, I should be congratulated—I whittled it down to three novels. And two magazines. And one non-fiction book and—

Yes! Okay. I do plan on stopping by the bookstore as I stroll out to the terminal. Just in case.

"I guess it's time," says Mom again. What's with her? Suddenly I'm yesterday's buns, and she's parceling me out to the neighbors.

Jas has tears and I reach for her first. "If Milton gives you any trouble, you can always come live with me." She laughs. Milton reddens. I wink at him, though, and for a second, everything ugly between us shatters and only the love for Jas remains. It feels pretty good.

I move to my mother next. She holds me tight, and when she leans back, she has tears, too. "Take care of yourself," she says softly. I feel my throat tightening up, cutting off my breathing.

"'Bye, Mom," I say, but it sounds like my voice is in Ethiopia. A rush of panic slices through my veins. What if Mom, or Dad gets sick, or even, *dies* while I'm in Russia? What if Jasmine does get pregnant and I miss out on all the fun? What if Chase finds another Amazon girl, right in Gull Lake, someone who is willing to wash nappies in the river and follow him across the world?

Okay, that chance is slim, especially in Gull Lake, and that fact brings me back to reality, reboots my lungs. We have e-mail. We have IM. And, if God is especially generous, my cell phone will work.

"I'll write when I get there," I announce to the crowd.

Then, with a final smile that feels more Mona Lisa than happy, I add myself to the security line.

I'm immediately sucked into the Goodbye Vacuum. That place between warm goodbyes and actual departure. In Gull Lake, it is similar to the wave vacuum that occurs between passing vehicles. Wave too soon, and you're going to have to fill time inconspicuously, like checking if you have lipstick on your teeth in the rearview mirror. Or digging in your purse for gum.

Please, please just leave. I stand there, feeling their stares burning my neck. I glance back, give a small smile. My mother waves, though she is standing five feet away.

The line shifts; I move forward. *Leave!*

"Don't forget to write!" Jas says. I smile, nod. *Leave!*

Silence. More movement toward the checkout.

And then it begins.

"Did you remember your wool socks? You hate cold feet," my mother calls.

I grimace, smile at her, nod.

"What about your nasal strips? You know how you snore, and you don't want to wake your roommate."

I swallow hard, move forward. The guy in front of me glances over his shoulder, one eyebrow up. Yep, that's me the old lady is yelling at, Josey the Wheezer. I give Mom a *please, don't* look. But she's just trying to care, in her own special way.

"What about your Dr. Scholl's corn—"

"That's enough," I hiss through clenched teeth. I tilt my head, give my mother a tight smile. "I got it all, Mom."

But she has tears running down her cheeks and suddenly she rushes to me, leans over the black ribbon and grabs me in another squeeze.

Didn't expect that. And well, I forgive her on the spot for everything—the news articles, the Goodwill donation, the lasagna, even for shackling me with a curfew of ten o'clock the summer of my senior year (even if I did sneak back out once I checked in).

We disentangle just as the man in front of me vacates his spot. I can barely see, and I hike my carry-on/anvil into my arms.

My mother moves back to her troops and I don't look at them as I walk forward, plunk my carry-on onto the belt, unzip it and pull out my laptop. I stick that into another tray, saying a brief prayer for the hard drive, and toe off my shoes, putting them in another tray.

I don't look back as I walk under the arch. To my breath-snatching relief, it doesn't buzz.

I retrieve my shoes, laptop and bag (and nearly fall over when I put it over my shoulder—it takes a second or two to reestablish equilibrium), and when I look back, they're still there.

Mom has her arm around Jas. Milton has a wry expression. H is waving.

I take a deep breath, wave back.

It's this very last second that counts. The one I carry with me, as I trudge down the terminal and board the plane. The one I revel in over the next two hours (while consuming a blueberry bagel).

Shazam! Chase has appeared out of nowhere, and he is searching for me as he runs up to the group. Wearing his smashed baseball hat and a rumpled T-shirt, he looks haggard, as if he rolled out of bed a half hour after we left in a panic. (Yes!) H points me out and for a second our eyes lock. *Cha-ching.* I can hear the echo in my heart. He gives a solitary wave. And the barest of smiles.

Chase! *What am I doing—*

Then the guy behind me tries to scoot past me, jostling me. My carry-on crashes to the floor. Uh-oh…can anyone say laptop?

I scoop it up.

And when I stand up and look back, the magic has broken. They're regrouping. Turning away. *Leaving.*

Leaving?

Turncoats.

I swallow hard and shuffle down the gateway.

I've never been to New York City. I have two words to describe it as I look out the grimy windows onto the tarmac, waiting for them to call my next flight.

Big.

Fast.

And that's just between the Northwest wing and the Delta wing. I took a conveyor belt and stood there while people flew by me with their fancy rolling carry-ons.

I want a rolling carry-on. Nearly enough to stick out my foot and send one of those business travelers flying while I snatch the bag and run. My shoulder is bruised, my arm hanging like a dead walleye at my side.

I admit to feeling a slight bit of melancholy that I don't get to see the Big Apple. I would have enjoyed a day checking out Central Park, Broadway, the set for the *Today* show. Katie Couric always has good hair. Second benefit to living in Russia, right after starvation, is no beauty parlors. I'll grow my hair out, and no one will be around to see me in that "oh-my-*do*-something-with-your-hair, please!" stage. In my defense, I should interject that I had great hair in college. Straight and long and very Jennifer Aniston.

Then I sheared my hair close to my head during my

"professional"-look era and discovered that Halle Berry I am not.

I looked more like a Mexican hairless. Since then, it's grown out, given me a sort of haphazard, I-don't-care-what-my-hair-looks-like-because-I'm-a-hard-nosed-reporter look.

It was a bit difficult to pull off in Gull Lake, land of big hair and high volume VO5.

But now I'm a missionary, and well, we grow our hair long. It's part of that deprivation thing we're so good at.

I listen to people eat their R's around me, the dialect of the Apple in the ever present static of conversation. Digging out my cell phone, I call home, but it rings five times and I figure I must have beaten the convoy to our destinations.

Had I really seen Chase? I'm looking for confirmation from Jas, because deep inside, I'm a Doubting Thomas. It is not beyond my mind to conjure up, in a moment of emotional angst, Chase tracking me down at the airport in a last ditch, *Friends*-episode attempt to keep me from leaving.

Still, even if it was a dream, it was a nice one that makes my stomach feel warm and gooey. And not hungry. So, maybe it's good Jas isn't home yet.

They call my flight and I check my ticket. I'm in row 16, seat B. I'm hoping that isn't the middle. Across from me, an elderly couple rises, shuffles toward the gate. Maybe I'll get to sit by them. They'll sleep, maybe read a book. Maybe it'll even be a good book and I can read over their shoulder.

Or even better, maybe I'll end up with Matthew Fox over there, the one with short brown hair, lazy eyes, who's wearing a sharp brown suit. Sure, I could somehow pass twelve hours sitting next to Matthew.

See, what a loser I am. I'm supposed to be pining for Chase.

No, he's supposed to be pining for me.

Whatever.

Still, the thought tightens my chest. What if Chase does find his own curvy brunette in Gull Lake...and I'm in Russia, eating kasha because I threw away Matthew's business card after declining a night out at the Bolshoi, or a walk through Red Square under the lights of St. Basils all for the sake of Chase?

That Chase! How dare he do that to me? Matthew liked me, I know it. And we could have hit it off. Twelve long hours we spent together while Matthew, because he found my life fascinating, looked into my eyes and listened to my dreams of changing the world. And, because I am a missionary, he trusted. He poured out his heart to me, and told me that he'd just broken up with his girlfriend. The poor guy.

Yeah, well, I know the feeling, I said to him, noticing again his pretty eyes.

"Are you going?"

I hear a voice behind me, turn.

Grunge 'R' Us stands behind me, and I think it is a naturally acquired fashion when I catch a whiff of him. Dreadlocks, tie-dyed shirt, chains, torn pants dragging beneath his Birkenstock sandals. Please, let that be a tan on his feet....

I see Matthew moving into the gangway. Argh! So much for a chance meeting where my carry-on (sorry, Mr. Laptop) falls and wow, do I feel embarrassed, and that's okay, Miss, can I help you—

"Maybe I can just go around you?"

"Sorry," I mumble to Grunge and move forward, handing the flight attendant my boarding pass.

I wrestle the carry-on down the gangplank, greet the captain and troop of flight attendants, and then realize that the carry-on and I won't fit into the aisle together. I carry it in front of me like a birthday cake and nearly take out a woman in a hot pink sweater who looks like a Pamela Anderson knockoff.

Where is Matthew?

I squirm through first class, smiling at the already seated patrons when I spot him. Last row. First class. Aisle seat. Looking at his laptop, which is already open on his seat.

I'm trying not to feel robbed. Really. I don't look at him. Which is probably my folly because a gal who was watching out might not have hit him in the face with her elbow.

"Oh, I'm sorry!" I truly am! I make an apologetic face to prove it. He holds his perfect cheekbone, frowns at me.

"Watch where you're going."

Jerk. Good thing we're not stranded together on an island.

I struggle by and suck in my breath as the aisle tightens like a corset. Happily the elderly couple isn't as touchy as Matthew the Jerk because I nearly land in their laps. I finally struggle to row sixteen, and wouldn't you know it, the overhead bin is full.

"You can stash your bag in the back," says a helpful voice standing a few rows down. I glance at the flight attendant, and she looks about the size of an angel-hair noodle. Big smile, perfect blond hair piled on her head and no tear-smudged makeup. And you just know she doesn't right-hook people when she walks down the aisle. Instantly, I hate her.

"No thanks, I'll put it under my seat."

She surveys me, my bag. Up goes one perfectly groomed eyebrow. You can tell she waxes. I tried that once. Put me in a very, very bad mood.

I fling the bag down on the seat. It makes an ominous *whump*. And when I then push it to the floor, I know that I'd have an easier time fitting the Titanic under the minute cubby they've allotted my feet for the next ten hours.

"Let me take that to the back for you," says a voice I now recognize.

You lay one hand on my bag and you will lose every one of those red fingernail tips. I need my bag. Not only does it have ten bagels in it, but also my laptop and my reading material. And I still haven't decided what I want to read. "No, that's okay," I purr. "I might empty it out some." I smile. *Back away from the bag, honey. Slowly.*

They must give lessons in psychology of stressed-out, recently dumped Midwesterners in Flight Training school because Perfect Eyebrows moves away. But I know she'll be back, so I haul the bag back up on the seat. There is still some room in the overhead bin and I know I can fit the bagels in, as well as at least three books. Maybe even the bag of red licorice. Oh yeah, I didn't mention those, did I?

I pull these items out, shove them overhead, way in the back, leaving the bagels most accessible. Then I remove the laptop, tuck it overhead and, with a grunt, push the bag into the abyss under the seat. Ahh, see? The bag fits. No need to get into a lather, sweetie, I think as I glance at Perfect Eyebrows carting another victim's bag to the back. We missionaries know how to think on our feet.

I sit down in the middle seat (Didn't the airline know about my bladder?) and wait for my compatriots.

Each face I see holds promise. A cowboy in a Stetson, an elderly woman with the look of couture, a college student still wearing her NYU sweatshirt. No takers.

I am staring the tarmac, listening to the jets whine when I feel movement. And then…a smell.

Oh, no.

Throwing his backpack on the floor, he kicks it easily under the seat. Then, giving me a glare, Grunge flops down, throws his grimy, knotted-hair head back and turns up the volume of his MP3.

Reggae.

I didn't see the ocean. Even though I scooted over to the window seat and pushed my face against the glass. First it was the NYC skyline, then the clouds. Then, darkness. As in *night*. I would be more than ambivalent about this little detail if exhaustion hadn't slugged me like a sledgehammer fifteen minutes after takeoff. I grabbed a scratchy synthetic airplane pillow, jammed it up against the window, and then, despite the entertainment and odor emanating from Grunge Boy, hit full slumber in about thirty-five seconds.

I think I even drooled.

I missed supper, which didn't upset me too much (I mean, a choice between baked chicken leg and Salisbury steak? Hello?), but when breakfast rattled by, I roused myself and forced my gritty eyes open. "Wait!" I say, glancing at Grunge Boy's plate. Fruit, a cinnamon roll and eggs. Okay, not Jas's *kringle,* but it'll do.

The flight attendant—oh, no, it's Perfect Eyebrows!— looks at me with a faint smile. "Oh, you're awake."

I *did* drool. I see it on her smug face. I nod, aware that my hair is probably doing its 1920s skullcap impersonation, and there are pillow lines etched into my face. "I'm awake. Can I get some breakfast?"

"Of course." She hands me the tray. "Coffee?"

"A gallon, please?" That was supposed to be a joke, but she just gives me a courtesy smile and pours me a cup. I've had bigger shots of whiskey. I thank her and she rattles off.

"Sleep well?"

The Grunge speaks! I try not to spill my OJ as I open it,

and look at him. Underneath that rats nest hair, he has pretty hazel eyes and they're glancing off me as if I make him… nervous? I must have a sort of missionary presence.

"Yes, thank you. Did you get some sleep?"

"Naw. I can never sleep on airplanes. Watched the latest Ben Affleck thriller, though, on the movie options."

Movies? I missed *movies?*

No one mentioned movies. Not fair.

"Do you know how much longer it'll be?" I ask. I dig into the eggs, and despite being rubbery, they fill a few gaps. The cinnamon roll is what I expected. Sahara dry and sickly sweet. But it accompanies the eggs nicely.

"Oh, an hour or so. We're over Poland."

Wow. I slide up the shade. Sure enough, dawn pours through the window and the sunrise is breathtaking as it spills out like OJ onto the clouds. "Wow," I say again, this time aloud, because God deserves it.

"Yeah. I love traveling east."

I add sugar and cream to the shot of coffee. "You go to Russia a lot?"

"Yeah," he says, while crumpling up his napkin and wadding it in his juice container. "I do some computer consulting for a company in Moscow."

Grunge-Man/Computer whiz. Of course.

"Why are you going? Tourist?"

Do I look like a tourist? I wore my black linen capris and a white blouse, with a pressed (well, it was!) suitcoat. Sort of a rebound from the fruit-skirt fiasco, but I wanted to enter my new world with a touch of class.

Except I just dripped coffee on the blouse. I bite back a word that might give me away and dab at the shirt. "I'm a missionary."

Silence. He raises one eyebrow, then a slight smile. As if humoring me. I feel my hackles rise like Godzilla.

"That rocks."

Oh.

"Thanks. I ah, am going to teach English for Moscow Bible Church."

He nods, like he knows exactly where that is.

"Maybe you should stop by sometime," I say, because we missionaries are supposed to invite people to church.

He smiles wider, and I see just a hint of a blush. "Yeah, well, I'm a member."

I don't know what to say. "That rocks," comes out of my mouth.

He holds out his hand. "Caleb Gilstrap."

I feel something warm, something besides a coffee stain, heating my chest as I shake his hand and introduce myself.

As it turns out, Caleb has a Ph.D in computer science and the consulting he's doing is for an NGO project (Non-Government Organization: meaning humanitarian aid). He's been awake for two days, jetting across the country from California, (hence the smell) and after an hour of conversation, I feel like a slug.

Caleb the Grunge: nice guy. Josey the Missionary: slug.

We finally part the clouds and start our descent into Moscow. I see tiny houses on miniscule plots of land spiraling in the closer we get to the city. Caleb leans over me. "Those are dachas—little summer cabins on garden plots. Most of the Muscovites live in high-rises and come out on the weekends to tend their land."

"There are a lot of them."

"There are a lot of people in Moscow. It's bigger than New York."

Oh. If I push my eye up to the glass, I can see the airport, a tiny speckling of gray buildings.

"You'd better buckle up and hold on," Caleb says as we hear the engines start to whine, the landing gear clunk down.

"Why?" But I obey. I cinch the belt tight and hook my feet around my carry-on. Please, let my bagels stay in their bag overhead.

"Because Moscow has the worst landing strip in the northern hemisphere."

Thanks, Caleb. I needed to hear that. Especially since I'd done a great job of muscling the bogeyman of flying into the recesses of my brain. But, no, here he comes, with a roar and a wash of sheer ice in my veins. I white-knuckle the armrests.

We touch down. Once, twice, three, now four times. And when we get all three points on, I can feel the teeth rattle around my head. Caleb grins at me, but he's a blur of motion.

I close my eyes, and the bogeyman slinks back into hiding. Sometime soon my lungs will begin working, too.

We taxi near the terminal, but stop far enough away for me to ask why.

"Oh, we have to disembark on the tarmac and hike in," says Caleb as he releases the belt. "Say goodbye to the land of conveniences."

I'm not quite sure what he means by that because Dwight said I'd have running water. But now that I think about it, he did follow that with "most of the time."

Hmm.

I stand on the seat, unlock the overhead bin. A bagel falls out. I scoop it off the seat and hold my hands up, catching two more.

But I'm here. In *Russia*. Russshhhhaaa. Russia, Russia, Russia!

And more importantly, it's been thirteen hours and I'm not even missing Chase.

Much.

Chapter Six:
The Gray Pony

To: Jasmine Snodbrecher [JMSnod@mn.usa]
Sent: August 27, 2:47 p.m.
From: Josey@mail.com
Subject: The Lowdown

Dear Jas,

I've been in Russia for six hours, and if this e-mail finds you, ever, it is only because God has seen my day and decided to extend a smidgen of mercy.

I'll start by saying that I made two mistakes in my trip over to Moscow.
1. I ate breakfast.
2. I didn't use the lavatory on the airplane, thus making it a necessity for the airport.

I'm pretty sure the bathroom hadn't been cleaned since it housed rebels from the Bolshevik Revolution. And, no running water. Which didn't bode well for my flagging spirit. But I am rushing ahead, giving you the punch line first. Let me back up to the place where I am standing in line with the other passengers as we ponder our future with customs and passport control. The first thing I noticed after lugging my carry-on/anvil down the stairs and across the cold and windy tarmac of Sheremetova 2, Russia's International airport, was that gloom preceded us. Like an x-wing fighter, it strafed the gray buildings, chipping the cement and souring the air with the odor of oil and dust. A woman dressed in the gray-greens of the Russian military held open the door for us, and I couldn't help but wonder if she was waiting, like the Gestapo, to yank one of us (me!) from line, and send me to gulag for an eternity of gritty kasha. She scrutinized me for a long moment with narrowed eyes, during which my heart, the coward that it is, leapt from my body and fled.

So, there I was shuffling in behind the other gulag potentials and we lined up in a cement-and-brick hallway that had no more light than Uncle Albert's root cellar and all the cheer of a morgue. The expressions worn by my compatriots convinced me that I had sinned, greatly, by smiling, so I feigned (sorta) calm. But, really, I'm here! I'm here! I remember thinking. In retrospect, that excitement was premature, and I should have done a mental head slap when I looked up at the ceiling and saw dust hanging like Spanish moss. Running water *most* of the time? It was then my gut started to twist. (For a long while, I thought this was excitement. Probably my most glaring mistake for the day.)

Among the smaller mistakes over the last six hours were:
1. Making a joke with visa control in which I told them I was

here to make Russia a better, brighter place. (They obviously need to lighten up.)

2. Packing *two* suitcases (a sin that I now confess! But I called the airline and they said I could bring two. I foolishly believed that the "one suitcase" rule, now broken, was instituted by the mission to make me think...missionarish, and well, I already said that just because I'm a missionary doesn't mean I can't have decent footwear.) because they don't have any of those nifty carts and I'm telling you, in Russia, chivalry is a cold, dead corpse. Thankfully Granny Netta's poppy-orange bag is built like the Titanic. I kicked it through the concourse with little mercy.

3. Choosing the red line, which at the time seemed to be a wise option, due to the fact that there were only three people occupying spaces. What I didn't know was that they were merely placeholders for the Mongolian Horde. Thirty Asian shippers, with bundles roughly the size of Mount St. Helens wrapped in blue-and-red nylon shrink wrap muscled right in front of me. I thought maybe I could take two of them, after all I have a good twenty, (okay, thirty-five!) pounds on them. But they just kept streaming in, like the agents on *Matrix Reloaded*, so I surrendered with a loud sigh. Which no one heard because the cement immensity of the terminal swallowed all sound, a design, I am sure, calculated by the KGB officials I spied lingering along the recesses of the terminal. (And by the way, the Russian movies with soldiers with big guns—all true.) Meanwhile, the green line, some twenty passengers long, clipped along at a reasonable pace.

I held out hope until the green line shortened past me. Then kicked the poppy bag and her fellow Tubby over to the green line.

That's when the customs control agent spotted me and went on his lunch break. Not lying about that. Left us there to sit on our suitcases for an hour. Meanwhile, well, remember that excitement in my stomach? It turned into something nasty, and moved south. I started hunting down the bathroom. I spotted what looked like the sign for a woman affixed to the wall next to an open door. Where was Grunge Buddy when I needed him? (Oh, yeah, I forgot to mention him. I met this nice guy named Caleb, who happened to be my seat mate on the airplane. Turns out, despite his attire, which mimics Gooch Riley's [remember him? Drummer in H's first band, the Uglies?], Caleb is a nice guy, a computer programmer and a Speaker of Russian.) Deciding not to leave my bag for the next available thief, I abandoned my spot in line (I mean, really, does it matter?) and kicked my bags to the open door.

Words can not describe the atrocity inside this tiny five-by-eight-foot room. Out of three possible sinks, one was actually lying cracked on the floor, the other two as dry as the Sahara at high noon. The stalls—well, sis, I'm here to tell you that Russia must be so poor it can't afford stools, because there were…(I'm nearly afraid to tell you)…holes in the ground where porcelain should be. Holes…and well, you can guess the rest.

I backed out slowly, pretty sure that was a memory I didn't need.

I returned to line, and for the first time since setting foot in Russia, brought God back into the picture.

4. Not putting my shampoo in a zip-lock bag. (But it serves the customs official right for pawing through my things.) Matthew Winneman, my contact, (I'll get to him later) met me

on the other side of the glass barrier. (I forgot to mention that humanity was pressed up against this barrier like human wallpaper. Matthew stood in the back, unaffected, holding a small sign with my name. I wanted to throw myself in his arms.) By this time, I was crying openly, my stomach in knots. He thought it was stress. I threw pride to the wind and ask him where the nearest clean public bathroom was.

He *laughed*. Grabbed one bag and hauled it outside.

I remember thinking, what, exactly, did that mean?

Moscow airport is located one hour, thirteen minutes and 47 seconds from my new *flat*. (Isn't that cool? My first foreign word! By the way, it is code for apartment.) I'm on the fourth floor. And, yes, there is an elevator, but we didn't use it (so I hauled the Teletubbies up the stairs—are you so very proud of me?) because Matthew said he wasn't feeling lucky.

Not sure what that meant, either.

He let me in my flat, which I'm sharing with a girl (not with Mission to the World) named Tracey Mylander from Ohio. She is gone at the moment, but I picture her as sorta like me, short blond hair, nice smile, someone out to change her corner of the world. She works for an NGO (another new word!) which stands for Non-Government Agency (code for humanitarian aid). Which makes her sorta like a missionary, in a nonevangelistic way. I expect we'll be close friends.

The flat, by the way, is three rooms (aka, a two-bedroom apartment) roughly the size of your new place over the restaurant. Except the walls are gold and the furniture black leather. The kitchen is the size of our closet (you would die) with a tiny linoleum table and a couple of stools pushed underneath and bright red wallpaper that is peeling around the edges. It's okay, I don't plan to eat here much. Even the floor is gold, by the way. Gold linoleum that runs the entire flat. With a black and brown throw rug beneath the leather sofa and easy chairs and under a glass coffee table.

Most importantly, I don't see a television. You *will* tape *Lost* for me, right? Right?

Matthew showed me to my room and told me to "wait for instructions."

(Yes, I'm in the middle of a Le Carré espionage book. But wait—all his characters die at the end! What does this mean for me, exactly?)

Back to Matthew. He's tall. Curly black hair, dark blue eyes, a warm smile. And, like I said, he carried one of the bags. He's wearing a ring, but it's on his right hand. Not that I noticed, really.

By the way—was that Chase I saw at the airport when I was leaving?

Anyway, I locked the door behind Matthew and took stock of my surroundings. I have an exotic view of a...dusty yard. And four other apartment buildings that blot out the sky. No nod toward aesthetics here. The buildings look like card-towers, and about as sturdy, painted the oh-so-very lovely color of gray. Each flat is a box, with two windows, and there are probably a thousand of these cubicles just within my view. (Which means that a girl could get swallowed up here very easily.) Each flat has a tiny balcony (can they fall off?) and a few host geraniums, others, old refrigerators or bicycles.

My room is about as big as my old bedroom, a double bed (fun!), an armoire, a saggy desk, a hard wood chair and a lovely brown throw rug on the gold linoleum floor. Okay! It needs some work. But it's only been six, no, now seven hours. Give me a couple days, in between meeting with Putin with my suggestions about the airport (I mean, please, aren't they trying to encourage tourism?) and starting a public bathroom petition.

I jest, of course, about meeting with Putin. But maybe a well-written letter to the head of the International Airport?

After scooping shampoo out of my suitcase and rinsing out my underwear as well as that cute lime-green cardigan I stole from your closet (I figured you'd find out sooner or later, so yes, it's in Russia), I ran a bath.

Ever wanted to bathe in sun tea? Didn't think so. Well, let me tell you, it was warm, wet and if I closed my eyes, I could imagine it was a mineral bath in the tropics.

I have a great imagination.

Aren't I adapting well? I know you are surprised, but really, I can do this!

Oh, and by the way, there is more to this electric-converter stuff than just changing our flat plugs to the European round ones. I made fire come out of my hairdryer today.

So, I'm sitting here in my wool socks (see, I told Mom the truth!), my jammie bottoms and my University of MN sweatshirt. I have exactly seven bagels left. It is 2:00 p.m. and I feel like I've been run over a couple times by Lennie's street sweeper. And, the King of all Tragedies—there is *No Signal* on my cell phone. I thought I got an international plan. I guess that means France.

You must do two things for me.

1. Call Myrtle and ask her if she wants an editorial from Russia. I don't know why I didn't think of this sooner, but I'm thinking I could find something to write about.

2. Follow Chase. Okay, I don't mean go overboard or anything, but you know, just drive by his house twice a day, keep a journal of where you see his car (he's driving a Bronco these days), run into him in the grocery store, and if you call over to the police station, I've always found Pete a good resource for general happenings around town. He should be able to give you some dates and times for Chase's social life if he stays in the Gull Lake vicinity. Not that I'm expecting him to have one without me, but you know, just in case. Oh, and keep an eye on Missy down at the Holiday gas station. She and Chase were "friends" once, and I suspect that she'll try and get her claws into him now that he's back. (And she broke up with Mike Bellow a month ago, not that I pay attention to that sort of thing). Anyway, it's not like I care, but she gets off at 10:20 on Friday nights, so if you happen to be cruising by there around then and see a Bronco...well, you know what to do.

I miss you. I miss Mom and Dad. There are also others I miss, but well, I listed the most important for the moment.

I think I'll go to bed now. Maybe I'll wake up in Gull Lake.

Love,
Just Serving God Josey

I'm sitting in a café, watching foot traffic. Already, I love Moscow. I feel the sunshine on my face as I walk down the sidewalk, listening to the sounds of foreign words, the scent of lilacs overhanging green wooden fences. I am looking svelte, having already lost ten pounds. Then I hear the voice. "Josey! Josey!" I turn, and there he is—running! Sweat drips down his temples, into the collar of his white polo shirt. He's wearing his faded jeans and his Birks, and he looks flushed. Worried.

Come to think of it, it is a hot day. I feel sweat bead on my forehead.

"Josey!" he says. "Wake up!"

Huh?

"Wake up!"

But I *am* awake. I frown at him, but he's fading fast—no! I reach out— *Thwack!*

"Hey, c'mon! I'm just trying to help!"

Pain shoots up my arm as I claw toward consciousness. My eyes feel like sand, and my body has refused to join reality as Chase vanishes.

"You're Josey, right?"

I hear the words, but all I see is a window painted with gold trim, a lace curtain, a wilted African violet. A breeze is pushing around the edge of the curtain, and brings in the smell of dust, exhaust.

I stare at it, by brain whirring, my eyes wide. Okay, excuse me but *where exactly am I?*

"Josey?"

I want to turn and look, I do, but my body feels as if it's been at the bottom of a mosh pit and all I can do is groan. So the voice behind me does the moving and I see hair first— glorious, long roan-red hair—then the face, hazel-green eyes, lots of lips. "Hi. I'm Tracey."

Tracey? And—*who is Tracey?*

I can nearly hear the gears clicking as my brain races through time to the present. Then, with a body-slamming *whump,* truth T-bones me. *Russia.* Tracey, my roomie from Ohio?

"Hi," I manage and disentangle my body from the web of fatigue. I roll over, and Tracey straightens for all her glory. Oh, boy. If she's from Ohio, I'm Charlize Theron. Five-foot-bazillion, and wearing a clingy short black skirt and a top that might fit my right thigh, she's got the body of an Amazon and a tan to match.

Good thing I'm a missionary or I might be jealous.

I sit up and casually wipe a line of drool from my face. What is she doing here, in my room? And so what if my hair is, well, mussed. At least it is clean. Sorta.

"I'm sorry to wake you," says Tracey the Ten. "But you have to stay awake or you'll be up all night pacing and you'll never break the jet-lag cycle." She smiles again—wow! she must have had years of ortho work—and holds out her hand. "C'mon, get dressed. We're going out."

Out? The only place I'm going is back to Chase, who is still standing in the middle of the sidewalk. What if he ran all this way to declare his undying love?

Then again, I'm not completely ready to jump forever into his arms, am I?

Chapter Six:
The Gray Pony

To: Jasmine Snodbrecher [JMSnod@mn.usa]
Sent: August 27, 2:47 p.m.
From: Josey@mail.com
Subject: The Lowdown
Dear Jas,
I've been in Russia for six hours, and if this e-mail finds you, ever, it is only because God has seen my day and decided to extend a smidgen of mercy.

I'll start by saying that I made two mistakes in my trip over to Moscow.
1. I ate breakfast.
2. I didn't use the lavatory on the airplane, thus making it a necessity for the airport.

I'm pretty sure the bathroom hadn't been cleaned since it housed rebels from the Bolshevik Revolution. And, no running water. Which didn't bode well for my flagging spirit. But I am rushing ahead, giving you the punch line first. Let me back up to the place where I am standing in line with the other passengers as we ponder our future with customs and passport control. The first thing I noticed after lugging my carry-on/anvil down the stairs and across the cold and windy tarmac of Sheremetova 2, Russia's International airport, was that gloom preceded us. Like an x-wing fighter, it strafed the gray buildings, chipping the cement and souring the air with the odor of oil and dust. A woman dressed in the gray-greens of the Russian military held open the door for us, and I couldn't help but wonder if she was waiting, like the Gestapo, to yank one of us (me!) from line, and send me to gulag for an eternity of gritty kasha. She scrutinized me for a long moment with narrowed eyes, during which my heart, the coward that it is, leapt from my body and fled.

So, there I was shuffling in behind the other gulag potentials and we lined up in a cement-and-brick hallway that had no more light than Uncle Albert's root cellar and all the cheer of a morgue. The expressions worn by my compatriots convinced me that I had sinned, greatly, by smiling, so I feigned (sorta) calm. But, really, I'm here! I'm here! I remember thinking. In retrospect, that excitement was premature, and I should have done a mental head slap when I looked up at the ceiling and saw dust hanging like Spanish moss. Running water *most* of the time? It was then my gut started to twist. (For a long while, I thought this was excitement. Probably my most glaring mistake for the day.)

Among the smaller mistakes over the last six hours were:
1. Making a joke with visa control in which I told them I was

I'm drying my hair (upside down, which doesn't help the schnapps spinning thing) when the buzzer rings. I see Tracey do an orangutan waddle across the room (she's moved on to her pedicure) and then hear a male voice.

At least I'm dry, if not fashionable. I emerge and— Ooops! Didn't need to see that. Roomie draped around…Rick? I avert my eyes and they laugh.

"Josey, meet Rick," Tracey says and disentangles herself, going back to the sofa. His gaze follows her, then—Uh-oh!—lands on me. Yep, that's me, the dowdy missionary from Minnesota.

"Hi," I say. Rick's gaze passes over me, and I can see curiosity in his eyes.

"Tracey says you're here to teach English?" He is wearing all black, and it gives him an exotic gangster look. Black dress shoes, black pants, black silk shirt, black leather coat. Black hair, dark eyes. Oh my! I've just met Neo! He looks at me without a smile.

"Yeah, for Moscow Bible Church."

He gives a little snort. "Yeah, well, good luck."

I raise one eyebrow, but Tracey breezes past me. Wow. She's wearing ten-inch open-toe black spikes and I'm wondering if she needs oxygen at that altitude. I slink out behind them, a nondescript shadow of fatigue, hearing my bed whimper as I close the door.

I don't remember much of my apartment building on the way in, but now, it looks like one of those Bosnian documentaries, with the chipped, graffittied walls, and the smell of cigarette smoke seasoned with animal droppings embedding the halls. Dusty light angles from filthy rectangular windows. I follow Tracey and Rick into the elevator and hold onto the wall as it shudders down four flights.

Rick owns a black Mercedes. Figures. He clicks off the alarm and we slide in—me in back—as he unlocks his "club" from the steering wheel. I notice the car swims in his cologne. As if I needed any help with the head spinning. He pulls away from the curb and out onto the Moscow streets.

I should cut away here and mention that most of what I've seen of Moscow hasn't been pretty, but I attribute that to first, fatigue and stomach distractions, and second, daylight.

I feel like it should be midnight, but the streets are bright, the sun shining. I glimpse darkened stores, some boarded, some simply gated. People with heads tucked against a swirling wind hustle down sidewalks, their hands shoved into the pockets of their leather coats. It's August, right? Why the jackets?

I lean forward to ask, when suddenly we hit a pothole. My head explodes against the roof of the car. "Be careful," Rick says, but I'm not sure to whom.

"Is Moscow always this light?" I ask.

Tracey turns around. "Have you ever heard the song, Moscow days and Moscow nights?"

Do I look like a connoisseur of Russian folk tunes? I shake my head.

"It's a pop hit from the sixties. Moscow is so far north that it gets dark pretty early around here in the winter, but in the summer, it can stay light until eleven p.m."

"What time is it?"

Tracey checks her watch. Oh sure, it's a Cartier. "Ten."

My bedtime, for sure. Just how late does she want me to stay up? And, when will I receive my next set of instructions from Matthew?

We cut a right, weave between two squatty buildings and pull up to a long, low building distinguished by a sign of deformed stallion in midrear. "The Gray Pony?" I ask.

Tracey nods.

I'm not sure how to read Tracey. So far, I find her pushy, exotic, intriguing and maybe friendly. And way too pretty for Neo/Rick. He has his hand on the small of her back, proprietary as we walk into the…what is this place?

Uh-oh. I'm pretty sure Matthew isn't going to like this. My mother might call it a night club. Dwight would call it a den of sin.

I slouch in, and suddenly my headache erupts with a roar, the pulsating beat keeping rhythm with the thud in my brain.

"Want something to drink?" Tracey yells as we slide onto high-top stools. My gaze is caught on the couple in the middle of the dance floor. She's wearing red leather and he's wearing John Travolta black stretch pants and a frilly shirt, and guess what? Disco hasn't died, it's moved to Moscow! A silver disco ball dangles above the floor, and I just know the next song is going to be "Night Fever." I can't help but smile.

"No, thanks," I say. She shakes her head at Rick, who slips away. Yeah!

Tracey leans over the table. "I know that you missionary types don't hang out in these kind of places, but I thought you needed something loud to keep you awake."

Oh. Yes. Loud would be the operative word. But I appreciate her sentiment.

"So, you work with Rick?" My voice echoes a couple times in my head.

"Yeah," she hollers back. "Actually, he's my boss. We run an anti-trafficking program, dealing in the trade of women. We offer grants to organizations who offer training and employment alternatives to the flesh-for-sale profession."

I blink at her, trying to catch all the words as the tune

changes to a Donna Summer song. "What kind of things do you teach them?"

"Aside from business and computer classes, we also have classes on self-esteem. We want them to see themselves as more than a commodity, but a person of value."

I know all about that kind of teaching, and I can't help but smile. She is speaking my language, well except for the... "Did you say Rick is your boss?"

She blushes slightly. "Yeah."

"But, well, are you...dating him?"

Her smile dims. "He's nice once you get to know him."

Oh, I'll be looking forward to that. But, her boss? Even I can hear the sirens.

Rick returns with my nothing and what looks like a gin and tonic for Sheena. The music rolls over me, soothing in its own raucous way. I don't have to think, I can just let the sounds, the smells, the colors wash over me. Lull me. I lay my head down on the table. Rick and Tracey aren't paying attention to me anyway.

And there's Chase. Where have you been? I ask as he slides up to me and puts his arm around my shoulder. I don't lift my head. "I'm stuck in this bar—"

"If it isn't Josey the Missionary!"

I jerk awake, clawing my way to reality. *Where am*—

"I never expected to see you here. Trying to stay awake?"

Grunge Boy! I want to hug him. He is smiling broadly, and holding what I think is a Coke. He's dressed up for his night out in a pair of cargo pants, flip flops and a WWJD T-shirt.

"Caleb," I say, pretty proud I can remember his name. "I lost you at the airport."

He offers me his drink, and yes, it's soda. "That's why I

travel light. No baggage claim for me." He eyes Tracey. "Who is Safari girl?"

I glance over at Tracey and Rick, who definitely have no problem with any employer-employee taboos. "She's my roomie. Works for an NGO." (I'm pretty excited to use that word, but unfortunately, Caleb doesn't notice.)

"She talked you into going out," he says without question in his voice, which assuages my guilty conscience for being a missionary in a bar. "It's an unspoken ex-pat pledge to help all newbies over the jet-lag initiation."

"I'd rather be pacing at two a.m.," I mumble. He laughs. He has really pretty hazel eyes, and now, his smile makes me produce one, also.

"Let me take you home. I'll give you your first subway lesson."

I eye him for a long moment, and then I realize I have no idea where I live. He must be able to read my mind because he leans over and taps Tracey. She disengages herself from Rick and sighs. "What?"

"I'm taking your roomie home. Where do you live?"

Obviously Tracey has no problem handing me over to a complete stranger for she rattles off our address and returns to her lip lock. Caleb leads the way out of the Gray Pony and onto the litter-strewn street. Wind scrapes up dust and old soda cans and scurries them down the street. Not a bistro in sight.

Darkness has oozed across Moscow in the hour or so I tarnished my reputation in the Gray Pony. I walk beside Caleb in silence, listening to the rustle of drying leaves, seeing a few stars poke out of the night. I wonder if the sky looks the same as it does from the beach on Berglund Acres.

"Do you go there a lot?" I ask Caleb.

"Sometimes. It's the ex-pat watering hole, even if you don't like the atmosphere. They play American tunes and serve soda with ice—a winning combination." He waits at a light, even holding out his arm in case I might leap forward. How sweet. "You caught the Pony on a bad night. Jazz night is fun. And Mondays they have karaoke night—even carry the entire Elvis collection."

I smile. Oh sure, I'll make sure and keep that night free. But I'm wondering if they have Karen Carpenter. Caleb just grins at me and he feels sorta like my brother, Buddy. Easy not to fall in love with. Safe. Protective. We descend down stairs—the Metro entrance is off the street-level sidewalk—and I feel the air turn cold. He stops in front of what looks like a vending machine and extracts a couple tokens. "Metro fare," he says, then pushes me toward a turnstile.

I drop my token in, walk through under the scrutiny of another uniformed guard—or wait, was that Gestapo woman from the airport?

I hustle faster and find myself on an escalator.

"Don't look down," he says. Of course, I do. And nearly lose my lunch/breakfast/whatever—oh, bagel! It's a couple billion miles to the bottom. I sway. Caleb grabs my shoulder and laughs. "Trust me, you'll get used to it."

We hit bottom and he knows exactly which way to turn. It isn't lost on me that I am at his mercy. Garbled conversation hums around me, and for the first time I realize that I heard mostly English in the Gray Pony. I see other late-night travelers, holding bags, leaning against the ornately carved posts. They look as tired as I feel.

"The Metro system used to be a bomb shelter, and it runs throughout the entire city. Around the center is a ring, and from this ring runs every other line. It's easy to understand once you get the hang of it." He hands me a Metro map and I study it for a second. It's written in Cyrillic, but it's color-coded, and Caleb runs his finger around the gold ring in the middle. "You live on the green line." He runs his finger out. "And we're here, on the purple line."

Okay, I can get this. Confidence rushes through my limp veins.

I've never been in a subway station before, but I can feel the train coming as if it is in my soul. A dull rumble that starts in my bones and moves out through my pores until it consumes my ears, my nose, my thoughts. I glance once at the rails below and calculate the distance if one were to fall....

I take a step back.

The train rushes in, bringing with it wind and the odor of dust and oil. It screeches to a stop, and I feel Caleb push me into a car. Inside, it is deathly quiet. As if this sacred ride under the crust of Moscow it is a private and religious affair, worthy of only whispers. I grab a handle, and a moment later, we are off.

The subway shakes, swaying from side to side, nearly frenetic as it whooshes to the next station. Caleb, I notice, isn't hanging on. He's got his arms out, and he's grinning. "I like to call it subway surfing. Try it!"

Uh, no, I'm having enough trouble standing, as it is.

But by the time we've transferred to the gold line, and then to the green, I've tried it, once. Laughed. Felt just a little like I've taken a piece of Moscow into my heart.

Caleb hikes with me to my building, and we take the stairs up without discussion. I fumble for the key and find it in my passport bundle.

"Don't take your passport with you again," Caleb warns

as he opens the door. "The last thing you want is to lose your identity in Moscow."

I walk inside my gold-and-brown flat, flop down on the black leather sofa and listen to Caleb leave, closing the door behind him. I have a feeling it's much too late for his warnings.

Chapter Seven:
We have no Bweestros
in Russia

I'm up at the crack of dawn. (Maybe that isn't exactly accurate. It's 3:00 a.m. and there isn't the faintest hint of dawn outside my window. And, if I've done my calculations correctly, it's noon Gull Lake time. But I've never been up "at the crack of dawn" before and I'm just going to bask in it, *okay?*) I'm buzzing. Ready to fly. The new and improved Josey, the missionary, rising early like the Proverbs 31 woman to meet with God and throw verve into her day.

Either that or there is more to this jet-lag thing than I want to admit. The flat is quiet, and I don't remember hearing Tracey return, which tells me that either she is very quiet and considerate, or...she's not here. Which leads to other thoughts, fertilized mostly from my last clear memory—that of her playing dentist with Rick.

Gross. Not the first thought with which I'd like to start my day.

As a missionary, I know a few basics. Like, we read our Bibles. And we pray. And we don't hang out in bars. So, I guess that means I'm going to have to do extra time in the first two categories if I hope to even out last night's activities in God's scorebook.

I find my Bible buried under my Gull Lake sweatshirt. Admittedly, I haven't spent too much time inside the pages since I returned from Missionary Camp. Not because I didn't want to. In fact, this summer, I've been closer to God than I've ever been, which probably accounts for the fact that I find myself in a foreign country this morning. But, over the past month, life has been about preparation, about gathering my resources, about embarking on a new journey.

It strikes me that perhaps a wise girl would have spent time preparing, um, *spiritually,* too. Whoops.

I crack open my Bible and it falls open to Ephesians, where I've stuck the bulletin from the fateful, "Call to Russia" day. I read it over, and listen to the missionary's words replay in my head—"For we are God's workmanship, created in Christ Jesus to do good work, which God prepared in advance for us to do." Verse 2:10.

Perhaps it would be wise to start at the beginning of the book of Ephesians?

Admittedly, my only experience with formal Bible study has been:

1. Sunday School lessons, mostly about Bible characters (but I'm really good, even with the obscure ones. For example, do you know the lesson about...Acsah? Didn't think so. That's why *I'm* a missionary.).

2. The memorization and theological comprehension of

the "Romans road," a gospel presentation of sin and salvation. (I know, I'm so Dallas Theological Seminary, but again, we missionaries know these things.)

3. A "Special Times with Jesus" devotional book my mother gave me in eighth grade.

But, really, how hard can it be? I'm a reader, and this is a book, right?

I cruise through the first chapter of Ephesians, but maybe my brain is fogged from the time jump because the words blur. As if I've just licked the first layer of frosting off the cake, not getting the full taste.

I grab my journal, feeling like a real scholar. I'll go verse by verse, and focus on the really deep ones. Maybe I'll even teach Tracey something. She seems like she needs a little Bible training in her life.

Now, I have to tell you that, since I'm a missionary, I got a really thick, heavy Bible. It's a deluxe study Bible, with a Greek and Hebrew concordance, red lettering, topography maps, timelines, Bible helps (not that I'll need it), an index to subjects, a weights and measures table and a reference concordance. And it's got a zippered light blue leather case with a carrying handle, a place for a pen, a notebook and even a couple of fancy ribbons/bookmarks. It weighs, roughly, 14.3 lbs, and I had to take out an entire bag of chocolate chips to accommodate it. (I know, I know, sacrifices, but that is what missionaries do). Yes, it's high-end, but like I said, it's like a doctor and his stethoscope. We missionaries rely on our Bibles.

I skim over the first two lines. Greetings. No problem. Even verse three seems manageable—praises to God for his blessings.

Then I get to verse four. "According as he hath chosen us

in him before the foundation of the world, that we should be holy and without blame before him in love; Having pre-destined us unto the adoption of children by Jesus Christ to himself, according to the good pleasure of his will—" take a breath, will ya, Paul? "—to the praise of the glory of his grace, wherein he hath made us accepted in the beloved."

Phew. And, excuse me, but *huh?*

When you spend $50 at my local Christian book store, you get a free gift. I got Hi-Liters. And I try out the pink one on the words that hit me—*chosen, pleasure, will* and *glory*. Those are nice words, don't you think? (A whole lot easier to get a grasp on, also, than "holy and without blame." I mean, who am I kidding?)

I flip to the back of my Bible, find the Greek equivalents and surface with these definitions:

Chosen—to select, as in calling out to go forth.

Pleasure—desires, delights.

Will—purpose.

Glory—revelation, honor.

I'm feeling like Martin Luther as I string together this new understanding: He's called me out, selected me before time to be (gulp) holy and without blame (who, me?), and to be-come His child through Christ (okay, I like that part), be-cause He desires me, (even delights in me?—whoa! Hold that thought tight!) and has a purpose for it (like, uh, Russia?), and through this purpose, He'll be praised and His grace will be revealed.

Okay, I know it's a rough analysis, but I'm feeling smart, bolder, richer…and I like that whole delighting thing. Imag-ine, the smile of God upon me.

That thought makes my heart fill, and strangely, the feel-ing I had as I watched Russian children on the television screen at Camp Will-you-be-a-Missionary? floods through me. As if, yes, God has a plan. And it's one He's smiling over. I want to ponder that whole, "to the praise of the glory of his grace," but I think I'm going to shelve that for the moment. My brain feels pretty sated.

I push off the bed and onto my knees, and feel oddly happy to be here, again. "Lord, You got me to Russia," I say, and a shiver of excitement races through me, buzzing my nerve endings (and no, it's not a jet-lag hum). "And I gotta believe it's for good. So, today, help me be Your girl. To do it right, whatever that might be."

I say a prayer, too, for Milton and Jas (I figure she needs it), and Mom and Dad and of course, Chase, and especially H. I have this gut feeling God's just getting started with her.

Finally, I pray for Tracey. I really want to like her. I *do*. I pray she wears something normal today, clothing that doesn't include paws.

The flat is still deadly quiet as I tiptoe out into the main room. Sunlight runs across the carpet, heating the leather sofas (or are they vinyl?). I'm really, really hungry, and my brain is fixed on having a bagel for breakfast. I counted the ones I had left behind last night—a garlic, a cinnamon and raisin, a poppy seed, a whole-wheat, a dried tomato and herb, an egg and finally, my favorite, a veggie bagel with carrots and broccoli and onions.

A veggie bagel toasted with a scrambled egg and I might be able to face the world.

My world slowly dissolves under my cold bare feet as I stare at the crumbs on the countertop. My bagel bag is crumpled, an *empty carcass.* I slam my hand down on it, and it flattens into the counter. No! I pick it up, stare inside, as if bagels might materialize. Hello? There were *seven* bagels in here. *Seven.*

I am sick. Nauseous. I grab the counter. Could I have dropped them? Eaten them in my sleep? Okay, wait, I do vaguely remember chewing late last night, but even if I did really eat that garlic one I am suddenly tasting, that leaves *six*.

Six stolen bagels.

I need to sit down, put my head between my knees. I barely make it to the chair and am breathing hard when...

"Josey?"

I can't look up, and I'm sure that my lungs have ceased to work because the voice...is...male.

Rick.

I look up, painfully aware that not only am I in my Taz jammies, but he's wearing a leopard skin bathrobe that I'm pretty sure isn't in his current all-black *Matrix* collection.

There is a scream coming. I can feel it. But it's trapped in my clogged throat.

Rick, I mouth.

He doesn't smile. "I'll make some coffee."

He'll make coffee? What, to go along with *my bagels* he's consumed? I hope the poppy one gives him gas. I am still trying to form words when Tracey appears. Wearing a pair of red silky undies and a matching camisole.

Oh, please, God, just strike me dead. Right. Now. I manage a quivering smile.

"How do you feel this morning?" Tracey asks, oblivious to the fact that I'm already mentally packing. How could this happen? Not only is Tracey trampling over, without a blink, every single moral and ethical line I've etched for myself (and not an easy thing to do at the University of Minnesota, School of Immorality, I might add!), but she has *consumed* like a *hyena* all my *bagels*.

I want to go for her throat.

She leans her perfect ten hip against the wall, and smiles, awaiting my answer.

"I'm…ah…fine." I lie. So much for that Holy and Blameless stuff. See? There were reasons I skipped over that.

"Good. I hope that you'll be getting picked up this morning, because Rick and I have to be to work early."

Hence the head start last night when he came "home" to our flat? I have no words so I sit there, watching Rick pour himself a cup of coffee. The smell reaches out and makes me ache.

"Oh, and by the way, I cleared you a shelf in the refrigerator and in the cupboard." Tracey pours herself a cup and glides back to her bedroom, Rick behind her.

Oh, good, my own shelf. So that, you know, our food doesn't get mixed up and you accidentally eat, say…my *comfort food* that I oh so badly needed this morning?

What, did she think the little bagel elves left them for Rick and her Late Night Afterglow Munching?

I pour myself a cup of coffee and retreat to my room to hide my smashed chocolate-chip butter cookies.

I don't speak Russian. I know that comes as a great shock. But aside from reading the Mission to the World "conversational Russian" book, I figured I would get it as I go. How hard can it be? Besides, I had other things to concentrate on as I prepared for my trip. Like, how many songs, exactly, would my MP3 player hold?

The language omission, however, is haunting me at the moment as I stare at the little old woman who has knocked at my front door. With fear and trembling (because I could barely see her as I stared out the peephole), I cracked open the door and found her holding a plate of what looks like a greasy version of my sister's Bismarcks.

She doesn't wait for an invitation as she pushes past me and stands in my entry way, talking.

Hmm. I close the door. At this moment, although I'd like to string Tracey up by her pedicure, I could use her Russian language skills. If, in fact, she has any.

The elderly woman beams at me, in-between the rush of words, and I see lots of gold teeth. Her face is gaunt, her figure the padded nondescript evidence of the it's-too-late-now mode of thinking, and she's wearing a gold-and-brown wrap dress in some sort of soft polyester. It sort of matches my apartment. I wonder if she belongs here. Her gray hair is piled on her head in a high bun, and the wrinkles around her eyes place her at a good sixty-five plus.

She holds out the plate. Gestures to me to take it.

I dive for my Russian-English dictionary and look up the word for "What." As in "What is it?"

"Shto?" I ask, grimacing.

Wrong thing to say. Because she launches off in a barrage of Russian that even includes some spittle.

I take the plate. Put it on the counter. Smile. Now, I did read in the Russian culture books that it is culturally appropriate to give a gift in return.

If I had a bagel, I might give her one. Might. But I have nothing, except…hmm. I keep smiling, then turn fast and open up one of the cupboards. Ah, jackpot. It's a Tracey cupboard and what do we have here? A year's supply of Splenda, a stack of Bubble Yum (sugar free), and an equally stunning supply of M&M's—the *three pound bag*. I recognize American contraband when I see it.

I grab the M&M's, shove them into the neighbor's grip. *"Spaceeba,"* I say. (That means *thank you,* by the way. Okay, okay! So I *do* know a little Russian. But don't ask me to say *please,* because that entire thing has me confused. Evidently, they use the same word for *please* as *you're welcome,* which would end up being, "Please, and please," wouldn't it? Or "You're welcome, can I have a pickle?" Weird. I'll stick to *Spaceeba.*)

She smiles. More gold glinting.

Yikes, now what? How rude is it to push an old lady toward the door? It's not like I'm going anywhere, is it?

I'm contemplating my next move—what would Lara Croft do now?—when the doorbell rings again. Wow, I'm popular, and I've only been here twenty-four hours! I open the door without peeping through the eye hole because, you know, I have another Russian in my midst so I must be safe, and I'm startled to see a young woman with long tawny brown hair and brown eyes, dressed in a turquoise suit and matching coat. And boots, the kind that I only dream about, all leather, over the calf, three-inch shaped heel. Wow.

"Hello," she says in sweet, clear English, and I nearly fall over.

"Hi," I say back. Silence, as if she might be expecting more.

"I'm your translator."

Oh, right, my contact! I grab her by the arm and pull her into the flat. "Hello!" I say again. "Can you help me talk to this woman? I think she's my neighbor."

"My name is Larissa," she says, glancing at the woman.

Yeah, yeah, we all have a name, but I want to *talk.* "Nice to meet you. Would you ask her who she is?"

Larissa hesitates a moment, no smile, and suddenly I'm feeling like a jerk. "Please," I add, in English because I want to get it right.

She shrugs, turns to the woman. It is amazing how effortlessly she speaks Russian. Like she's been doing it all her life.

The woman replies and Larissa turns back to me, armed with information. I want to yank it from her mouth. "She's your neighbor and she says you're to call her 'Totye-Milla,' which means Aunt Milla."

One day and already I have an aunt!

"I'm Josey," I say to my new relation, as if she can understand me, and Larissa translates. I catch my name. It sounds like *Zhozey*. Aunt Milla jabbers back and suddenly I'm in a riveting conversation. She's glad I'm here, and wants to welcome me. She wants to know where I'm from. She has no idea where Minnesota is and asks if it is near New York. She asks me what I'm doing here, how old I am, how long I'm going to stay. And if I'm single.

Why?

Larissa is listening to her, a grim look on her face as Aunt Milla begins to gesture. Wildly. Big arms, lots of gold teeth. Then she finishes and grins.

"She's got a grandson, just a bit older than you she'd like you to meet," Larissa says.

Oh. Um…wow. I'm picturing gold teeth, a gaunt wrinkled face. Padding. "Thanks, Larissa. Tell her I'll…be looking forward to that." Would that be lying? Or rather, a half truth because it's similar to my perspective on a typhoid shot. Looking forward to…getting it over with.

Aunt Milla beams. I've made her entire decade. She shuffles out, matchmaking deed completed.

"Oh," I say, catching her. "What kind of goodie did she bring me?"

Larissa translates, and the first hint of a smile appears on

Larissa's elegant face. Auntie Milla leaves and I close the door behind her.

Larissa grins, a glint in her golden eyes. "They're *peroshke*. Deep-fried sandwiches."

"Yum. What's inside?" So they aren't Jasmine's. They're puffy and made with butter and flour and inside could be strawberry preserves, or even—

"Liver."

Liver? I have no words for that. I just stare at the liver *peroshke* and something similar to grief pools in my stomach. "Want one?" I ask Larissa.

She raises one groomed eyebrow.

Okay, other missionaries can eat worms and bugs, I can eat liver, right?

Or, not. Diet, day one. No liver.

"Where are we going?" I ask as I gather up my backpack, sans passport. I'm wearing a jean skirt, a short orange Gap T-shirt and my classic brown Polartec, waterproof hiking boots, with the black rubber treads I got on sale for $95.49 at our local Ben Franklin department store last fall during the Moose Madness days. I'm feeling perky. Thin (sorta), and brave.

Larissa eyes my footwear. The eyebrow stays up.

"What?" I ask. I note that she's wearing three-inch heels. And looks fabulous.

"Nichevo," she says and turns to leave.

What? What? Oh, not fair speaking your native tongue!

I follow her out of the flat (we take the elevator—it seems to me I should be opting to take it *up,* and hoofing it *down,* but I'm in no position to argue. I'm pretty sure she and I aren't going to be soul mates.)

Russia doesn't look any different than last night. Crumpled wrappers swirl at my feet, and the smell of trash lingers in the air. I could use a glimpse of a bistro right now. Instead, we hike through a weedy field that is occupied by kids playing soccer with a watermelon, (Miss Hoity-Toity sure wishes she had hiking boots now!) and descend to the Metro.

I don't subway surf. Not only would Turquoise Woman probably backhand me, but the subway is standing room only, and I note a definite difference in personal space. As in, Americans have it, Russians don't. I barely avoid a full body smush next to Mafia Jr. in a black leather jacket and crew cut, and opt instead to tower over a hunched babushka sitting on one of the seats. She pulls her purse in tight to her chest. Yeah, lady, I'm going to boost all twenty rubles and your bag of potatoes.

"Where are we headed?" I ask. I'm thinking that perhaps it might be wise to obtain this information prior to leaving the apartment next time. Just in case I offend her. Further.

"Moscow Bible Church. Matthew asked me to pick you up." She has one hand wrapped around an overhead bar. She's not even glistening in that silk suit. I, on the other hand, wouldn't lift my arm that high if my life depended on it.

"Do you work for Matthew?"

"Yes," she says, and gives a slight smile. Hmm. Am I reading something into this? Maybe Turquoise Girl has feelings for Matthew.

We fall out of the subway with the masses, ascend on the escalator and I gulp in fresh Moscow air as we walk the two more blocks to Moscow Bible Church.

The church building is three stories tall with lime-green stucco and ornate white trim. We walk through the front door and take the wide winding staircase up to a second floor. A corridor overlooks the entry way. I see displays, and advertisements, in Russian, for events. Pictures. An offering box.

"It used to be Comsomol HQ," Larissa says simply and climbs the stairs.

The Comsomol was the communist youth organization—think Russian boy and girl scouts plus brainwashing. I smile, liking how God works.

Upstairs, we knock on an office door. Matthew opens it and yes, he's just as beautiful today as last night. He gives me a warm smile. "Hi, Josey. I see you made it."

Larissa is all grins, and for a second, Matthew's smile lands on her. I see something in his eyes. Then it vanishes and so does my translator, but I don't need any help interpreting that exchange.

Matthew invites me into his office. It's a nice room, with bookshelves, brown carpet, a metal desk, two wooden chairs and lots of books. I sit across from him and we do the pleasantries.

Then, he hands me a schedule. I peruse it. It has "orientation" listed for this week, then a class schedule starting September 1st. I have two classes a day, one in the morning, one in the evenings. I'm listed as Matthew's assistant.

"I've asked Larissa to show you around town today, take you to the market, teach you how to purchase food, change money and find your way home."

Is this difficult?

And, oh, joy. I can't think of a better shopping companion.

"She'll also be your language teacher," Matthew says, steepling his long fingers.

"Language teacher?" I ask. I look at the schedule. Who is teaching whom?

"You'll take two hours of language instruction in the mornings."

Oh. "Why?"

He frowns. "To get a grasp on your host country. And to prepare you for further missionary service."

Further…okay, getting ahead of ourselves here. But, remember, God's got a plan, so I smile.

"The evenings you'll spend with me, teaching beginning English. We have a group of adults who are all applying for seminary classes at our sister church in Seattle, Washington, and they need a grasp of the English language to pass their entrance exam."

Adults? What about Mother Josey?

A knock at the door. Larissa pokes her head in. Her smile is for Matthew alone. "Ready to shop?" she asks.

Are you talking to me?

"Sure, I'm game," I say. Because, you know, shopping means food. And even I can deal with Turquoise Girl if she feeds me. I try out an idea that supernovas in my head.

"Maybe we can stop at a bistro? Grab a bite?" I saw blue sky and clouds on the way over….

"Bweestro?" she says, and her frown is the first sign of disaster. "We don't have any bweestros in Russia."

Anyone else feel that rush of panic?

Five o'clock p.m. Moscow time is two o'clock a.m. H quitting time in Minneapolis, MN, USA.

I'm loving my current luck. And the fact that only four days into this adventure I have figured out how to hook up to the Internet. Okay, okay, I asked Rick, but still, that took courage! Or rather, priorities.

<Wildflower> I can't believe you made it! What day is it there?

<GI> We're one day ahead, so it's Thursday.

<Wildflower> Is Thursday a good day? Ha Ha. I can't believe you've been there four days already. I'm so impressed.

<GI> Thanks. (Because I do deserve it. Not only have I not killed Tracey, but I asked her, as politely as I could, not to have Rick sleep over. She called me something in Russian. There it is again—the glaring need to speak this garbled language!) I'm adjusting.

<Wildflower> So, met any cute Russian men?

<GI> Cuter than Chase? (That's my way of saying, well, no. Because, although I have the opportunity knocking in Auntie Milla's daily offering of fried goodies, I'm less than anxious to meet Vovka, her grandson. Dunno why. A gut feeling maybe. The only hopeful is Matthew, but I haven't seen him since Monday. And I think that maybe that is a Larissa maneuver. But, he did call me once. Perhaps it was just because I hadn't heard English in about sixteen hours, but his voice sounded dangerously endearing. Gentlemanly. Suave. Are missionaries supposed to be suave?) No. All the men here dress in black jeans, black squared off shoes, dark shirts and crew cuts. It might help if I could understand a pickup line if I heard one.

<Wildflower>: Have you eaten all the bagels yet?

<GI> (dodging the question) I learned to shop at the market—think fruits, vegetables, the smell of barbecued meat, pig heads, raw fish, canned goods and a lot of people saying "Eta." Which means, "That." I know because I'm taking Russian lessons every morning. (Larissa could be a first cousin to Stalin himself. I'd like to teach *her* a few words. Oh, Josey, be nice!)

<Wildflower> When do you start teaching?

<GI> Next week. One lesson a night. In the meantime, I guess I'm supposed to hand out tracts, or something. Saturday I'm headed out to St. Basil's Cathedral and Red Square. I thought I'd get my tourist phase out of the way. (And I'm starting to get subway surfing down. Caleb would be proud. Hey, where's he been anyway?)

<Wildflower> Have you heard from Chase?

<GI> (feeling that question like a punch to my sternum) No. (It actually hurts how much I miss him. In fact, every time I close my eyes, he is there. Waving, running after me. In various attires and forms of angst. In all of them I turn, and then stand there, wrapped in invisible duct tape while he calls my name. Which means…what?)

<Wildflower> Too bad he missed you at the airport.

Airport? Airport! Tears prick my eyes, and I'm not quite sure why—angst, relief, sorrow, glee?

<GI> Well, if he wants to see me, he knows where I am. (I type it, but inside, I'm hearing a primal scream.)

<Wildflower> You go, girl.

I awaken at 6:00 a.m. Saturday morning, and it's the latest I've slept all week, which is a sign of hope, I have to believe. I lie there, letting the smells of a new morning rush over me, draw me to consciousness. I feel alone. I've been in Russia for a week, and as I take stock of my choices, my accomplishments, I realize that I've made no dents in my landscape. Yet.

But Ephesians 1:5 is still embedded in my brain. Here for a purpose, by God's delight. To the praise of His glory. It sounds good, even if I don't fully grasp it.

I dress, and sneak out and take the subway, surfing until someone joins my compartment. I'm wearing my jeans and a pair of Birkenstocks and my short-sleeve lime-green T-shirt and I've pulled my unruly hair back into a headband. It's seen better days. But today is about me. It's my one-week anniversary of leaving my homeland and I'm going to Red Square. The landscape of revolutionary revolt, the parade ground of grand beginnings. It is here, under the shadow of the red, green and blue copulas of St. Basil's cathedral that the Bolsheviks spilled blood. Here, seventy years later, a generation revolted again, this time bringing glasnost (which means freedom, another new word—see, I'm going to be fluent soon!).

I exit the subway and hike to Red Square. The sun has burned off the fog hovering over the Volga and is drying the puddles of dew lining the cracks between bricks. I march through the relative quietness of the square, watch the changing of the guard at Lenin's Mausoleum. I hear there is a petition under way to bury his corpse, alongside Stalin and Brezhnev and Khrushchev. Another sign of change. I'm all in favor of burying the dead. Especially those who've been gone nearly eighty years.

I spot an artist setting up his stand, and stride over. Gesture what I hope is the phrase, "Are you open?"

He understands my pantomime, nods, and asks me to sit. I pose and listen to the morning—pigeons cooing as they stalk the pavement, the sounds of traffic snarling nearby, the clanking of bread kiosks opening—while he paints a caricature of my face. I hear that these artists pick one feature and accentuate. I'm thinking it'll be my hawklike nose, and I'm suddenly regretting this move.

But when he's finished, I'm surprised to see he's found my eyes, Blue. Shining. Huge. And a slight Mona Lisa smile, as if I'm not sure, yet, what to make of my new life.

"*Spaceeba,*" I say and drop him a hundred ruble note. (Don't panic, that's only five bucks.)

I roll up the picture, put it in my bag, and wander into GYM—pronounced "Goom." It's a two-story department-type store—once the state store—complete with fountains and nooks and crannies for Benetton, Lego, Hallmark, the Gap (yeah, Russia!) and a few other notable western shops. The center kiosks are closed, but I look in the windows, feeling a sense of courage, being here, alone, as if I own the place. I hear the *cha-ching* of store fronts opening as I exit onto the street.

This is my first excursion to the center of Moscow. Well, except for my transfers onto and off of the gold ring Metro line. I'm wondering what I'd discover if I got on the gold ring and just surfed from stop to stop, emerging to street level to explore the different opportunities. I check my map. Arbat Street. Lenin's Museum. The Bolshoi! I find a smile.

I glimpse a Golden Arches in the distance and my heart leaps. McDonald's? I turn toward it, pulse pounding. French fries would never taste so good.

Except, *there,* across the street from Oh Happy American Eatery is…a *bistro.* Little tables with green umbrellas tilted toward the sun. Early morning coffee—or most likely, tea—connoisseurs perusing menus. I wait for the light, then stalk toward it.

We have no bweestros in Russia.
Yeah, right. Well, guess what, Miss Turquoise?
God is smiling.

Chapter Eight:
Declarations

Just call me Vanna. Really. Because as I sit here, day fourteen of our class, collecting papers, and pointing to words that Matthew has written on the board, I know that I am simply window dressing. Oh, joy, I came a billion miles overseas, live with Tarzan's Jane and have been reduced to eating carrots for breakfast so I could point to *the* and *and*.

"Matthew, do you think I could prepare a lesson?" I ask as we hustle down the hall toward his office after class. And yes, I'm carrying the lesson books, as well as all the overhead transparencies. I mean, that's why I'm here, right?

"Maybe." He turns, and I don't know what is wrong with me but all the anger that burned in my chest a second ago is doused with his white smile. "I just don't want to rush you."

Rush me, rush me! And I'm only sorta talking about the teaching part. But I'm touched by his thoughtfulness. "I appreciate that, Matthew. But I think I could do it. I mean, we follow the ESL book, right, and the lessons are basically prepared? I think I could add some creative twists. Maybe a game or two."

He considers me with those dark eyes, a half smile. I've decided that missionaries can be suave, as long as they do it chastely. That definition works for me as I lean against the doorframe of his office and offer my own version of a suave smile.

"Okay. Listen. I have to go out of town in a couple weeks. You plan the lessons and I'll let you handle the class while I'm gone."

"Who were you going to have lead it?" I ask, feeling slightly betrayed.

He looks sheepish. "Larissa. She's filled in for me on occasion."

Turquoise Larissa, Stalin's cousin? Over my cold and mutilated body. "I'll do it. I promise, I'll do a good job."

He looks skeptical and I give him my best smile, the one I used on Dwight when I convinced him that I had a calling, really, a calling! "Okay. We'll go over it, say, a week from next Friday evening, right before I leave and then Monday you can have the reins."

A Friday night? Is that a date, a *working* date? I glance past him, and see our students (doesn't that sound romantic? *Our* students. Like, our *children*) flood out of the classroom. We have twenty students, mostly college age, some my age and even a few in their fifties. I have to admire their spunk as they say words like *thank-you* (zank you) and *her* (kher). Of course, I must not sound any better, as I mangle the word hello. (*Dzrastvootya*—I mean, c'mon! How totally unfair is that?)

"Where?"

This is the sure test of a date. If it's someplace fun, like the

Gray Pony (although I'm pretty sure that Matthew wouldn't step a foot in the Gray Pony, not even on Karen Carpenter night—he's too "missionary"), or even Venetsia (my bistro off Red Square!), then we'll know…date. If it's at his office… well then…yuck.

"There's a new restaurant opening in Moscow underground—the mall off Red Square. It's supposedly Italian. How about meeting me there, around seven?"

A date! It is a date! I smile, but can't help feel a twinge in my gut, something that feels a little like guilt.

Go away. I'm fair game. And Chase hasn't written to me. At all.

But he came to the airport.

Did I say go away?

"Sounds great. You won't be disappointed," I say, about the lesson.

"I'm sure I won't," and he has a glint in his eye that makes me warm down to my toes.

I admit that I didn't attend church my first two Sundays in country. I know, I know, that's a missionary sin, but for one, I knew I wouldn't be able to understand a word. For two, at the time I couldn't quite remember how to get to the Moscow Bible Church, having only visited once (with Larissa). And, I didn't have Caleb's telephone number.

I'm starting to miss him.

But I'm game for church today. I'm even looking forward to diving into this new cultural experience and fellowshipping with my brothers and sisters in Christ. I'm armed with my Super Deluxe Bible and my Russian/English Dictionary, and looking good in a pair of black suit pants (they're even loose on me, how about that?) and a sea-green cardigan set and a brand-new pair of black leather scuffs I found at Macy's on clearance. I leave in plenty of time, make my subway connections and surf with confidence to MBC. I open the door to the building, already hearing the buzz—

"Hey, is that the new missionary? Isn't she a cutie? I wonder how she's faring?"

"Oh, I hear that she's already taking over teaching Matthew's class. And her grasp of Russian is amazing. She'll be fluent by Christmas."

"She'll probably lead a Bible study, too. Oh, I hope so! I want to be her class."

I march into the MBC sanctuary with a triumphant smile.

I'm nearly flattened by a deacon. Or someone holding offering plates. And right behind him, the congregation is streaming out. Happy people in conversation. I am a salmon, swimming up-river. What?

I stand there for a long while, trying to get a grasp of why I'm standing in a quiet auditorium watching the sound crew coiling up cables. A large golden paper cross is pinned to the far end of the stage, on bloodred curtains. I look up, and the familiar webs of dust hang from the ceiling. This room could house a Garth Brooks concert.

"Josey?"

I turn, half expecting Matthew, and see instead my favorite Grunge Man.

"Caleb!" I barely restrain myself from hugging him. "How are you?"

"Glad to lay eyes on you. I was wondering if you'd gotten sucked up by the Metro."

Oh, man, I'd forgotten what a great smile Caleb has. And he's dressed up for church today in a pair of cargo shorts, a tie-dyed shirt and a bandanna over all that hair. He's also wearing a leather necklace with a shark tooth tied in it.

"No," I answer, laughing. "You'd be proud of me. I can surf, and I even found the McDonald's all by myself." For some reason, I'm not telling him about Venetsia. It's my place. Where Chase finds me for the hour he arrives in Russia to declare his love for me. "I guess I still can't tell time, however."

He laughs. "We changed our service time. Sorry. I should have told you. How about a 'Big Mac With Fries' apology?"

I laugh, weighing the ramifications. It doesn't qualify for a date…which really shouldn't matter because Matthew and I are a non-item at the moment. But what if Matthew truly likes me? What if behind that white smile, soft eyes and pressed-khaki attire there lurks passion and adventure? What if he wants to sweep me off my feet, tour Arbat Street with me or even treat me to a night out at the Bolshoi? What if he's the guy I've come all the way to Russia to find… Okay, yes, I know that I haven't come to Russia to find a man, but what if that is a God-perk? A reward for a job well done? What if, with Matthew, I see fireworks? I can't have Grunge Man lingering on the outskirts, right?

But…McDonald's isn't a date, even in Russia. Moreover, it is food. This fact should never be dismissed, especially by a gal whose sum total of food in her cupboard consists of a bag of carrots, a hunk of scary yellow cheese, a few softening cucumbers, a piece of hard sausage, two apples and three bottles of a kind of lemonade (I know because there is a lemon on the label). Lest you think this is meager, I want to point out it took me a good two hours to gather these products as I "*eta*-ed" my way around the market. But, I had to focus on items that one does not have to cook. Because, well…I don't know how to work my stove. It's gas, but it doesn't seem to have an on switch. I fiddled with it for a couple days, but I haven't been able to ascertain the magic steps since Tracey doesn't eat, ever. (Except for her dwindling supply of Bubble Yum—yes, I've been checking. Hunger does that. And, I still owe her for the M&Ms, which she seemed pretty big about so far. But, who knows when PMS hits?)

A stampeding herd of rhinoceroses couldn't drag the request to teach me to use the stove from my mouth. Not to Tracey and especially not to Rick or Larissa. Food ranks below Internet in priorities.

Besides, I think I've lost a couple pounds.

Which means I can afford some French fry indulgence. "Yeah, sounds great," I say to Caleb.

We surf down the red line to the ring and get off. The pigeons scatter as we stroll down the Garden Ring road toward the Golden Arches. Fine dining, ex-pat style.

"So, how's teaching going?"

I shrug. "Not the glamour job I thought, but I get to take the reins in a couple weeks, so I guess I'm excited."

"Well, bear in mind that the people taking your class are depending on you to help them change their lives. They need you, and your help, if they want to get the education they need. After seminary, they'll return to Russia and go to work as missionaries or Christian workers in tiny communities. In a way, you're the first step toward the salvation of hundreds, maybe thousands."

Stop it, Caleb, you're freaking me out. But a warm feeling has started in my heart at his words. Josey Berglund, seed-planter, equipper. "Thanks for that reminder, Caleb."

"You missed a good sermon today. It was on Philippians

2:13. 'For it is God in you who works in you to will and to act according to his good purpose.'"

Hey, that sounds a lot like the Ephesians stuff I've been reading. I'm up to verse eleven, by the way, which talks about God working out everything according to His will. A comforting thought. Sorta. I mean, if His will is going my direction. I mention this to Caleb.

"I love Ephesians," Caleb responds with a chuckle. "I love how it starts with the basics—God choosing to reach out of heaven to love us and then to give us a purpose. In fact, the entire book is about God's grand picture, and how we fit into it."

"I hope that is a good thing," I say, remembering Chase, the way his hair tangles in the wind off Gull Lake, his particular Chase-scent after a round of catch. I mean, I *hope* God knows what He's doing in sending me here. Because, without a letter from Chase, I have to admit I'm slightly panicking.

"It's a good thing, Jose. God is for us, not against us. He is ultimately about showing Himself and His unbelievable love to us, and through us, as He takes us through life."

I smile. I like to think of God giving purpose and being a part of the grand picture. And, it feels freeing to be walking along the streets of Moscow, strange words in stereo around us, the smell of street vendors' greasy fried sandwiches tingeing the air, and blue sky beyond the Yellow M...talking about God without hesitation. Caleb makes his faith feel easy. Something that is an extension of himself, that isn't confined to his attire, or his persona. Who woulda thunk it?

We pull into McDonald's and true to his word, Caleb treats me to a Big Mac and fries and even adds a vanilla shake. I could kiss him on the spot. The places is packed, and it feels weird to order a Big Mac in Russian (Beeg Maak). I decide to save my wrapper because it's written in Cyrillic. Maybe I'll send it to Jas.

Whom I miss. I haven't received one letter from her, and this bothers me nearly as much as not hearing from Chase. What, have I dropped off the planet? Good grief, I only moved to Russia!

Caleb and I spend the day walking through Gorky Park. From the Ferris wheel that overlooks the city, he points out the Kremlin—right off Red Square…now why didn't I figure that out?—and a few other landmarks. I especially take note of the U.S. Consulate. I imagine it's only a matter of time before they invite me to a ball or something. We eat ice cream on a bridge overlooking the Volga and feed the pigeons our soggy cones. And, as he walks me home, I tell him about Larissa (Turquoise Girl), Auntie Milla, Tracey and Rick. He asks me about home, but I don't mention much. It feels like the bistro information…too far into my world.

"Watch out for Totye Milla," he says as we climb the stairs. (Again, elevator up? Stairs down? I need to get my rhythm right!) "She's probably after a visa."

I frown at him.

"You marry her son and she's got a ticket to the states."

Whoa back there, Bucko. "I never said I was going to marry him."

He smirks and I'm not sure, suddenly, how to read him. "Russians can be…persuasive," he adds.

Not sure how to take that. I give him an eyebrow up, but we're at my door so he jots his telephone number onto my hand. "Call me if you need a memory jog on what time the service starts."

Then he's gone. My Grimy Hero.

I let myself in, interrupting something PG-13 on the sofa.

I turn my back on Rick and Tracey and enter the kitchen, help myself to a carrot. I stare at the stove, feelings of longing welling inside as I hear Rick and Tracey murmur in the background.

Rick says nothing to me as he leaves.

Tracey thumps back to the family room, lands on the vinyl (yes, unfortunately) sofa. "Hey," she says.

Words from the Tiger Woman? It piques my interest. I so don't want to fight with her, and it makes me more than sad that we're not bosom buddies, in an abstract, roomies-should-be-buddies way. I walk into the next room, crunching my carrot. She's leaning back into the cushions, arms across her ample bosom. I have a similarly ample bosom, but it's pretty much swallowed up by lots of ample other stuff.

"You have a package," she says.

A package? A package! My heart leaps and I nearly bite the inside of my mouth. "Who from?"

"Not so fast. Who told you to use my PO Box?"

What? I frown at her. She gives me a CIA interrogator look (I can spot them now, after the summer with my mother) and apparently decides I'm truly baffled because she sighs and I see some of the fight leave her face. With her foot, she nudges a shoe box sitting on the top of our black glass coffee table. "They do that sometimes—just see the English writing and stick it in the closest American's box. I stood in line for an hour today to get this, and it wasn't even for me."

Oops. "Thanks, Tracey. That was really nice of you."

She considers me. Doesn't smile, flops back on the sofa. "Where have you been all day?"

"I went to McDonald's with a friend from church." I'm looking at the package, dying to open it, but feeling that it might be sorta rude. So, with great and admirable restraint, I set it on my lap. "Then we hung out at Gorky Park."

She takes a hunk of her hair, starts to separate it. "Rick wants me to move in with him."

My gut reaction is *no!* Then, shamefully, Yes! Yes! Yes! But, I'm a missionary, and it's not about me. "Are you sure that's the wisest thing to do?" I try and say it gently. Because I don't want my rebellious feelings of joy to bubble forth.

To my utter surprise, she sighs. What? No jumping to her feet in defense? No appalled Russian comments about my overly moralistic stance? "I'm not sure he loves me."

Uh, that's a big no-brainer. Because even I can see that it's all about Neo. He's constantly checking his hair in the mirror behind our door, fixing his sunglasses (before he leaves the house? *Please.*) and giving Tracey a long look over before they leave, as if assessing her worthiness for his company. And, a guy who loves her wouldn't be playing house before he put a ring on her finger. Because, true love respects, cherishes and *waits*. And that's not a line.

But I don't say all this. "I would miss you," I hear instead. And then I search the room for *who said that*. Me, miss the Bagel Burglar? But, maybe I would. Because I've been praying for Tracey for two weeks, and maybe God is giving me a glimpse past the animal skins into her world. My gut says she seems just a bit…unhappy.

"You'd miss me?" she repeats, as if she, too, is unsure if those words came from my mouth.

"Yes. And besides…well, do you see anything incongruent with you running an anti-trafficking program and…ah, setting the example you are with your boss?"

I've hit a nerve because she flinches, looks away, at the encroaching darkness outside our window.

I'm scraping up all my courage here, ready to launch my final volley. I owe it to my roomie to speak the truth, right? "Rick…might just be out for a sure thing, Tracey. And, well, you're worth more than that."

She looks at me, eyes wide. Then they glisten and suddenly she's standing. Is it to give me a hug? Finally, a true friend, who will speak the tru—

She storms into her room and slams the door behind her. Oops.

Custom's Declaration

1 1-lb. bag Reese's Peanut Butter Cups
2 pair of wool socks
1 bag Tootsie Pops
1 small bag coffee
1 magazine

Dear Jose,
I know that this isn't much, and it feels so weird to be sending this package when you're right across the yard, packing. But I don't know how long mail is going to take overseas and I want a head start. I'm sending this to your mission, and I hope that they forward it. Besides…well, the truth is, I'm not sure I can figure out this e-mail stuff. You know my strengths, and well, if I can't put it in an oven, I'm fairly sure it'll flop. Milton says he'll help me, however. He's been uncharacteristically quiet since your declaration of moving to Moscow. I think he feels he's to blame, but I know better. You've always been the adventurous one, and I probably shouldn't be surprised by your decision. Still, I'm so

proud of you. I know you're going to change the world over there. You probably already have a million friends and are winning souls for Christ with every breath. As for me, you've already made me think about my life and my walk with God. Maybe there is something to this calling stuff.

A couple things:

1. The socks are from Mom. I know you think she's not on your side, but yesterday I overheard her telling a guest that her daughter was going to Russia as a missionary, and even I could hear pride in her voice. Don't doubt it.

2. Just because I am sending you a *Lost* magazine doesn't mean you're a groupie. (Although I don't believe you when you say you don't have a thing for Sawyer.)

3. Do you remember the summer we drove to Montana? The Tootsie Pops brought back memories. I still have my collection of wrappers with the Indians on them. What are we supposed to do with those anyway?

I love you.

Jas

I eat the entire bag of Reese's cups. They're a little salty, due to the tears, but they make a great supper—all that peanut butter protein.

Chapter Nine:
Tattoo Me

One would think, living in a resort community in northern Minnesota, that I might have learned to fish. Gull Lake is a magnet for anglers looking to score and we have more than a few pictures on our restaurant wall of grubby patrons holding the leviathan of the freshwater ponds. I mostly don't like to fish because I don't like to *touch* fish. They're... well, did you know they salivate through their skin? Now, imagine *that* touching your hands. My point exactly. And, well, I can't get their glassy eyes out of my head. On a few joyous occasions I've walked in on my mother cleaning fish, and the smell is enough to make a possum run.

The sad irony in all this is that I really enjoy the taste of fish. A walleye fried in butter is a delight that probably should be on God's lists of sins. Usually, if I enter the process of fish preparation at the point of presentation—pan-fried walleye with a glaze of glorified butter and a side of fresh broccoli—I'm fine.

I should have recognized danger the moment I opened the door. No, before that, actually, from the smell seeping under the front door. And then hurled myself from the balcony.

Instead I gape for a half second while Auntie Milla launches herself across the threshold. She's obviously upped her ammo from liver Bismarcks, which I'm starting to sort of look forward to, in a way a person might enjoy their daily ingestion of bran. But, until my Hot Date (and food!) with Matthew, I'm subsisting and liver Bismarcks are better than, oh, say…air?

She's grinning. I know, because I'm nearly blinded from the sun off her teeth. *"Pashulsta,"* she says, and I now understand enough of the code to know it's *please* she's saying, not *you're welcome.* She holds out a carcass of something wrapped in newspaper.

I take it like one might accept the remains of roadkill. I lay the offering on the counter. Maybe it'll just…decay right there and some day I can sweep away the bones.

"Spaceeba," I lie.

"Pashulsta," she says. (Get the code? You're welcome? I'm deciding that if I only have to learn a few words, maybe this is a good one? Sorta double duty?) She then stands there and smiles. She's wearing a turquoise-and-brown housecoat, gold slippers and her hair's coiled atop her head.

Uh-oh. I'm fresh out of Reese's Cups, bagels, and my carrot supply is dwindling quickly. She's got me over a barrel. Which, perhaps is exactly where she wants me. Without a return gift I have to *meet her grandson!*

In a flash of brilliance, I see her thinly veiled plot. I may talk like a pre-schooler but it doesn't mean that I can't comprehend even the most sublime of ploys.

I am not without my own resources, however.

Tootsie Pops.

I hold up my hand in a sort of "wait here" gesture and dash for my room. I'll give her a brown one. To match her attire? But guilt grabs me around the throat and at the last second I grab a grape. That innate Minnesota niceness gets me every time!

She looks at it with an upraised eyebrow. I unwrap the brown one, and then, showing her, put it in my mouth.

She mimics me, and a second later, I get an approving smile. Just call me Josey the Diplomat. See, they should invite me to the embassy!

I motion her into the flat, not sure where Tracey is. Since my revelation two days ago, she's been avoiding me like SARS. I have a feeling she might be giving Rick's proposal a trial run.

Auntie Milla sits, runs her hand over the vinyl, all the while slurping her Tootsie Pop. I'm wondering what the grape is going to do for the gold teeth. Not a pretty visual.

I'm not completely helpless here, by the way. I've taken Russian classes for nearly three weeks. And used a bit of it at the market, so I decide to launch out to new pastures.

"Kak dela?" I ask. It means "how are you," and while I'm slightly terrified of the answer, the Norwegian inside me can't help but ask.

She rattles off a litany, of which I think I make out, *medicine, Putin* and something I think just might be a swear word. Oh, boy. I nod, though, and add concern on my face. The medicine part could be bad.

We sit there, more silence, more slurping.

She asks me a question. I stare at her, pause as if in thought while I fight to find even one word I might latch on to. It only takes one. I can conjure up all sorts of options from one word. For example, the word *rabota* might be a question about my work, and I could respond with a *horosho* (meaning good), and then maybe give her a tract. Or, the word *doma* (home) might be something about my feeling comfortable here in Russia, or better yet, a question about Gull Lake. At which I can produce a few pictures and try out some new words, and then eventually show her my church. And give her a tract. (See how I think like a missionary? Everything boils down to evangelism.)

However, I can't find that magic word in her sentence. She smiles, slurps, asks again. Oh, I hate surrender. But I finally utter the magic *"Ya Ne Panimiayo."* Which means… you guessed it—"I don't understand." This phrase, however, is misleading. Because, if I can say, clearly, in Russian, that I don't understand, it sorta lessens the impact of my words, right?

She nods, then rises, and out of me gusts a nearly audible whoosh of relief. As much as I want to tell this woman Jesus loves her, I can't find my hook. But the sudden grip of despair feels nearly suffocating as I realize how fully I've failed her. Aunt Milla, lost forever in the abyss because I can't latch on to her babble. I should give her a tract anyway.

Only, she doesn't bee-line toward the door, but for my kitchen. Opening the newspaper, she parks her Tootsie Pop in her cheek like a gopher and stares down at her offering. It's a fish, all right. I grab the door handle and nearly fall over from the smell. But she pays the fainting American no mind and rifles through my drawers until she finds a knife.

Who is that knife for, anyway…?

She's…not…going…to…

How rude would it be for me to run to my room and hang my head out of the window?

She guts the fish in one surgical move, then with two fingers, rips out the innards. That I didn't need to see. Then, two more chops and the head and fins are off. She sets them aside on the paper.

Chop, chop, chop, I have fish steaks.

She opens a cupboard, (not Tracey's! If only!) and finds a plate. She scoops up the steaks and plops them on the plate.

Slurping the Tootsie Pop (not an especially comforting sound given the moment), she examines the innards. Okay, I feel like I'm in science class and my head gets woozy. But she's on a hunt and a few moments later she grabs a coffee cup and in it goes a pouch of...oh yuck, eggs.

I'm needing to sit down, put my head between my knees. But, mercifully, she wraps up the carcass into the newspaper, then drops it into the garbage under my sink.

A garbage I'll have to empty, thanks.

But Auntie Milla isn't done, and I'm pretty sure that God knows my desperation, (after all, I finished off the cheese this morning), because she grabs a fry pan from under the counter (which suddenly begs the question—how does she know my kitchen that well? Has Tracey already been a fish victim? Or worse...a *Vovka* victim? Yuck. Now I am so not meeting him. Even with the fish gift.)

She fills the pan with a scant amount of water, and then... *turns on the stove.*

Yes. I nearly fall into a faint, and am feeling quietly stupid as I rewind her actions for later emulation. She opened a drawer, found matches (who put those there? I thought Rick had left them!) and lit one over a burner. The stove burner flamed with a whoosh.

And then there was fire.

I feel like Neanderthal girl, marveling, mouth half-open.

Auntie Milla plunks a fish steak into the water, adds a cover. She turns back to me with a smile and a look of kindness in her face.

I love her. Truly. I can actually feel tears welling behind my eyes.

Ten minutes later, I'm looking at a piece of boiled something—it looks familiarly like salmon. She puts it on a plate, gives it to me.

I can hear my stomach clapping. *"Spaceeba,"* I say.

She shrugs, and *now* she moves toward the door.

But as I let her out, she turns back, and the smile I get is pure KGB Victory. And I want to cringe. I've been had by the chief of spooks.

I owe her big.

Vovka better know how to cook.

I smell football air as I kick aside scattered, decaying leaves in my trek toward the Metro this late Friday afternoon, on my way to my Hot Date with Matthew. It's homecoming weekend in Gull Lake, a fact that seems to be dogging me all day, tugging out recollections like one might pull out old pictures and become tangled inside the memory of sweet smells, and the calls of old friends. I wonder if Jas and Milton will go to the game. Jas was never a fan of the gridiron, but found her niche playing the flute in the marching band.

I played the blow horn. Which isn't exactly an official MB instrument, but worked for me. It had one pitch, *loud*. And it could be used as a drumstick against the bleachers when I ran out of breath. Yes, I was a dyed-in-the-wool Gull Lake Seagulls booster. I wasn't above painting my face in two greasy stripes of gray and black, wearing a fake gray mane and standing at the top of the bleachers with my long plastic blow horn—which sounded more like a frustrated Brahma bull—and making a fool out of myself. I told myself then that I did it because of Chase. He played wide receiver, and something akin to pride would well up inside me when he jogged onto the field in his silver warrior's garb. He'd turn, wave to me in the stands and I'd blow my horn. It was our finest hour.

Now, I wonder, if it was these moments that made me shift weight, ostracized like a leper on the sidelines of the homecoming dance. Unfortunately, teenagers don't think far enough ahead (three hours?) to the grim circumstances of their actions. Thankfully, now that I remember it, Chase usually came to my rescue with at least one dance and a quick getaway.

I wonder who he's going to rescue tonight.

Ooh, that thought hurts, like a knife in the sternum. Perhaps I should remember I'm on my way to a date. A *date*. During which I will not think about Chase, about how he might look in his old letter jacket, the soft gleam in his blue eyes, especially when he smiles, one side up, sorta cute and lopsided…

I said don't!

I cut down the Metro, and being the pro I am, I breeze right through the turnstiles, and don't even glance (okay, once!) at Gulag Woman standing guard. I know she works for the KGB. I can feel it in the small hairs standing on end on my neck.

I'll just say it out loud, fast and quick, like ripping off a scab. Chase hasn't written. It's been nearly six weeks since I left Gull Lake and nada. Nil. *Nichevo*. (See how fluent I am?)

And, you know, it's okay, because I don't think about him anymore. Not really.

Okay! I'm lying. It's so not okay that the fact he hasn't

written has only become an ember in my brain. What's his deal? Doesn't he know I'm serving God over here? Sacrificing? I can understand Jasmine. After all, while she can run a food processor in all speeds, and knows the use for every attachment, she still thinks a mouse is one of those things that you put peanut butter traps out for. But Chase—he's an anthropologist. Which tells me he knows humanity can not exist without their PC, especially this five-foot-three, slightly (but not as much as before!) pudgy humanity. And, accordingly, he learned to accommodate my addictions by installing AOL Instant Messenger and adding me to his contacts list. So what is his problem?

But this trip isn't about Chase. I promise to not think about him anymore.

In fact, I'll use this angst for self-reflection. How much of this trip really has been about him? Which means, by him not writing, I'm learning…what? What exactly is God up to here?

The Metro has a hushed hum to it. People don't shout in the Metro, no one wants to get rattled and suddenly end up in the pit. I've learned a trick about the escalators, too…I turn sideways. Thus, not looking down. Caleb would be proud.

Caleb's called me twice, by the way, and once we strolled down to the American Bar and Grill and stared in the windows. We can't afford to actually eat there. Then he took me to the circus, a much more affordable event that included popcorn and dancing poodles. He even picked me up for church last week (oh, he of little faith!) and translated for me during the sermon.

Don't read anything into it. He's just a friend. A grimy little pal who makes me laugh and feel warm and happy inside. And frankly, since Tracey has decided to wear her skin prickly side out, I need all the warm and happy I can find. She's moved in, mostly, with Rick. Keeps enough skins in her closet to recloak herself like a trapper coming in from the hunt once a week.

I get on the green line and surf toward the ring. Moscow Underground is a hot new mall built a stone's throw from Red Square and the Kremlin. Three stories of glitter and lights, it houses all the hip shops from Europe and America and on the mezzanine level, a pianist and an occasional jazz band. A gal just might think she's at the Mall of America if she doesn't listen to the babble of foreign language around her.

Wait! The babble of foreign languages *is* the Mall of America. I'm home, Toto!

I know all this about MU because Caleb and I prepped for this date. Because, you know, you can do that with *brothers.* I told him about Matthew just to confirm that this was an, *ahem,* date. We found the Italian restaurant and peered in that window, too.

Red-checked tablecloths, hurricane lamps, the smell of pizza. Not the height of elegance, but then again, I haven't had a pizza in nearly two months and any version of tomato sauce on a slab of bread will do it for me.

Russians do, by the way, sell pizza, via street vendors. Sort of. I let my expectations manhandle me one day and got sucked into a pizza line, only to discover it was tuna fish on a piece of Georgian *lavash* (think focaccia bread without the spices), covered in ketchup and mayonnaise and topped with a hard-boiled egg.

Someone nearly got hurt.

If I even get a whiff of tuna fish tonight…

I jump off the green line and surface to *Ohotniy Ryad.* The

Kremlin and St. Basil's cathedral send long shadows across Red Square, and a gust of wind off the Volga swirls leaves around artists and other vendors holding court at the fringes. I cross the street and head past the eternal flame and down the boulevard toward MU.

This is a spoon. (Zhis iz a spyewn.) I am running over my class notes in my head, trying to focus on the stated *why* of this event. Matthew, playing coy, hasn't hinted any further of the covert truth of our meeting—to know me better, to discover why I'm here, what makes me smile. He's been all business these past two weeks. But it's a front. Because really, we shouldn't cross any lines at work. Besides, he really is leaving on Monday, and I do have to prove I have this class well in hand. I'm positive I'll stun him with my teaching ability. I've made flashcards, games and even a song. I told you this teaching thing was a piece of cake/*kringle.*

But tonight after we have the preliminaries covered, I imagine Matthew will reach across the table, his elegant hand on mine, and he'll tell me what a great job I'm doing. Even more, he'll compliment me on my outfit (as he should, because I'm wearing a nicely conservative long black skirt, and a V-neck blouse with frilled cuffs. And a pair of thick-heeled pant boots in black suede, purchased from a catalogue I found in the *Gazette* bathroom. Hot is me. Well, Missionary hot. I don't want to go overboard or anything).

In fact, Matthew will be so overcome by my, well, *hotness,* that he'll rise to his feet the first moment he sees me, delight in his dark brown eyes. He's smitten, the entire restaurant can see that, and he pulls out my chair. "I've already ordered," he says. "Pepperoni and green peppers?"

Oh, see, we're meant to be! I smile demurely, because I don't want to give anything away, but I'm thinking, Josey

Winneman, Mrs. Matthew Winneman, Mrs. Josey Winneman. Lucy Winneman, Joey Winneman, Cindy-Lou Winneman. And no one will wear poppy at the wedding, which we'll have in Gull Lake, the reception on the front lawn of Berglund Acres with the wind teasing the clouds, and the smell of lilac in the air. Of course Jas will be the maid—er, matron (ha! Doesn't that sound old?) of honor, and well, Milton…he'll wash dishes…no, no, be nice. He'll be an usher. That's thoughtful of me, right?

I wonder where Matthew is from? He seems Italian, in that dark mysterious sort of way. But I don't sense a New York accent (not that I could tell one from, say, a Scottish accent. So twang placement isn't my specialty! Sue me!).

What if he wants to live in Moscow for the rest of his life? Do I want that? Maybe we can strike a bargain? Two years in Moscow, a few in Gull Lake raising the kids, then back to Europe. I'll have to be sure and nail that down tonight.

I cross the street and walk down the ramp to the MU doors. The wind whooshes out, as if the cavern of shops takes a gulp of fresh air as I round the revolving doors.

Maybe we should invite some of the members of our English class to the wedding. Because, you know, they knew us *when*. Definitely Evgeny—he's got beautiful liquid brown eyes that make me forget my verbs. No, don't jump to any conclusions, it's just that I love eyes. They're windows to the soul, and Evgeny's soul is sweet and gentle and heroic. And we'll have to invite Vera and her sister, Lera. Vera and Lera, cute huh? Vera is studying Christian education, and Lera wants to be a Bible translator. Short brown hair cut cropped, twinkling hazel-gold eyes. Smashed together they're a size four. But they seem so close it makes my heart feel squishy and soft to see them giggle together. I call them the Sugar Twins.

And we'll invite Sergei. Sweet Sergei, who pronounces iron as I-ron. He's so skinny I feel like Helga the Amazon next to him, but he wears a kooky smile and offers to walk me home at night, which I find pathetically sweet. Because, well, I'd be the one defending *him* from the Moscow street gangs. But the thought counts on my tally sheet.

I hear piano music soaring from the mezzanine level as I descend down the escalator. I wonder why Matthew wanted to meet me here. Why didn't he pick me up, date style? We could have ridden the subway together (or, well, would he have let me surf? Or is he too refined for that? Uh-oh, this may be a glitch!).

The smell of Italy—oregano, basil, baking bread—beckons like a Frank Sinatra ballad and I feel excitement swell inside me. I didn't come to Russia to find a man, but I have to say, this is a nice accessory. A sort of reward for a job well done. God likes me, He really does!

I stroll into the restaurant, stand in the entrance for a moment, my eyes adjusting, and spot Matthew sitting on the end of a booth. He's looking fine in a black pullover and tweed jacket. He catches my eye, lifts his hand, beckons me over. Why doesn't he rise to greet me? Well, maybe his chivalry is a bit rusty. (I mean, it's hard not to let it die in the land of eat or be eaten.) I easily find a smile as I maneuver around table groupings toward him.

I see his mouth move. Is he talking to me? His eyes are on me. I glide up to the booth, pained that I didn't hear his question.

But he's *not* talking to me. My pulse hiccups only slightly as I see, sitting next to him, a woman with long golden blond hair, brown eyes and a white smile. She's dressed in a nicely conservative blue corduroy jumper, with a starched white peasant blouse and large purple beads at her neck and ears. I can't see her shoes, but they've got to be red flats from Payless.

I'm trying not to hate her, really, because she seems nice, in a schoolteacher from the eighties sort of way. But who is she, and why has she sabotaged my date?

I stand there, my legs sort of not working, like icicles (only not quite as thin), wearing my Mona Lisa smile. I look at Matthew and I hope I have "who's your friend," in my eyes because he better make this good, the two-timing weasel. And after I'd invited Evgeny and Sergei to the wedding!

"Josey, I'm glad you could make it." Now he rises. Numb-skull. He pries himself out of the booth, and gestures to the interloper. "I'd like you to meet Rebecca."

I hold out my hand, She wraps a tight grip around mine. "Rebecca," I repeat, but my voice sounds like it's trapped in Siberia, along with the rest of my body. "Glad to meet you. Are you a fellow teacher with Moscow Bible Church?"

She laughs. It's more of a loud cackle. Whoops, I'm lying again! Her laughter is sort of a sweet, bouncing giggle. A Buffy-the-Amazon giggle.

"Oh, no," she says, and somehow I feel the world spinning as she looks at Matthew, something proprietary in her eyes, a look that all women can spot from across the room. "I'm Matthew's wife."

Of course.

I must have idiot stamped on my forehead.

5:30 p.m.
From: "Josey Berglund" <Josey@netmail.moscow.ru>
To: "H" <OnlyH@.mn.usa>
Subject: I'm so stupid

Dear H,

He's Married. I can't believe it. He never mentioned a word in nearly six weeks. Pond Scum. No worse, Sewer Sludge. I'm glad today is Saturday, or I'd have ripped his eyebrows out in class. "Hair, class, can you say Hair?" (Khair!)

How could this have happened twice? Do I have a tattoo on my body somewhere that reads, "fool me"?

Josey

3:50 a.m.
From: "H" <OnlyH@mn.usa>
To: "Josey Berglund" <Josey@netmail.moscow.ru>
Subject: Re: I'm so stupid
Dear No Tattoos Josey,

Not yet, but like I said a few months ago, we could arrange it. It might have been easier than flying halfway across the world. So that's two rejections in six months, not some sort of record or anything. Besides, Matthew was too stuffy for you.

H, the Wise One

6:03 p.m.
From: "Josey Berglund" <Josey@netmail.moscow.ru>
To: "H" <OnlyH@mn.usa>
Subject: Re: I'm so stupid
Dear Wise One,

Too stuffy? He was tall, dark and Italian—and aren't they known for their, um, expressiveness? Besides, I like Italian. I love pasta and pizza and even calzones, (although I hate French bread pizza, but then again, that might be French, not Italian). Most importantly, he was a missionary. Having "like goals" counts for a lot. I read that in our "finding the perfect mate" class at church.

By the way, you were all for this idea, remember?
Wondering Why I Listened in Moscow

3:23 a.m.
From: "H" <OnlyH@mn.usa>
To: "Josey Berglund"<Josey@netmail.moscow.ru>
Subject: Re: I'm so stupid
Dear Wondering,
I was for you changing your life. Tattoos were included in that
advisement. And having like goals *does* count. Like—I'll meet
you at Big Joes for ribs on Friday night. And let's pick up a
couple Schwarzenegger movies tonight. Or even, wanna go
see the Painful Dozen play down at the Howling Wolf? The
rest is beyond my purview to answer. But I can say that WinnA-
Man is not a last name for you. Josey Wins a Man? Yuck. Consider yourself saved from fifty years of mortification.
Maybe you should let love come to you. (Oh brother, see what
you made me do? I sound like Air Supply. It's too late for these
conversations. I'm going to bed.)
Snoozing

7: 24 p.m.
From: "Josey Berglund"<Josey@netmail.moscow.ru>
To: "H" <OnlyH@mn.usa>
Subject: WAIT!!!!!
Let love come to me? What if I end up like Myrtle, collecting
lawn art, or like Uncle Albert, sleeping in my barn with cattle
to keep warm? Shouldn't I be just a little panicked? So far love
has done an end-run around me and someone, no names
here, has forgotten I exist. I am Vapor Josey, the not quite
woman, not quite ghost. I can't even haunt someone with
memories!

By the way, speaking of, did you go to Homecoming?
Love,
Vapor Girl

4:39 a.m.
From: "H" <OnlyH@mn.usa>
To: "Josey Berglund" <Josey@netmail.moscow.ru>
Subject: Re: WAIT!!!!!
Dear VG,
Yes, I went. For some reason, Jasmine's wedding started this
cosmic nudge back to Gull Lake. I went to the game. Wore
silver paint (oh, thank you so much for that addiction), and res-
urrected the blow horn. We won, 17-12. Good game.

7:58 p.m.
From: "Josey Berglund" <Josey@netmail.moscow.ru>
To: "H" <OnlyH@mn.usa>
Subject: My Favorite Person!
Please, please, please!!
??
????????

5:11 a.m.
From: "H" <OnlyH@mn.usa>
To: "Josey Berglund" <Josey@netmail.moscow.ru>
Subject: You're in Moscow, remember?
Yes, he was there. I'm going to bed.

8:26 p.m.
From: "Josey Berglund" <Josey@netmail.moscow.ru
To: "H" <OnlyH@mn.usa>
Subject: Why don't you just drive bamboo under my nails?

He was with her, wasn't he? Missy, the Holiday Girl. I knew it,
I knew it, I knew it!

5:40 a.m.
From: "H" <OnlyH@mn.usa>
To: "Josey Berglund" <Josey@netmail.moscow.ru>
Subject: Don't Panic!
I'm sure it's a fling. A rebound. He's pining for you. Really. Re-
ally. Just, he's doing it in a very medicinal way.

8:53 p.m.
From: "Josey Berglund" <Josey@netmail.moscow.ru>
To: "H" <OnlyH@mn.usa>
Subject: You're my Very Best Friend Who Speaks the Truth
What if I was the rebound and she's the real Shazam? I knew
this would happen. I've lost him again.
…Quietly Dying in Moscow

6:10 a.m.
From: "H" <OnlyH@mn.usa>
To: "Josey Berglund" <Josey@netmail.moscow.ru>
Subject: Seriously, Don't Panic
1. You weren't the rebound. Because, well, you weren't around
long enough.
2. Refer to #1 + you can't lose someone you never had.
3. Do you want me to run over her? I still have my dad's
pickup in storage.

9:27 p.m.
From: "Josey Berglund" <Josey@netmail.moscow.ru>
To: "H" <OnlyH@mn.usa>
Subject: My Hired Assassin

Not yet. Let's save that for last. But don't let her slip from your sight. Maybe a little incentive is needed, here. Can you get a message to him, via the Gull Lake grapevine? Let's consider it a litmus test.

6:42 a.m.
From: "H" <OnlyH@mn.usa>
To: "Josey Berglund" <Josey@netmail.moscow.ru>
Subject: Consider it done.
Content?

9:53 p.m.
From: "Josey Berglund" <Josey@netmail.moscow.ru>
To: "H" <OnlyH@mn.usa>
Subject: Vovka
Just that. Let him wonder.

I am not here to meet men. I am not here to meet men. I am not here to meet men.

The flat is quiet, only the dripping of water into the sink. My social life consists of rereading the dog-eared *Lost* magazine Jas sent me (I am not a groupie) and slurping down the last of the grape Tootsie Pops.

There could be worse things. I could be sitting in the homecoming stands, silver paint on my face, watching Chase cuddle up with Holiday Girl.

Gulp.

I climb into bed, wearing wool socks and Taz jammies and unwrap my Tootsie Roll. No one will, ever, ever, upon pain of death, know this is how I spent my Saturday night. Not even Caleb.

I make three decisions:

1. I will meet Vovka. Because it is my diplomatic duty. And, because Auntie Milla left a jar of pickles outside my door and this is getting embarrassing.

2. I will pour myself into my students over the next two weeks Matthew is gone. (He approved my lesson plan despite my rather stuffy presentation—I mean, how am I supposed to unglue my tongue from my mouth while I watch Rebecca hang on the man who was supposed to give me cute little Joe, with his unruly black hair and dark blue eyes? Home wrecker)

3. I will focus again on Ephesians and maybe figure out a few of those lingering questions about why God sent me here when I could have been perfectly happy and useful in Gull Lake.

I think.

Chapter Ten:
The Distaff and Spindle

I keep getting bogged down by one phrase in Ephesians that bears inspection. "To the praise of His glory." I'm sitting cross-legged on my bed, the sun coming through the window warming my legs despite the crisp chill in the air. Tracey informed me during our last three-sentence exchange that the heat for the city doesn't come on until November. I might start burning my English books pretty soon. Start a little Gull Lake campfire. On my bed.

So I'm not having a good day. Which is why I'm here, trying to find some perspective in the quagmire of the book of Ephesians.

"To the praise of His glory." Still confused, but I have managed to make more colorful additions to my Bible. (Blue is my Hi-Liter choice for the day, because, well, it matches my mood). This phrase occurs three times in the first chapter and since three is a special number in the Bible (like, three days in the grave, three persons of God, three strands not easily broken—wonder where I got that? Look it up!), I've decided there must be something of import here.

The Greek for *glory* = *apparent*, as in *revelation*.

So, translated that would be the "praise of God revealed." *Huh?*

This concept is way too deep for a Monday morning. Or is it? Maybe it's just about grace. As in I need it, He gives it, and because of my cracks, everyone can see it. God revealed…yeah! (The "saved a wretch like me" thing is coming to mind, and I'm not going to break out singing or anything, but the phrase seems especially applicable here.)

In fact, at the moment, I can't think of anyone more in need of grace. Okay, maybe that is overstated, but still, if God is looking for someone to prove His grace, *over here, over here, me, me!*

My inadequacies + God's grace = to the praise of His glory.

That works for me, especially since I have to face Matthew this evening, his first day back. Oh, fun. In fact if I take a good hard look at the past few months, taking in my abundance of friends, my stellar evangelism abilities, my fluency and stunning perception into character, I need all the grace I can get.

Still, the question I have to ask is, if God knew I was such a pathetic grace-leech, why did He send me here, and where are the "good works, the ones God prepared in advance for me to do?" When do we get to *that* part?

My Vovka ploy worked! It worked! It worked! I am so very wise, oh, the cleverness of me! (And don't you dare call me a liar. I intend to meet Vovka. I truly, truly do. Someday. Maybe next June, an hour before I leave…)

I arrived home from class today (week three without Matthew, who called and left a message for me saying he was delayed! See, Grace! Grace!) to two pivotal events.

1. A note from Tracey: *Dear Josey. Moved in with Rick. I still have my key, so don't rent my room out.* (As if. Hello, I could get someone worse. Hard to imagine, but possible.)

2. *A letter from Chase* in my e-mail in-basket.

To: Josey <josey@netmail.moscow.ru>
From: <ChaseAnderson@mail.com>
Sent: Oct 28; 7:23 p.m.
Subject: A note from Gull Lake
Dear Josey,
I got your address from H, who was in town last weekend. She said she'd corresponded with you, and since Jasmine or your mother couldn't find your e-mail address, I was glad she had it.

Which means what? That's he's been stalking them around town, asking for it? Or, that he's wanted to write to me but couldn't? C'mon, I'm not that hard to find! He could have called Dwight down at Mission HQ. And with a little stiff-arming, Dwight would have talked.

How are you? Gull Lake seems…quiet without you. Lew Sulzbach said that he felt safer driving through town at night, knowing that you weren't there to egg him. I told him that you only did that once—on homecoming our junior year—and at least they weren't rotten. I don't know why he was so touchy. (Except that you did have great aim.) Myrtle misses you. Contrary to your opinion, Karen can't write as well as you. She buries the lead and she gets her facts from Pete down at the

Sheriff's office, and you know how reliable he is. Wasn't he the one who accused you of skinny-dipping our senior year? I told him you'd never do that, but I don't think he believed me.

Whoops. Just to set the record straight, and not that Chase needs to know, but yes, that was the truth. In my defense, however: 1. I thought I was alone. 2. It was a dare, and 3. Sometimes a girl has to do one memorable thing, just to prove she can. Probably wasn't the best choice of challenges however. Might have been better to say, hike the Grand Canyon or something.

I'm enjoying teaching more than I realized. I'm still not sure if I'll apply for next year's position, but for now, there are a few areas of research I'd like to explore here—

Uh-oh, those wouldn't center, for example, around the mating habits of Gull Lake singles, would it?

—like the language of the Ojibwa near Gull Lake Reservation, or the thread of the Danish population that still colors our area.

Oh, phew.

Your mother has invited me over for Thanksgiving. It's still about a month away, I figure it's better than hanging out with Rodney Anderson and his six-pack.

I should interject here that Chase's mother died when he was sixteen, and his father, who already had an intimate relationship with his whisky bottle turned fully toward it for comfort. Chase might as well have moved in for the time he spent at our house. Another possible reason for my second-cousin feelings about our relationship.

I'm looking forward to some real food, especially some Jasmine-made dinner rolls. I'm hoping she's well enough by then—she's been looking pretty white lately.

What? White? What?

Although I hear that's normal in the early stages.

What?

Sorry I missed you at the airport, by the way. I meant to get there...but it doesn't matter now.

Stop, wait! It matters! Because I have to know...does it mean what I think it means? And if it does, is my tendency to swoon into that moment indicative that I wasn't actually jealous of Buffy but have real, romantic type feelings for Chase? Is my angst because I truly love him, and it's not about being green, and perhaps just a little too proprietary? What does real love feel like?

I...wish you well in Moscow. Be careful.

Honey, Careful is my middle name. Which is probably part of the problem between us. Okay! Maybe I'm just selectively careful.

Chase

P.S. I started going to your church. I thought, well, since you were so set on doing this, maybe I could figure out what all the fuss what about.

Oh, isn't that just sweet? I leave, he moves back to town AND starts letting God in his life. Hello, is that fair? Anyone, anyone?

Be home, be home, be home!

I listen to the telephone ring. Once, twice. It feels a little like it is ringing through one of those corrugated sewer grates they bury around Gull Lake every summer.

According to my watch, it is seven a.m. Gull Lake time. *Surely someone is home.*

"Hello?" Milton sounds like a frog. I'm not going to make any further comparisons.

"Milton! Is Jasmine there?"

"She's sleeping."

Duh. But how often does she get a telephone call from *Russia*? "Sorry, Milton, um, can I talk to her?"

I hear snuffling, then a soft murmur. I don't let my mind linger on what that picture might look like. Hurry up, Mil!

"Hello?"

"Jasmine, are you pregnant?" I can't hold it in any longer. I mean, *good grief,* I waited an entire hour since reading Chase's e-mail.

I hear a pause, and in it I hope she feels my hurt, and that a thousand, okay, maybe only a *hundred* needles of guilt pierce her soul. "Yes. Did you get my letter?"

What letter? "No."

"Oh, no! I wanted to be the first to tell you! I sent it a couple weeks ago."

"Jasmine, please, learn to use the computer."

She laughs. *Laughs*. Because you know it is just hilarious that all of GULL LAKE knows my little sister is pregnant before I do. Talk about a chainsaw to the pride. Man, a girl moves to Russia and the world acts like she's walked off the planet. It's only over the ocean, people!

"Sorry, Josey. I've just been busy, and not feeling real well. I promise, I'll do better. But I did send you a letter the day I found out."

Okay, I feel better. I sigh. And taste a couple salty tears. "I wish I were there."

Pause. "Me, too. But there isn't anything you can do. Just promise you'll be back for the birth."

I do some quick adding (on my fingers, because, you know, it's late and we English majors didn't take Calculus for good reason) and make that promise.

"Good. Now, how's life?"

Hmm. Not sure how to answer that as I sit here in my wool socks, my needing-a-wash jammies, eating something called *Padushkie* which is sort of like Shredded Wheat cereal filled with chocolate. It's my latest culinary find, right after Nutella, which is a chocolate-hazelnut spread. I eat it straight from the jar (because, well, I can't figure out how else to eat it…). My hair is starting to turn, um, burnished gold, from all this mineral water, my hands are red and chapped from washing my clothes out by hand in the tub (yes, there is no washing machine here, but why get worked up by the trivial?) and last but not least, Auntie Milla left a bottle of deodorant outside my door as she moves on to personal hygiene items as bribes. Or maybe it's some sort of hint. Oh, and one can't forget that tonight, my roomie officially moved out, which means that if one of the Russian

Mafia thugs I squish up next to every day on the Metro decides to follow me home, rape and murder me and leave my
body in the bathtub, no one will find me for at least a week,
if not longer due to the fact that Larissa, his lap dog/what-
ever will probably tell him I've ditched them all. So, I'm fine.
Just. Fine.

"I'm good," I lie. *"Horosho,"* I even add, and she laughs.

"Oh, Josey, I'm so proud of you. You're amazing! Are you
fluent?"

Oh, yes. And Putin calls me for advice every morning. "I'm
doing okay."

"Do you get to come home for Christmas?"

Christmas! It's bad enough that I'll miss Thanksgiving
(do they even have turkeys in Russia? I mean, I've seen pig
heads…) but I'm going to miss *Christmas,* too? Was this in
the contract? Because I don't remember that. It seems to me
that they should print that in bold, so it stands out. Christmas! And what if Chase is there, looking sleep-tousled and
handing out presents? Who will get my gift? In my absence
will he give it to Holiday Girl? "Jas, I gotta run. The call is
fifteen dollars a minute. I'm sorry."

"No problem." But I hear a catch in her voice, which is
good, because I can no longer talk, and I'd hate for the angst
to be one-sided. "I'll try and learn how to use e-mail, I
promise."

"Yeah. I know. I love you."

I hang up on "Love you, too," because although I'm
Minnesotan and can do the long goodbye, my chest is seiz-
ing up and I think someone has flushed carbon monoxide
in the room.

Okay, needing that grace, now, Lord.

I wanna go home.

★ ★ ★

Matthew Winneman has grown a mustache in his absence, and if he doesn't stop chewing on it, I'm going to rip it from his face, one whisker at a time. This is all I can think about as I watch him grade the first trimester papers from our students. No, *my* students, because the crumb has been gone for nearly a month, having called me from, get this, Vienna, *Austria*, where he was attending a conference.

He's also a little tan. Can anyone say, the south of France? I know he set this up. I feel it in my cold bones.

"I appreciate the hard work you put in during my absence," he says in a low tone as he looks up and smiles. I'm positive he bleaches his teeth. They can't naturally be that white.

"Sure, no problem," I say, shrugging, because you know, one of us has to be dedicated to the task. We have an important job here. The future of the spiritual life of Russia is in our hands. Not a time to go gallivanting around Europe, hmm?

"Unfortunately, well, we have a problem."

Like, maybe, you're married and a weasel and you forgot to mention both?

"All the students failed their exams."

"What?" I am leaning forward now against the desk, my hands braced on it as the earth crumbles beneath my boots. (They're really neat, too. I found them at this Italian store in GYM. They're black leather, slim line heels and go halfway up my calves. Turquoise Girl has nothing on me. Sadly, I'm pretty sure I'd be called a number of interesting names if I wore them down the street in Gull Lake, but here I fit right in. Which says what?) *"Failed?"*

He puts the papers into a neat pile, then purses his lips and nods. I could do without the pursing. Because he sort of looks like Tom Selleck now, and it makes me want to smack him. "Yes, *failed*. I'm sure your lesson plans were fine, but did you follow the textbook? They had to know their pronouns, and contractions and be able to carry on a simple dialogue. What happened?"

Textbook? Just great. I…well, who knew there'd be tests? "They can sing 'Happy Birthday'? Would that be considered dialogue?"

He shakes his head and I see disappointment on his face. I guess now he knows how it feels, doesn't he? "Josey. I know you are trying to help them assimilate into our culture." (What am I, the Borg? I just wanted them to have fun!) "But they need to pass some very strict entrance exams. We're going to have to work overtime to help them catch up."

Gulp. Oh, do I feel like a wart. Here I thought…well, I mean, most of them can name the table settings, and they can perform a rousing rendition of "God Bless the USA" by Lee Greenwood (I labeled it under geography…maybe that isn't something I should mention right now). But shouldn't learning be fun? And culture is a part of learning, right?

"I guess this means I can't go home for a Christmas visit?"

He stares at me, part disbelief, part sadness. "Josey, you signed a contract to teach for a full school year. I am assuming you will honor that contract, or the mission will ask you to repay all they've invested in you."

Invested? *Invested?* Like…what, teaching me how to cook, or use my nonexistent washing machine? Maybe helping me negotiate the Metro system without being mugged? Oh, I know, paying for my daily humility class with Larissa. Right. the mission hasn't invested in me—they've digested me!

"In my defense, I thought you were only going to be gone two weeks. I had to really punt the last two weeks."

He doesn't like this answer. He looks away, out the window. "I'll ask Larissa to step in for my next trip."

Oh, ouch. A line drive, right to the kisser.

"No, Matthew, listen. I promise, I'll stick to the lesson plans next time. Really. I didn't know."

He takes off his glasses, rubs his eyes with his thumb and forefinger. I remember when my father used to do this. It was a sign that meant "brace yourself" and didn't bode well for the rest of the conversation. I straighten, cross my arms over my chest, (which, by the way, doesn't seem to be decreasing at all with my latest find—"Viola." Softened American cheese with chives and onions that tastes really good on the Russian version of French bread.).

"Josey, I want to give you as much leash as I can here. I'm planning another trip in February. If you can prove to me between now and then that you can plan these lessons and execute them, as well as devote your extra time to bringing our students up to speed, I'll hand the class over."

Done. I can't believe the relief that fills my chest. Another chance! And this time, Matthew old-boy won't be disappointed. "Thanks, Matthew," I say, wondering how, suddenly, I could feel so grateful. What happened to my brain? A minute ago I had the chance to quit, to jump a plane back to Gull Lake, land of bagels and Chase. And I let it slide through my fingers.

Or did I? Maybe it was the thought of Evgeny, his sweet eyes turning sad as I tell him I've failed him. Or I-ron Sergei, saying, "Zats O.K., Zhozey." Nope, I owe them. They're my students and I'm a Norwegian. We don't fail.

"Good," Matthew says, and gives me a fatherly smile and I feel about six years old after being dressed down by the principal. "Oh, by the way, Rebecca wanted me to invite you over for Thanksgiving. We're having an informal event, and we'd love to have you join us."

Rebecca, as in your wife Rebecca? Oh, fun. Somehow I hear my mouth saying "Yes," despite the fact that my brain is waving a yellow flag. "I'd love it."

No one listens to me anymore.

It feels very strange to be carrying a Jell-O salad to a Thanksgiving Day party when all around me, Russians are hurrying off to work or school. Hello? Don't they know it is a national holiday? Pilgrims? Squanto?

I am protecting my mandarin orange salad in an embrace, so I don't surf through the Metro. Thankfully, Matthew and Rebecca only live three stops away on the green line, and by that time, my Jell-O salad has had a chance to warm, just slightly, so I can slide it onto a plate. Yes, I did say Jell-O. Just call me resourceful.

Okay! I went to the French grocery store and bought a pack of what I thought *might* be gelatin (due to the orange box and the picture of a parfait on the outside) and a little can of mandarin oranges (also revealed by their picture). And I paid about $15 for both, which makes this not only a feat but a real gift.

I hike up to the third floor (still don't have my elevator rhythm down) and push the buzzer for Matthew's flat.

I hear voices, then the inner door opens. All Russian flats are protected by two doors—the inner wooden door and the external, vaultlike metal door with a window cut out at the top. Think: prison cell and you'll land on the right image. "Hello?" I ask.

"She's here!" a squeaky voice yells and it makes me smile.

Matthew appears. He's wearing a nice Lands' End sweater

and he's shaved his moustache. Obviously Rebecca has some taste.

"Hi, Josey," he says as he unlocks the door.

"I brought you some salad." I hand him the Jell-O.

"Oh, dessert!" I hear from another room, and I assume it is the non-Minnesota description of my offering. Then, Rebecca appears.

June Cleaver is alive and well and living in Russia. Rebecca is my mother, subtract thirty years. She's wearing another jumper, and blue flats (I think I have a pair of those from senior year somewhere). Her hair is long and braided into a long strip in back. But her smile is bright and she sweeps me into a tight hug like we're old friends and not at all like I stared at her the last time we met with a look just short of animosity.

I feel sick. Not only that, I'm feeling like a loser in my jeans and U of MN sweatshirt. Hello, Matthew did say *informal*, did he not? I'd hate to think what formal might be.

"Josey, so glad you could join us." Despite her words I see wariness in Rebecca's eyes. Oh no, can she see through me to the fantasies that once swirled in my mind? I have purged them, I promise! But she holds the smile and pulls me past the kitchen into their family room.

I notice two things, first off.

1. They have wall-to-wall carpeting. Don't gasp, I'm serious. I have yet to be in a Russian home with wall-to-wall carpeting, or even a Russian building with wall-to-wall carpeting and I would probably lie down and do a carpet angel on it if I didn't fear upsetting the eight-piece table setting and crystal on their oval oak table.

2. I have stepped into Country Home, USA. Frilly curtains with tie-backs in the kitchen (and is that stenciling along

the ceiling? It is! My mother would be thrilled!), and a swag over the living room window. Overstuffed floral chairs with knickknacks on a shelf behind them, and a wicker table between the chairs holding magazines and a lamp. Where am I? It even smells like middle America.

On the table in the middle of the room I see a turkey, stuffing, a tossed salad (where did she find lettuce? Oh, wait, silly me, she probably grew it on her balcony with heat lamps), homemade rolls and broccoli. And my orange salad. At least it adds color.

Matthew calls the children, and they almost materialize from the walls. Pressed white shirts on the two boys, a homemade Laura Ingalls style dress on the girl, and she even has a cute floppy hat with a fabric flower. Of course.

I'm today's only entertainment and the children want to sit beside me. That feels good as I try not to think about who is sitting next to Chase. We hold hands, pray. And then I have my first decent meal in three months.

I can probably like Rebecca if I try.

Sometime after dessert (banana cream pie. Sorry, Jas does better, but this was a close second) and the basic quizzing, Rebecca slides down to my end of the table. The turkey carcass is being removed by Matthew, who has rolled up his sleeves and is wearing an apron.

"So, Josey, tell me, really, how is Russia?"

See, people are always asking me to lie. Because, really, she doesn't want to know. I think suddenly about Caleb, the only one with whom I can reveal the truth. He's been oddly vacant in my life since the episode when I took him to check out the restaurant for the Matthew Event. I saw him at church once, but lost him in the crowd.

Hmm.

"It's good. *Really.*" Forgive me, Lord.

"Matthew says you're a bit homesick. Someone back there you miss?"

Ouch, wow, she goes for the jugular. Oddly, I find myself nodding. I told you that my brain decides to defect at inappropriate times. Please, not now!

But Rebecca's drawn me in with her smile, the way she's turned toward me in gentle anticipation, as if we're at the cusp of a budding friendship.

"What's his name?"

"Chase," my mouth says. Inside, I'm screaming, *Over sharing!*

"Chase," she repeats and gives me an eyebrows-up, conspiratorial smile. "He sounds intriguing."

"We're not dating or anything. We're just friends."

"I see." But I can tell by the look on her face that she doesn't see. Or maybe she sees more than she should. "Matthew and I started out as just friends, at Bible School. Maybe Chase just needs a nudge."

Or a kick. Or maybe he's not the one who needs the push. I'm so confused! I shrug.

"Maybe he just needs to know that you're not looking around. That you'll come back to him."

Will I? Am I not looking? I feel like I'm looking. But why am I looking? Answers to these questions might help me respond to her in some way. But I open my mouth and nothing, *nichevo,* emerges. She laughs.

"I know. We'll make him see what he missed when you were gone."

We will? "How?"

"Well, you obviously know how to cook…."

Oh, yeah, the Jell-O salad was a dead giveaway.

"But can you sew? How about tend a garden? A good Proverbs 31 wife is a manager of her household and when you go home to…Champ?…he'll be amazed."

"Chase. And I kill plants. And well, I sort of considered the Proverbs 31 woman as a test model, not for distribution."

She laughs again, but I'm not kidding. Have you read that chapter? Seriously. "Rises early and is clothed in fine linen and purple?" I look washed out and pale in purple—it's right up there next to poppy on my no-no list. The one thing I can agree with is, "When it snows, she has no fear for they're all clothed in scarlet." Up in Gull Lake, the Ben Franklin has a fall sale on snowsuit gear. Moms stock up every year, and every kid in Gull Lake has a Michelin suit, adequate for the -30F once-in-a-century cold snaps. While the snowsuits are usually orange (due to the hunting season), I figure that's close enough to scarlet.

"I'm not sure. Chase isn't really the domestic loving type."

She pats my knee. "Take it from a woman who knows. All men love their woman keeping the home fires burning. Who knows but that God sent you here to prepare you for marriage?"

Well, it's a good thing I ran into Rebecca then, because I'd hate to go into holy matrimony without knowing how to use a distaff and spindle.

Most of all, I wish the Almighty would clue me in. Because up to now, I was getting the distinct impression that there wasn't a *Bride's* magazine subscription even in my distant future.

Chapter Eleven: Vovka

To: Josey <Josey@netmail.moscow.ru>
From: <ChaseAnderson@mail.com>
Sent Dec. 12, 8:52 p.m.
Subject: Thanksgiving
Dear Josey,
I'm glad you had a real Gull Lake Thanksgiving with the Winnemans. We all missed you, especially Jasmine, who said that you would have loved the French Silk pie she made. (Or shouldn't I tell you that?) She's feeling better, by the way, although I can't tell that she's pregnant. But what do I know?

Before it gets around, I should tell you that I brought Heidi Blackburn to dinner. (Your mother saw us in church and said I should.) I know you and she had that fight in sixth grade, but she says she's over that and you should be, too.

Fight? Excuse me? She took my underpants at Girl Scout camp and shoved them into the stove! Of course she's over it. She didn't have to walk around with sooty undies for a week. So very funny, *hardy har har.* What's she doing going to *church?*

We're not really dating or anything, but we did go into Brainerd to see the new Bond movie (which proves it wasn't a date) and out to Jerry's Pizza.

And he's telling me this—why? So I don't find out from Pete (whose e-mail I tracked down by the way, and he's proving a nice source) or worse, is he covering up something…more incriminating? Sorta, throwing me a bone so I won't find the real loot? Arrgh!

She thought what you're doing in Russia is really cool, and I told her all about how God called you to be a missionary (just like you told me) and we both decided that we might like it if God talked to us, too. As long as He didn't ask us to be leprosy workers in India or go serve gruel in Somalia. I have to admit, Jose, that I never saw you, in my wildest dreams, as a missionary, but now that you are, I am really proud of you.

Proud? Wow. Okay, that sentence right there makes it all worth it. All.

I wish you were going to be here for Christmas. The town is starting to decorate. Langs put up the Christmas tree in their store window and they've hung garland on the hanging streetlight in town and candy canes along the strip. The annual lights contest has begun, and I think the Rylanders are going to take the prize again—they've added two blow-up snowmen to their already postage-stamp yard. I think they have it covered—the nativity scene, a menorah, Santa and his eight merry reindeer, Rudolph, Frosty, candy canes and a huge twinkle star. They've drained the power for the city twice already. I think they should retire them in the hall of fame or we won't make it through the season.

This is making me painfully nostalgic because, now that it is the second week in December I'm not seeing one twinkle light, one candy cane, not even a reindeer appearing anywhere in Moscow. We did get a light snow, however, that froze over immediately and turned the terrain into a sheet of sheer terror ice. I wonder—if I mention the fist size bruise on my hip will Chase feel really bad about going out to pizza with Heidi-the-underwear-thief Blackburn.

I hope you are seeing a lot accomplished "for the Kingdom" as Pastor says when he prays for you. I miss you.
Chase.

I'm not sure if this is a sad joke, or just pathetically sweet. I'm standing in the auditorium of the Moscow Bible Church while Bing Crosby croons "White Christmas" over the staticky ancient speakers from the stage. The Russian students have thrown us Americans a Christmas party, complete with tree trimming and karaoke. Rebecca just did a version of "O Holy Night," and Sandi Patti she is not. (But wants to be, bless her heart.)

I'm pasted to the fringes of the room. No need to call attention to myself and get sucked into, say, a Dolly Parton rendition of "Winter Wonderland." On the bright side, I've discovered what *peroshkes* are *supposed* to taste like—the non-Auntie Milla version have jam, or fried cabbage and onions and I could easily become addicted. I'm thinking "new recipe," for Jas. That, and salmon cutlets and *chebureki* sandwiches and even fried potatoes, served with *smytena*.

I'll start my diet in January.

Still, all this frivolity two days before Christmas has started a low, deep pang in my stomach. I'm on the lee edge of tears as I listen to Evgeny mangle "O Leettle Tune ov Vethleeheeeem."

My apartment seems dismal, at best. I bought a string of lights and draped them over my window. They play a tinny version of "Jingle Bells," and flicker in succession. But there isn't a tree to be found in the entire city, and when I finally screwed up the courage to ask Matthew, he said Russia doesn't celebrate Christmas.

How immensely sad. Even if they don't buy into the religious significance, the world needs the spirit of generosity and giving once a year, sort of like a booster shot to keep away the bacteria of despair.

I see Matthew and Rebecca and their three children clapping at Evgeny's song, and Rebecca's gaze sweeps the room, lands on me. I raise my glass of *sok*—prune juice—and smile.

I'm not approaching, however, because I haven't finished the counted cross-stitch ornament she gave me to work on. Mostly because my fingers hurt from the pricks, but also because a person can only rip out stitches so many times before the fabric frays. I never liked candy canes anyway.

Rebecca's flat, on the other hand, is decorated like a *Better Homes and Gardens* issue, complete with home-made garlands, strung popcorn chains, the smell of mulled cider and home-made knit stockings under the tree (in the absence of a hearth. Frankly, if I was a Winneman kid, I might start asking panicked questions....). I know all this because last week we had the staff party at the Winnemans, and again, I ate a decent meal. I might just survive this year if I celebrate every major holiday at Rebecca's house.

"Holding up the wall?"

I turn toward the voice, and I feel a smile building all the way from my toes.

"Caleb!" There is enthusiasm in my tone, and frankly, it's all I can do not to jump into his arms. Where has he been? "How are you?"

He smiles. He's wearing a bright red shirt, like Santa, and a pair of camouflage pants with black suspenders. His idea of festive, I guess. "Good. You're looking nice tonight."

Oh, isn't that sweet? Because, despite my sleek Italian boots, I am feeling frumpy in my black skirt and fuzzy white sweater that I picked up at the market. It looked so good on the sales lady, but admittedly she was a size 3, and, well, I'm not. It hits me right at the hips and makes my upper body look like a snowball. But I smile at the compliment/lie anyway. "What have you been up to?" (That's code for *Why did you abandon me?!*)

"I was out of town. Had to go to Khabarovsk, where we have a sister church, and help them set up their new office."

Out of town. Oh. Well, then. "Glad you're back." *I missed you,* I nearly say, but can't bring myself to fling my emotions that far out of my body.

"Yeah, me, too." He holds my gaze for a second longer than necessary, and suddenly I'm wondering if there is more to his words, also. A warm feeling passes between us. He breaks the magic by glancing around the room. "Wanna get out of here? I have something to show you."

Oh, honey, do ducks swim? I nod, and a familiar feeling squeezes my heart. How many times has Chase said that to me?

Can't I escape *the boy I can't forget* for just one night?

I set my cup down on the windowsill and steal behind Caleb as he stalks toward the door without looking. I can feel Rebecca's gaze on me. I know she wants me to sing.

I grab my coat from the hook and button up tight. Moscow has turned ferociously cold over the past month, and I've graduated to my ankle-long blue parka. Yes, I feel like the Pilsbury Dough Girl in it, but I'm warm, and frankly, I can't afford the mink coats that the entire population of Moscow seems to wear. No issues with protection of animals here.

Caleb holds the door open for me, and the frigid air nearly takes my face off. We bend into the wind and I think I ask, "Where are we going?" but the words are sucked away to Siberia the second they leave my lips.

I follow him to the Metro entrance, and as we descend, the bowels of Moscow warm us. I see the homeless lining the corridors and stop to hand out rubles to a young mother with two children. Caleb has his own change, and is doing the same.

We then pass through the turnstiles, and I impress him by turning sideways on the escalator. "You're catching on," he says, and I hear pride in his voice. "How's your Russian?"

"Horosho."

He laughs. I update him on English class, Tracey (who I haven't seen for nearly a month), Auntie Milla (who left a hard-bristled toothbrush and mint paste in a floral bag hanging over my doorknob—I'm starting to take this personally) and Matthew. Matthew's recent matrimony comes as a shock to Caleb. "You mean he was married all this time and didn't tell you?"

"You know, I sorta knew this in a women's-intuition type of way. He was just too perfect. Still, I saw the way he looked at Larissa. There's something going on there. He gives me the creeps."

Caleb smiles at me, one eyebrow up. I notice suddenly he's gotten said eyebrow pierced since the last time I saw him.

I give him a suspicious look. "You didn't know, did you?"

He shakes his head. "I don't hang around the MBC staff. Besides, as a friend I would have warned you off. You should have figured that out by now, babe."

Somehow his words make my entire night.

We exit onto Ploshad Lenin, and Caleb strides past the imposing stance of a Father Lenin statue. "Where are we going?" I ask, keeping up.

"It's a surprise," he says and gives me a sly grin.

We pass a video kiosk, advertising the hijacked movies from the States. I see a collection of *Lost* episodes and remember Matthew Fox from the airplane. Has that already been four months ago? A shiver runs up my spine.

Caleb stops, waiting for me just a few paces ahead, and as I catch up, a familiar scent finds my nose, tugs at my memories. We are at a café, and as I decipher the lettering on the door, my heart does a double flip.

Caleb is grinning, like he's delivered me the moon.

No, better. He's delivered me…bagels.

"Canadian bagel," I say, reading the words again, confirming my joy. "Canadian bagel? Here in Moscow?"

Caleb reaches for the door. "They just opened." He puts his hand on my back, pushing me in. "Merry Christmas."

I'm surrounded by happiness. Little round, holey tubes of joy. Caleb has helped me haul home goodies—poppy seed, garlic, veggie, plain, whole wheat and egg bagels, enough to withstand even a Tracey attack.

But she isn't here, is she? Ha! Only, despite the relief I feel in that, melancholy settles over me as the night ticks toward Christmas Eve Day. Jasmine will be up early, baking cinnamon rolls. My mother will be cooking clam chowder soup, laying out the relish tray. Tonight they'll go to the Christmas Eve service, sing carols, watch the children tramp around in towels and bedsheets, proclaiming joy to the world. And Chase will be there, probably dressed up in khakis and a dress shirt, smelling musky and sweet. The thought of him taking up space in a pew, of seeking God like I had to find Him, well, it stirs up feelings of joy that dwell in the deepest places of my heart. Chase finding God just might be the best Christmas present ever.

And, while my family spills out into the magical star-strewn night in Gull Lake, I'll be here with my bagels. If Tracey decided to show up, I'd share. Especially since I can get more.

To the praise of His glory. The words I've been pondering ripple through my mind as I rise, go to the window and stare into the darkness. A few people are still up, their squares of light from apartment windows pushing back the darkness. Overhead a sliver moon hangs like a lopsided grin. I lean my forehead against the glass, feeling the cold bite my skin. It sends a shiver down to my toes, back up my spine. I've never felt more alone. And I haven't particularly made a dent on the world here. I'm hoping the New Year looks a lot more fruitful than the past four or so months.

What, exactly, God, are You doing here, with me?

I wonder, did Mary share this view of the world as she held Jesus in her arms? Marveling at his tiny hands, the open tender mouth, the blinking eyes adjusting to light. What are You doing *here,* Lord? With *me?*

To the praise of His glory.

I sink to my knees, and suddenly tears burn my eyes. This trip has been about me, as much as I've wanted to deny it. It's been about jealousy, and wanting to be something more. It's been about running from inadequacy, about wanting acceptance. From Chase. From God. Most of all, it's been about Josey's hunt for significance, the gold ring prize.

"Lord," I say. "Please forgive me for making this all about me. I want it to be about You. About Your grace. To the praise of Your glory. Help me to stay the course, whatever it takes and to do this year right." I take a deep breath, and in the silence of the flat, I feel that sweeping tingle that I know is the touch of heaven. A tear drips off my chin.

Chosen. Saved. To the praise of His glory. You know, that sounds pretty significant to me.

And He even gave me bagels. Little Gold Rings.

Merry Christmas from God.

I nearly killed my roommate. No, she didn't eat the bagels.

But again, I started at the punch line. Let me back up to 3:00 a.m. Christmas night. I'm still full from dinner at the Winneman's and having a hard time sleeping, which is why I hear the door latch wiggle, then the *thwump* as it opens and bangs against the wall.

I sit up in my bed, my heart already in Jersey and headed west, fast.

"Hello?"

And then I hear it. Ew, that's not going to be fun to clean up.

I peel off the covers and run into the family room. Oh good, she made it to the bathroom, but she's looking like she's been chased by a herd of buffalo, sweaty hair, streaked makeup, oh, and now I know why—she's wearing a fuzzy hide of one of their clan, a sort of over one-shoulder wrap and black stretch pants. "Tracey?" I say, just in case it's her twin from the jungles of Africa.

"Help," she says, a split second before she takes another dive for the biffy.

I wince. Okay, I'm having to reach back into my dark past, but I manage to find empathy for her and grab a washcloth. She leans back, emptied, so to speak, and runs the wet cloth over her face. "Thanks."

I crouch beside her (not too close, but enough to show that I care). "What happened?"

Her chin quivers, and in a second her face crumples. "Rick!" she wails.

Oh, him. So, I take it I should stop using her room for my craft supplies?

"He broke up with me."

Yeah! Yeah! Oh, whoops. I stifle my cheers and nod sadly. "Are you going to be okay?"

"Why? What's wrong with me?"

Oops, not ready for the acceptance stage yet. Still stuck in denial. "I don't know, Tracey. But he doesn't deserve you." Well, sort of doesn't. He wears leather, she wears skins, I'm seeing "match made in heaven" but maybe I shouldn't say that. I do want better for her. Really.

"No, he doesn't!" she says and she blows her nose on a huge wad of toilet paper, throws it near the garbage. "I do everything for him, everything. I write the grants, give his speeches, even train our clients. He does what, shows up for the parties? The events at the embassy?"

Embassy? Hmm, he's single now, right—

"Tonight he told me that I didn't fit his style. Fit his style? What style does he have? I'll tell you what kind of—"

Okay, she's kinda scary when she's mad, because she's shaking and her lips aren't moving as fast as her words. And she's unrolling more toilet paper in clouds around her.

"His style is a girl who doesn't ask too many questions, who doesn't think past his lips, who doesn't care when she sees him at the Gray Pony with someone else."

See, and I don't want to say it, but I knew all that.

"Trace, he's a jerk. You do deserve better." And I mean it, now. "You need a man who loves you for who you are, for your dreams and your fears and everything great about you."

She stares at me, blinks. And then a soft smile curves her mouth. "Really, you think so?"

Me—you're asking me? "Yes!" I say, because I want my words for me, too. They sounded so good, don't you think? "You want someone who thinks you're so incredible he'd cross the ocean just to spend one hour with you."

We both smile.

"C'mon, get cleaned up, and then get some sleep. Tomorrow I'll treat you to lunch at my favorite little bistro."

Oh, well. I couldn't keep it a secret forever. Besides, I think Tracey needs some bistro in her life, even if the little tables have been moved inside for the winter. They still sell great instant coffee.

I am an awesome roommate. Here I am, declining a New Year's Eve party at the Winnemans so I can stay home and keep Tracey company. She's turned out, under all those leopard skins, to have a sweet Ohio smile. A treasure that I would have never appreciated had Rick the Slime not sent her packing. I'm quietly thanking him, for so many things.

For example, tonight, two days before New Year's Eve, she's *cooking*. Spaghetti, and she's made it from scratch. "My mother is half-Italian," she says, "but my father is Irish, which is why they live a couple states apart."

And I now know where all that lush red hair came from. I'm just a boring Norse woman.

She comes out of the kitchen, bearing two plates of noodles and sauce. My stomach wants to burst out in the Hallelujah chorus.

"I have an idea," she says as she puts the plate in front of me on the coffee table. I've poured us a couple Diet Cokes, finds from the central market. I'm feeling quite the accomplished hunter-gatherer.

I say a quick prayer, then dive into the sustenance. "What have you been thinking?" I finally respond.

"Let's go to the Embassy party," she says.

Embassy? *Embassy?*

"When is it?" I ask casually, doing my Lara Croft.

"New Year's Eve. They have a big party. Could be fun."

Ahh, oh wise me can see through this. I narrow my eyes. "Will Rick be there?"

Her chin starts to quiver. Uh-oh—danger, Will Robinson, danger!

"Maybe we should just stay home," I say, quietly dying.

"Yeah," she says.

Phooey.

"Or, we could get really dressed up and show Rick what he's missing."

What, who said that? Oh, no, that was *me!* What am I thinking? *She* can get dressed up. I have nothing to wear to an Embassy party. Again, see, mouth doing its own thing.

Tracey brightens, and the quiver is gone, replaced by a slow smile. "Love that."

"I don't have to anything to wear," I say, neatly opening

up my insecurities. But she's my roomie-pal, and we do these things.

"No problem. I know just the place."

Uh-oh.

And, my predictions are worth the sleepless night I tossed away because I find myself at high noon staring at a rack of shiny leather.

"I'm sure we can find your size," Tracey says, and she's being so very nice I give her a genuine smile. She pulls out a leather miniskirt, with a slit to the waist. Uh, *no.* I'm a *missionary,* remember?

The store smells of leather, and the shades aren't confined to black, but white, brown, turquoise and even red. A bomber jacket catches my eye and I can't help think of Chase.

He wrote to me on Christmas Day, which was his Christmas Eve Day, and not only said he missed me, but gave a two-page rundown of the event at Berglund Acres.

And he didn't bring a date to Christmas dinner. Whoo hoo!

Suddenly, all I want to do tonight is sit at home and IM with him. We'll reminisce on old times, I'll impress him with my Russian, and maybe we'll talk about the future....

Only, what if he is going out? With Holiday Girl or Panty-stealer?

"How about this?"

I turn and see Tracey holding up a pair of low-rise black leather pants that flare at the bottom. "Find me a top," I say and grab the pants. If Chase can go out, so can I. Aren't I important enough to miss *one* night cruising the Gull Lake strip?

I half expected some sort of tiger skin, but Tracey produces a white silk wrap blouse, V-neck with a tie at the bottom. Yeah, this could work.

I'm not sure I recognize the girl in the mirror, but according to this three-way, she's lost a few pounds, and frankly, despite the fact that Pudgy Woman I've grown to love/hate still hovers with a sick grin, I can see Leather Girl, someone sleek and fun and just a little exotic peeking out from the inside, smiling.

"I'll take it."

The Embassy. Say it with me. Emmm-Ba-Seee. Only, we're not going there. We're going to Spaso House, which sounds much less glamorous…until I find out that this is where the American ambassador resides. And not only that, but we're going by private taxi (not a limo, sadly). But it beats surfing the subway in my heels.

Located a mile or so from the Kremlin (I wave for old times sake), we have to take the Ring Road to get there and we pull up next to what looks like a mini White House, complete with white columns and bright twinkle lights. A marine, looking oh-so American, stoic and strong, guards the door. Tracey goes in first, standing inside the glass while I wait in my frumpy parka outside on the stoop. But under the frump is sheer glitter. If only Chase could see me. I am wearing my boots under the leather pants, and Tracey swept up my hair into an inverted bun-thingie that makes me look like a runway model.

They wave me in and I have to show my passport and deposit my valuables and take off my coat, and what, are they going to frisk me? They run a wand over me, and I don't beep (phew!), then I sign the register and I'm in.

I drop my coat off with a coat checker then follow the sound of jazz and the tinkle of glasses down a red carpet to the source.

I can feel the elegance radiating off the walls. I did a little research (because I was a reporter in my other life, remember?) and discovered that Spaso House was built in 1914 for a wealthy merchant and has been used since the 1930s as the Ambassador's residence. I'm momentarily swept back in time to the era of Russian mystique as I approach the edge of the ballroom. Nearly 100 feet long, with a three-story domed ceiling, the walls are creamy white with ornate light blue etchings across the ceiling and along the second-floor balcony. An enormous blue-glass chandelier hangs from the ceiling. I can hear my heartbeat swell as I watch Americans and other guests swing dance around the floor.

"I see they're using a Moscow band," Tracey says over the hum. She's looking like a tigress tonight in a tight black-and-brown sweater with fur at the cuffs and neck, and a miniskirt that just might be against the law in America. And she's so, so very tall. I look up about three miles to meet her eyes. "C'mon, I'll introduce you around," she says, scanning the crowd for You Know Who. She can't fool me. "I have a surprise for you," she says, but before I can follow up on that, she glides off and I'm her little penguin friend, waddling along behind her.

We garner little attention. Well, I do. Tracey attracts eyes like a magnet. She's smiling demurely, but I know it's an act. She took the entire afternoon to get ready and her room looks like a hurricane hit.

"Do you see him?" she asks, keeping her smile and her glide. Wow, is she good. I shake my head, but admittedly, I'm not trying too hard. I so don't want her to hook back up with Neo/Rick.

We take positions next to a column and she signals for drinks. I'm not sure—if I take the champagne, is that stepping foot over the missionary line? I decline and instead ask for a Diet Coke, feeling pretty proud of myself. The waiter, a man in white gloves, returns with my soda in a champagne flute. Cute.

Tracey gets a fresh glass. Uh-oh, she's fast. I'm going to have to keep an eye her.

"What's the surprise?" I ask her before she forgets she said it.

She just smiles at me and spikes one of those eyebrows. For some reason, it only generates a sort of queasy feeling in my stomach.

The song stops and I see Tracey work the crowd as it streams past. In a moment, she's handing me her champagne and heading out onto the dance floor.

Okay, I took swing dancing lessons once, and, well, my instructor compared me to a hippo. I didn't think that was so nice. And what's worse is that Tracey has the moves I long for. She's be-bopping and twirling and I know I need to leave, now. I'm in way over my head.

Only, she needs me, right?

Yeah, right, like the Lone Ranger needed Tonto.

I sigh, decide to circle the room. I stop for a moment, watching the band play. There are six or so violinists, two saxophonists, clarinetists, a trumpeter and a pianist. An eclectic bunch, but they're pulling off "In The Mood," with recognizable clarity.

I return to my position just in time to greet Tracey. She's smiling and she finishes off her champagne in two swigs.

Gulp.

"That was Craig. He's married to Cari Ann." She points to an elegant blonde talking serious shop with a group of men. "He works with me, and he says that he hasn't seen Rick all night." She signals a waiter. "So, I guess we can relax."

Yeah, right. Not with her tossing back the bubbly.

Another song, another opportunity to be a coaster. This time I wander out into the recesses of the hall, toward one of the balconies.

It's quieter here, and I hear voices, the low tones of clandestine meeting that happens on the fringes of these events. I feel like I'm intruding, so I turn, but not before I see the couple. She's standing against the wall, trapped slightly by his arm braced over her shoulder. She glances my direction and goes white.

That's okay, because I've already gone deathly pale, I can feel it. And, of course, I'm frozen, watching while she whispers something to the man hovering over her. He turns, looks at me, and I feel the sudden rush of heat.

Matthew. And Larissa.

I knew it, I knew it, I knew it! Mr. Innocent he is *not*. I lift one of my glasses—the soda one, because you know, someone needs to act like a missionary here—and stalk out.

Excuse me, but wasn't I invited to a New Year's Eve party *at their flat?* I'm so angry that I barely see Tracey return.

"That was fun!" she says, and I hear more than fun in her voice. Disappointment, and perhaps a little too much hooch. Just what I want—to spend the night watching her sink into inebriation while I ponder just what to say to Rebecca.

"You ready to go?" I ask, and regret the snip in my voice.

"What? It's not even midnight yet!" Tracey giggles and finishes off her champagne. This just might be the longest two hours of my life. "Besides, my surprise isn't here yet." She looks away with a worried look on her face.

Surprise? Here? I think I've had my quota of surprises tonight.

I glance toward the entrance to the balcony and see Matthew slink back in, alone. I wonder if Rebecca is somewhere in the crowd, or did he leave her and the darlings at home? I surreptitiously scan the room for her. *Nichevo.*

I want to karate chop him. He glances my way, and I send him my best death-ray glare, hoping to turn him to ash.

"Finally! He's here!" Tracey grabs me by the elbow and (what choice do I have, she's bigger than me!) we're shuffling across the floor toward…whoa, my heart be still. Tall and leathered, with long, burnished blond hair, and the slightest hint of whiskers, he's wearing a silk poet's shirt to go along with those shiny pants and, on top of that, the aura of suave. In fact, this guy has smooth down to a science as he perfectly times his smile at our approach.

Now, where did I leave my breath?

Suddenly, I can think of much better things to do tonight than dwell on Matthew Winneman and his weasely ways.

"Hi!" Tracey says, "Guess who this is?"

Wait! Is she talking to me?

"Who?" Fabio answers, and his eyes are on me. They're dark, and liquid, in a sort of bubbly-caldron-dangerous type of way. *Who* is a very good question at the moment.

"This is my new roomie. The one your grandma was telling you about?"

I'm getting a feeling, the kind that I got when Jasmine sat me down and told me that she and Milton were about to be married. A sort of tickle in my stomach, followed by the slightest hint of impending change, like the smell in the air before a storm.

"Zhozey?" He smiles, and there is something familiar about his angular face, the twinkling eyes, the conspiracy in his expression…

"Jose, this is Vovka."

Yes! Yes! Yes! There is a God and He likes me!

"Hi," I say. But my words stop there. Because, like I mentioned before, my body likes to betray me at inappropriate times, and right now my brain is ducking out.

"Would you like to dance?"

He speaks such beautiful English, with a twang that produces a curl of delight in my chest. Now I'm so, so very glad Auntie Milla gave me toothpaste and deodorant, contributing to my personal hygiene. I owe her big.

Except, don't forget, I have the rhythm of a hippo. I see our future crest, then fizzle…. "I'm sorry, I can't dance."

"Nyet problem." And then in a move that sweeps the breath out of my chest, he takes my hand and escorts me away from the dance floor…and toward the balcony overlooking the moonlit gardens. "It's too hot in there anyway."

I could swoon. Wait, I *am* swooning. The music drifts out after me, a faint accompaniment to the moment of magic. "So, Zhozey, my *babushka* tells me you're here to save Russia."

Oh yeah, sure. But the way he says it, with slight mocking, slight hopeful smile, well, I can feel myself warm down to my toes. Yeah, maybe. "I'm just teaching English."

"Think you could teach me a few words?" he asks in his low, accented English. Oh sure, he needs *so* much help. He leans against the wall, holding his…wait, is that soda?

"Why aren't you drinking champagne?" I ask.

He shrugs. "Religious reasons."

Oh, hold me back. I raise my glass. "Me, too."

"How about a tour?" He holds out his arm. I can't believe how easily mine fits into the loop. Wow, he smells incredible, in a leather-meets-cologne-meets-toned-muscles sort of way.

He tells me a Russian joke, and we watch dancers from above the balcony, laughing at a few who get out of sync. He has his hand on the small of my back, and I don't shrug it away. And, although I don't have the rhythm of Ginger Rogers, my heart is doing a wild rhumba.

Vovka. Who would have thunk it?

Happy New Year!

Chapter Twelve:
Trouts and Valentines

<Wildflower> Hey! I thought they put you in gulag or something! Where have you been?

<GI> DATING.

<Wildflower> What? Who?

<GI> You'll never guess. (Okay, I should interject here, that yes, I have been slightly secretive about my sudden new…activities, because well, H is hooked into the Gull Lake Grapevine, and I'm not so sure I want Chase to know. Yes, I can admit there are some purely selfish motives behind that decision. Still, I'm not required by law to tell him or anything? Right?)

<Wildflower> Evgeny?

<GI> Nope. (Although that thought suddenly finds a tender

place. But, well, I need more from a relationship than "this is a spoon." Other than window decoration, I don't see Evgeny in my future.) Vovka.

<Wildflower> NO! You surrendered.

<GI> Yeah, well, I consider it a victory. He's…amazing. We met at the ambassador's New Year's Eve party, and evidently Vovka works for the consulate as an interpreter and tour guide. More than that, he has manners, drives a Mercedes and has brought me flowers every single time we've gone out.

<Wildflower> How many times has that been?

I do some quick calculations. It's been nearly a month, and the time I'm not with him seems less than when I am. I'll round down, just to keep her calm.

<GI> Maybe ten?

<Wildflower> TEN? And you haven't said a word? That's a significant number. In Gull Lake you'd be buying *Bride* magazine and looking at diamonds. Is he a good kisser?

<GI> (feeling a slight blush) I haven't kissed him yet.

Long, long pause. Yes, I'm seeing the cursor blink and, with each flash, the question. Why? Why? Why? Why? The Answer? Because, well, we're not there yet. That's so…personal. I've never even kissed Chase and he knows me a gazillion times better than Vovka.

Although, honesty compels me to add that I've *thought* about kissing Vovka. In fact the concept follows me like a shadow. But kissing isn't the only way to communicate romance, is it? It counts that Vovka reached over during the ballet last Friday and found my hand, rubbing his thumb over it the entire second act. Or that while we were crossing the street, he tucked his hand under my elbow. He also calls me after our dates, and when he says, *Maya Sladkaya (my sweet one!),* in that low, rumbly voice, it makes all my senses sing. Most importantly, he opens doors, buys dinner and laughs at my jokes, with a warmth in those sweet molasses eyes.

<Wildflower> Is there something wrong with him?

Huh? I feel a rise of defense for Vovka. He oozes masculinity, despite the leather and the black turtlenecks. He's got a confidence and demeanor that says he doesn't have to impress. He just appears and the world swoons. *I* swoon.

But, despite my knee-jerk defensiveness the question tugs at me. Is there something wrong with me? Am I so repulsive that he has to work up the guts to press his lips to mine? This seems like an issue, suddenly, and well, something too close to my heart to ponder with H.

<GI> No. He's a red-blooded male, I'm sure. But he's also a Christian (he has even attended MBC, three weeks in a row now, and I have to say, I've never enjoyed the sermons more.) which means that he's not just going to throw his lips around.

<Wildflower> Calm down, Jose. It was just a question. But maybe I touched a nerve?

<GI> Did I tell you that my roomie moved back in? (When in a corner, change the subject.)

<Wildflower> Tracey? No! Did Rick move in, too?

<GI> No, thankfully, but I feel sorry for her. She's the one sitting home Friday nights while Vovka and I go out. She seems to be handling it okay, however. She's been spending a lot of time on the Internet, and I think she's looking for a new job.

<Wildflower> Speaking of new jobs, I'm moving to Gull Lake.

<GI> What? Since when?

<Wildflower> Since the Howling Wolf needs a new manager/bartender. I'm moving this weekend. So, I'll be able to give you the Chase report, live.

Chase. Wow, it's amazing the rush of emotions one word can dredge up. He's written to me three times since New Year's, and I've kept up the correspondence, dodging the Vovka tidbits, but so enjoying telling Chase about my class. Which is going well, by the way. Matthew the Weasel has decided to let me take over the class in February (after he approved all my lesson plans). I've tried to keep a twenty-meter pole distance from him, but he has guilt in his eyes. Obviously my laser gaze has some effect.

I'm feeling sick every time I see Rebecca. I do an end-run around her in church and haven't accepted her cooking class offer.

<Wildflower> Speaking of, I heard that Chase went to the Community Church all-night prayer meeting on New Year's Eve instead of hanging out at Lew Sulzbach's party. What's with that?

<GI> (staying calm, because I really didn't know that) Really? Wow. (Okay, I'm having more than a little guilt right now over the fact that Chase is alone, and I'm…not. But would I rather he be hitting the hot spots with Panty Stealer? I think not. Double standards work for me, okay?)

<Wildflower> I'm just going to ask it aloud…what's holding you two apart? Seems to me that Chase is gravitating toward your way of thinking.

<GI> Did I tell you that Vovka took me to the Bolshoi twice? And once to Lenin's museum.

<Wildflower> Whatever. Just don't get a tattoo without me.

I should have known it was coming. Who else does she have to cry on? As I open my apartment door to the sounds of sobs, I quickly deduce two things:

1. Rebecca has discovered Matthew's shenanigans.
2. I am going to be caught in the middle.

"Rebecca!" I say, and pull her into an embrace. "What's the matter?" (What am I supposed to say—"Oh, I'm sorry your husband is such a jerk?" What if she doesn't know the full extent? Oh, phooey, I suppose I should just be honest!)

"Matthew."

I hate it when I'm right. Because, deep inside, I would have been glad to be wrong about this. I draw her into the apartment. She looks…unraveled. Her hair is down (unbraided, gasp!) and in tangles, her eyes red and puffy (or maybe that's from the cold).

She pulls a wadded Kleenex from her pocket and blows

her nose. "I'm sorry. I shouldn't have come here. It's just that I don't know anyone else, and well, I thought maybe you'd seen them at school, and could tell me the truth."

Gulp. I pull her over to the sofa, hating Matthew with all the fibers of my being. Even my mitochondria hate him.

She sits down. Wrings her hands. I think back to Tracey's break-up and I'm suddenly profoundly thankful Rebecca doesn't drink. She'll probably bake a cake or something. "I never thought he'd actually, I mean, Lera is so innocent-looking. Who would have thought she could do this?"

Wait, whoa, back up. What? Lera, as in one of the Sugar Twins?

"I'm sorry, I don't follow."

"She, well, she told me that Matthew had tried to kiss her. Why would she try and hurt us like this? We've done so much for her." Rebecca's eyes suddenly turn hard, and she scares me with their intensity. "She and Vera were in our kids club three years ago, and we are practically paying for their English classes with the amount we spend on babysitting and housecleaning."

Housecleaning? Rebecca uses hired help? I take a deep breath. To the praise of His glory. And right now, I need God to be the One seen in me, because the Josey that wants to surface isn't going to do anyone any good.

"Matthew tried to kiss Lera?"

"No!"

Whoa, okay, I think I lost skin. I back away, pat her hand. "I'm sorry. Matthew is accused of kissing Lera?"

"*Trying* to kiss Lera. She told me tonight, after I got home from the market. Evidently he came home after school to-night and well, I don't blame him for firing her. She was wait-ing for me in the stairwell with her baseless slander."

So why is Rebecca here, upset? I shake my head, and it looks like I'm aghast at what Lera has done, but it's simply disbelief that Matthew has so completely pulled the wool over Rebecca's big brown, happy homemaker eyes.

"Why are you upset, then?"

"Because Matthew is! He's leaving in the morning and you are the only one who knows the truth. You have to go to school tomorrow and tell them that this didn't happen, that Lera is lying. I know it'll be hard to face her, but you must!" She takes my hands, and suddenly I know why her children obey her without a peep.

Why me, please, Lord, why?

I swallow, then in the softest, gentlest voice I can muster, I say, "Lera might be telling the truth."

I could have slapped her with less effect.

She yanks her hand from mine and accusation rings her eyes. "Lera already got to you," she snarls.

Suddenly, Tracey appears at her bedroom door, and dressed in her silky bathrobe, she looks like a ninja ready to karate chop Rebecca. My hero. I shake my head at her and she folds her arms over her chest, leans against the door.

"No, actually, I didn't know anything about Lera," I say. I shoot a glance at Tracey, and well, since she already knows what I saw at the party, as well as my penchant for speaking the brutal truth... "I actually suspected that there was something going on with Matthew and...Larissa."

Rebecca's mouth opens, just enough to let out a gasp. Then she closes it and swallows. "Why?"

I've never wanted to hurt someone so much as I want to hurt Matthew. I am quite sure that these aren't the feelings a missionary is supposed to have, but at the moment, I've forgotten I'm a missionary and I'm just Jilted Josey in a poppy dress at Jasmine's wedding, watching Chase glance over at Buffy, feeling my world crumbling to dust.

I should probably remember that moment more often, especially when I'm trying to untangle my mixed feelings about Vovka and Chase.

But it's Rebecca's world that is oatmeal at the moment, and I take her hand, gently, as I decimate her life. "Because I saw them together at the ambassador's New Year's Eve party. And they weren't, um, translating…"

Rebecca's face twitches. Then, suddenly, she turns and looks at Tracey, as if she might be the Purveyor Of All Truth. Tracey nods, and she has her feelings for Matthew and All Men Like Him (read: Rick) on her face.

"Oh!" Rebecca says, then her expression crumbles and she hides her face in her hands. I feel like a louse. But I pull her into my arms as she cries. At least she's not throwing up. Yet.

Opera always makes me sad. Which sorta fits my mood over the last few days, especially after Rebecca spent the night on my sofa, crying. The music is cathartic, and it doesn't matter that I have no idea what they're saying or anything about the story. All I know is that I am here, dressed in a glittery black dress, a white rose across my lap, in swank close-toed French spikes I found at GYM, and next to me lounges a man who could easily have glided right off *Esquire* magazine.

I should be feeling giddy. But in truth, I am feeling lucky.

No one pinch me. Or they're going to get hurt. Vovka leans back and puts his arm across the back of my chair. He smells magnificent tonight, and I am still in disbelief that I have scored so well this Valentine's Day while Tracey sits at home redoing her pedicure. See what happens when you wait for the right man?

Don't answer that. Because no, I'm not sure Vovka is the right man. But I like the way he makes me feel. Elegant. Beautiful. Especially when he leans against my doorjamb with a suave smile and white teeth, and says, "*Maya Sladkaya,* how about the opera this evening?" Oh, catch me! And all these feelings that seem to pile up when he's with me compel me to keep an open mind.

Which, late at night, goes something like this;

"Yes, Mr. Ambassador, I did come to Russia to teach English, but I guess God wanted me to meet Vovka. Yes, we're very happy, and living in an IKEA-furnished flat on Lenin Square. Oh, come to your Margarita Ball? And you'll send a limousine? Yes, I'd love to. And you want me to oversee a project to help teach English using the Bible to homeless children? I'd be delighted to, right after I take Vovinka to preschool."

So, you see, I'm open to all sorts of things.

We are in the Moscow International House of Music, and, as usual, I'm struck by the grandeur of the Russian estate. The two-headed Russian eagle adorns the arched doors, and the deep velvet curtains boxing the stage hint at opulence, even if they're a bit worn. All of Russia seems dressed to impress, and slowly I'm being wooed. And it only has a little to do with Mr. Wow sitting next to me. I also give credit to Sergei and Evgeny's eager smiles, to Auntie Milla and her liver *peroshke,* and even Tracey, who has made me feel like Solomon.

The only dark spot in all this Valentine's Day cheer is that Matthew has left for Europe, and no one knows if he's returning. Rebecca confronted him and it wasn't pretty, especially when she dropped my name a few times. I told you I was going to get sucked into this vortex of pain and despair.

And no one's talking at MBC, so I'm just trying to stay out of hot spots.

The final act finishes, and we endure twenty minutes of encores before we stand and join the press toward the door. And I mean press. I feel like baaing.

Vovka has his hand on the small of my back, however, and he stations me by a bust of Tchaikovsky while he retrieves our coats. My puffy Dough Girl monster is hard to miss and I shuck it on quickly. I'm slowly giving over to Russian styles, however—black leather skirts, black hose, black pullovers. I look good in black. It hides so much.

"How about a stroll down the Arbat?" Vovka says in that accented, rumbly voice.

He likes to walk, and I like the way he takes my hand and tucks it with his in his long, regal wool coat. He is wearing a suit coat and black pants tonight, his hair in a sleek ponytail. I never thought I'd like a man with a ponytail, but it looks good on him. Very Elegant French Model.

We turn down Arbat, and again, I'm struck by the architecture of the czars, tiny balconies and ornately trimmed narrow buildings that once housed merchants and artists. The street is cobblestone and during the non-snow months, artists set up easels and hawk culture. But tonight, the middle of February, there is nothing but the crunch of snow, the stars brilliant overhead, our breath streaming out ahead.

"You are beautiful tonight, *Maya Sladkaya.*"

"Thank you, Vovka." I smile up at him. Maybe I should kiss him. Because H's question has been simmering in the back of my brain for a full two weeks and now it's more like a three-engine inferno. Why hasn't he kissed me? Do I have repulsive lips? Am I too shy? I pull him closer, suddenly needing to get to the bottom of this. Will he curl his hands into my hair, kiss me gently, as if he's nervous? Or is he more of arms-around-the-shoulders, power-in-a-kiss type of guy?

In my dreams, he runs his fingertips down my face and I see his intentions in his eyes and he smiles a second before he kisses me, sweetly, perfectly.

I see a group of late-night sojourners shuffle toward us in the wan light. Among the group of students, who are dressed in all assortments of ragged attire, I'm surprised to spot Caleb. He stares at me, first a smile, then a scowl as he approaches. The group carries on past us, but I've stopped and so must he.

He shoots a glance at Vovka. Then back at me. "Hi."

"Hi," I respond, but I notice that my voice sounds much more cheery than his. He's shivering and he shoves his hands in his coat, what looks like a Russian army-surplus item. "What are you doing?"

"Oh, I'm just heading to the Metro after Bible study." His gaze ranges back to Vovka.

"I was at the opera."

He raises an eyebrow, then directs a statement in Russian to Vovka.

"Yes," Vovka answers in English. "We are."

Not sure why, but I feel a sense of panic, even fear. This is not the emotion I expected to have when I introduced Caleb to…my boyfriend? Okay, that feels weird.

"Caleb, I'd like you to meet Vovka. Auntie Milla's grandson."

He holds out his hand to Vovka, who meets it. The sparks in their silent gaze could power Moscow for a week.

"Vovka, this is Caleb. My friend." Probably my only real friend in Moscow, and I've done a superb job of cutting him out of my life for the last month. I feel slightly sick and I give Caleb my best apology smile.

"I'd better catch up to my friends," Caleb says, and gives me another no-smile look. "Nice to see you."

Okay, it may be cold out, but I can feel the numbing frost in those words.

"You, too," I mumble, but he's already gone. Why do I feel as if I've just kicked him in the teeth?

Vovka watches him go. "He likes you."

Oh, ya think? I'm firmly in denial however, at least in front of Vovka. "No. We're just friends," I say, my glance towards Caleb.

I feel Vovka's hand on my chin as he moves my face to his gaze. "He asked if we were together."

"Oh." So much for my sorry attempt to mask that fact. And now I am wondering why I tried to hide our status, because Vovka's eyes are on mine, so sweet, and I can nearly see his heart in them. My pulse is thundering, right below my skin as he searches my gaze. He has the slightest five-o'clock shadow, and it makes him looks elegantly rugged, in a Fabio-meets-Harrison-Ford kind of way.

And then he leans down and my heart just stops. He's going to kiss me! I haven't been kissed in—well, I can't remember when, and I've suddenly forgotten what to do. Hold my breath? Move toward him?

I close my eyes. That seems right.

I feel his breath close to my lips, as his hand moves around behind my neck.

Then he's kissing me. But oh, no! It's not gentle and sweet. It's…sloppy. Wet. And misaimed. I feel like he really *has* thrown his lips at me, and they slide off the side.

Panic wells in my chest. No! This can not happen. Vovka must be a good kisser, someone who makes me tingle, not reach for a towel.

Maybe it was nervousness? I'm willing to give him a second chance, so I open my eyes. He's wearing a slight smile and my heart goes out to him. "Vovka," I say, trying to set the mood, and step closer, reach up and tug his lapel. He reads my intentions and his arms move around me.

Trapped. This better be worth it. I rise on my tiptoes and let him kiss me again.

He's so…imprecise. And suddenly I'm realizing why Auntie Milla is trying to bribe me with food and perfume and most recently, an umbrella. Because under all her grandson's glamour and shine is…a trout!

No! No! No!

Certainly, this can be fixed? But it's not pretty as I pull away and a glaze of spittle nearly freezes my lips shut.

"Can we walk some more?" I somehow manage.

He smiles so sweetly, I just want to wail. He nods and tucks my hand again into his pocket.

Vovka the Fish. I stomp down the errant urge to turn and run after Caleb and his pals, but even if I did, I have a horrible feeling that I might have just burned a bridge.

What have I gotten myself into?

I find the package sitting on the table Monday after class. Tracey is at some sort of NGO function and the flat is quiet. I'm holding a jar of eggplant, or perhaps worms, I'm not sure. I found it outside my door, and I know it's from Auntie Milla, so she must not know I'm trying to sort out the Vovka dilemma. He's called every day since Saturday, and while I did have coffee with him yesterday after class, I avoided the *kissing* part, neatly ducking under his arm when he did the lean outside my door.

Certainly this can be fixed?

I grab a new jar of Nutella and a spoon and sit down on the sofa. The box is small, shoe-size, and while I am hoping for something from Jas, maybe a new *Lost* magazine (I am not a groupie) or a bag of chocolate chips, nothing can prepare me for the return address.

Chase.

Oh. My.

I put down the Nutella, and grab my scissors. This guy knows how to wrap a box because nothing sort of a neutron bomb is going to dismantle all this tape. I briefly wonder if this is some sort of cruel trick. But I finally get the wrapper off, the box open…and I want to cry.

A Valentine's Day card. Coffee from the Java Cup. A newspaper clipping of an article I sent to Myrtle. A CD of Point of Grace. And a very old, framed picture of Chase and me on his motorcycle.

So maybe he is pining for me!

I shuck away a tear and pick up the card.

Chase.

Writing me a card.

Dear Josey,
I know that you probably won't get this in time, but I wanted to wish you Happy Valentine's Day. I hope you had a nice one. I miss your smile.
Your friend,
Chase.
PS—How about I come and visit you sometime?

Chapter Thirteen: True Love?

I am a very good missionary.

1. I have bridged the gap with Sheena the Tiger Woman and she is now attending Moscow Bible Church. In many ways I think it is to meet eligible men, especially after I told her that I saw Vovka talking to one of his friends after last Sunday service. Still, she is there and that counts.

2. I sacrificed my pride and let Rebecca teach me how to make banana bread. I know, but really, the bananas were going bad, and she so needed to do something Proverbs 31-ish to remind her that Matthew is the fool here, not her. (Her words, not mine.) By the way, the bread turned out pretty good, and it makes a great supper, especially with Nutella on it.

3. I agreed to celebrate Auntie Milla's birthday with her and Vovka. At her house. Russian style, which includes a bottle of homemade prune cognac.

I'm staring at the cognac, wondering what St. Paul would

do. Be like the Romans, er, Russians and down it fast, with a prayer, or stick to my sense of, morals? taste? and decline.

Auntie Milla is dressed in her Birthday Best—a turquoise-and-brown dress with a brooch at the nape of her neck. I am pretty sure I saw that dress in a retro sixties catalogue, and someone in their late sixties shouldn't be wearing a dress that short, but I'm not going to comment. Especially since I'm also dressed in iffy duds—a black leather A-line skirt with a creamy white-ribbed turtleneck that clings more than I'm used to. Alas, I spotted it on a mannequin and, nudged by Tracey, bought it on a whim, remembering with fondness my Saks skirt, still hidden behind the poppy dress back in Gull Lake. Oh, if only! Because I know it would fit me now, since I've dropped a few more pounds. I also got my hair cut, Meg Ryan style, and highlighted. I was worried as I stood outside the beauty salon. It was called Dynamo, now wouldn't you be worried? What's worse, the Russian name for hairdresser is *"Pere-maker-skaya"* All I could think was Permanently Make Me Scary. But the highlights turned out fabulous. I barely recognize myself, this new hip Leather Girl. Which is good, or bad?

Most importantly, Vovka loves the 'do. Which matters, even if we still have the kissing issue hovering between us. I'm holding out hope that this can be fixed.

We are sitting around her tiny table, which is pushed up next to the sofa. Vovka sits beside me, and the table hits me at, roughly, the chin. Auntie Milla holds court regally at the end of the table. Vovka lifts his cognac, and I guess he's breaking his no-alcohol rule for the big day. Auntie Milla reaches for her glass. I'm still caught in indecision. Russia tra-dition says she's waiting to be toasted, in lieu of, say, a *prayer,* and I know it'll be a slap if I don't at least lift my glass.

And I want to be a good missionary.

Besides, as per Russian birthday tradition, she did all the work. White potatoes glazed with butter and fresh dill, liver cutlets, brown bread, cheese, dill pickles, cold herring, caviar(!), and most importantly, prune cake with walnuts.

Suddenly, my Nutella and *padushki* are looking pretty paltry.

And, out of gratefulness, both for the meal and for the fact that she's cast a little sunshine across the gray pallor of Russian winter in Moscow with her bribes, her *peroshke* and her rather hot grandson, I lift my glass.

"Baba Milla," Vovka starts, and then launches into a garbled Russian paragraph of which I get, "thank you," "love" and "happiness."

Sounds good to me.

They lift, shoot it back, and I smile, sip…and my lips turn to living fire. Ow, Ow, Ow! What is this stuff—kerosene? But I smile as I put down my glass…and realize there is nothing else to drink on the table. No water, no milk, no prune *sok* (they really love prunes here). Nada. *Nichevo.*

Yikes.

I take a piece of brown bread and attempt to sop the inferno from my lips. What if it had touched my throat? I'm sure I'd be in the ER right now.

Auntie Milla's eyes are just a bit watery as she dishes me up a cutlet, and frankly, I'm not sure if it's emotion or the atrocious home-brew she's served us. No wonder Russians are tough.

Thankfully, the food sops up the sting and Vovka translates as I finally, *finally* get to know his grandmother, my benefactor. I probably need to take notes, because as she unfolds her entire life story, I realize I am listening to a Danielle Steele epic, starting with the blockade of St. Petersburg/Leningrad during World War Two, moving on through the Stalin purges, then Khrushchev and the Bay of Pigs, and finally Gorbie and his wicked reforms. She's quite the chatterbox and long after the cutlets have turned cold, she's still motoring, occasionally shoveling one in her mouth in an effort to catch up to me (who has finished off the potatoes, the bread, the cheese and especially the caviar. Did you really think I was going to pass that up?).

She finally pulls out a photo album, and I put faces to stories. She's sitting on the arm of the sofa, leaning over me, explaining. (Why doesn't she just sit down? I've scooted over twice.) Vovka is on the other side, his low voice filled with emotion. He surely loves his Baba, and something my mother once said to me is running in the back of my mind. "Watch how he treats the woman in his life…that's how he'll treat you."

It's true. Vovka is such a gentleman, I feel as shallow as a crepe for not liking his kisses. So he's a little…soggy. With towels and training…

Finally, she finishes the last of the pictures, and I can see that in the fifteen or so hours I've been here (okay, I'm lying, it's only been four, but it seems like sixty-three!), the sun has begun to set, sending golden stripes across the brown-and-gold carpet.

Auntie Milla gets up, begins to clear the table. I also rise, grab a plate and follow her. But on the return trip, I'm shanghaied by Vovka, who is standing at the door to her bedroom. "Want to see my grandfather?"

What kind of heel would I be if I said no? I smile at him, follow him inside the room. I see a floral bedspread and, above the bed, a stately photograph of a young couple. Neither is smiling and it reminds me of my own grandparents' pictures. What is it with that generation that didn't like to smile? I wonder if it had to do with gold teeth? I step closer, along the side of the bed, to take a better look.

Vovka toes the door shut. I turn, and little hairs rise on the back of my neck. Um, this isn't going to work. But he's advancing and backs me up against the wall. I bump the lamp next to the bedside table.

He's got one hand over my shoulder, trapping me, but he smells so good, I might forgive him. And he runs a finger down my jaw line. "Now you know my family history, what do you think?"

"I think you've got an interesting grandmother," I say, wondering what he means. Was this a sort of interview? Caleb's words about visa ploys suddenly echo in my head.

But Vovka just smiles, and his gaze falls to my lips.

I swallow, but okay, I'm game. I lift my face, and he again cups his hand behind my neck and aims for my mouth.

Precision counts, as does control, and maybe he's been practicing (with whom? He better not have been!), but this time, the slobber level isn't quite as drowning, and in fact, he tastes slightly sweet and tangy, perhaps the remnants of prune cognac. I hear a soft sound in the back of his throat as his arms go around me. I surrender and kiss him back, glad that I gave him another chance. No, my skin still isn't tingling or anything, but the fact that I'm not leaping for a Kleenex is a good thing, right? And, this proves something.

Vovka still has potential.

He releases me and smiles. "I love you."

What?

I swallow, stare at him, mouth open. He has emotions in his eyes and they match his words, but I'm frozen. Vovka loves me?

What do I say? I love you, too? But do I? I don't think I do. I'm fond of him. And we're going to work out the lips thing. But do I want to spend the rest of my life with him?

Yes, Mr. Ambassador, Vovka and I will be at the opera this weekend.

I'm going to have to think about this.

I manage a quivering smile and he's just staring at me, those liquid eyes pulling me in. I feel like a worm and I just want to wiggle out of here. Now. But how can I not love Vovka? Isn't he what I want?

<Wildflower> He said he loved you?

<GI> Yes!

<Wildflower> What did you do?

<GI> Nothing. I just stood there. And then Auntie Milla knocked on the door. I ducked out of his arms just as she peeked her head in. I bee-lined to the living room, and grabbed a plate of pickles. When I came into the kitchen, he was up to his elbows in suds, grinning.

<Wildflower> Well, do you?

<GI>: I don't know. Maybe. What if I don't know what love feels like? What if I do love him, but I'm too afraid to say it? What if all this time, I loved Chase and just didn't know it?

<Wildflower> So, do you love Chase, or do you love Vovka?

<GI> I DON'T KNOW.

<Wildflower> Well, you better decide soon because I have it on good authority that Chase is on his way to Russia.

<GI> WHAT?

<Wildflower> You didn't hear it from me. It's supposed to be a surprise.

Be home, be home, *be home!* I had to wait until midnight here, 9:00 a.m. Gull Lake time, because I know Jas usually finishes her first batch of dough by now, and returns to the house for a shower and breakfast. But today the telephone rings off the hook. Where is she? And why didn't she tell me Chase was coming here? What if he meets Vovka?

I slam the receiver down, pace the room in tiny circles. Tracey is on the sofa, holding a pillow to her chest. She's very Flashdance tonight in an oversized ripped sweatshirt and a high ponytail. "So?"

"She's not there. Maybe H was kidding." Or not. H is as reliable as the CIA. I feel slightly sick, despite a coil of excitement.

Chase, coming here?

No, wait, that can't be. How could he find me?

Okay, I feel better now. It's not like I'm listed in the phone book. Besides, it's late and he's not going to show up in the next six hours. Right? *Right?*

I panicked for nothing. I know this because 1. I received an e-mail from Chase this morning and in none of it did he hint coming to Russia. 2. Although I suspect Chase could pull off coming to see me in Russia, we're not that far along in a relationship, despite what he mentioned in his Valentine's

Day card. I mean, yes, before I left he hinted that I stay in Gull Lake, but that wasn't exactly a proposal, was it? I need words. Spell it out for me. I hate reading between the lines.

I am walking home with Vovka, who surprised me tonight after my class. I saw him give Evgeny a long, narrowed-eye look, but it vanished when Vovka took my bag off my shoulder, put his hand on my back and we headed out of the building.

He's very sweet, Vovka is. And protective. He asked me about my day, listening and even highlighting details. Because, you know, he loves me.

It's hard to describe the feelings swirling in my chest. Warmth. Curiosity. Panic? Seems that I shouldn't feel that one, but I have to admit it. Am I ready for Vovka to love me? Because, there's sort of a punch-card limit to one admitting one's love for another. Say it so many times and it should be redeemed for reciprocal declarations.

But we haven't reached that limit, and I dismiss the panic as we hike up my stairs. (I've given up on *ever* riding *up* the lift. Besides, it's good for the thighs.) The hallway is dark, and I see someone has shattered the bulb hanging in my cement-peeling hallway. But, it's light enough to see that Auntie Milla left me something big at my doorway.

Something big…like a St. Bernard. Only, slightly hunched over, and holding a duffel bag, and wearing a Gull Lake letter jacket.

Chase. My breath actually clogs in my throat. *Chase?*

Oh, no! What do I do with Vovka? But fate must have its due and I take a deep breath and find a smile. Because, deep down, past the fear, and even the embarrassment, I'm painfully, excruciatingly, *delighted*.

Chase is here. In Russia. *To see me.*

What exactly does this mean?

He hears our footsteps, and looks up. I can't hide it now—my tall companion, my new hairstyle, the leather pants, the smile that's building. By the time he gets to his feet, I'm in his arms and he's got his face buried in my neck. "Chase!" I say, sorta breathless, because although I can't truthfully feign surprise at his visit, I am overwhelmed by my sudden rush of emotions.

And tears.

He looks so good, in a boy-from-back-home sort of way. His curly, dark blond hair is horribly mussed, and he is wearing my favorite version of his ripped-at-the-knees Levi's, and he's holding my hand, his incredible blue eyes on mine. I can't help but compare his smattering of whiskers with Vovka's, and have decided that Chase wins. On him, the fuzzy, unkempt look works, especially when he combines it with that little bit of smile he does so well.

"Surprise," he says softly.

I'm not recovering well at all, and Vovka notices as he shifts weight beside me. Chase cuts his gaze to my large, Fabio-style shadow, but I'm not ready yet for introductions.

"How did you find me?" I ask instead. Chase-Me, all the way across the ocean!

Chase shrugs, as if I should realize by now that he carries some sort of GPS-on-Josey device in his back pocket, and it reminds me of that time I was walking home barefoot and slightly punchy from Lew Sulzbach's July 4th bash and Chase drove up in his motorcycle. "I have a journalist friend in Moscow who did some hunting."

Friend, in Moscow? I suddenly hope she's not tall and blond and Buffy-built. Calm down, he's here to see me! Wow, that evil green monster rises from the depths quicker than I can blink.

"A spy in Russia," I say, trying to be funny, but now that I'm past the green moment, I am touched. He's pulled some strings, and hunted me down. "You constantly surprise me."

He raises one eyebrow. "That's funny, because you once told me I was predictable as your mother's sponge cake."

I grimace. I should admit to him right now that there's a lot I was wrong about. Instead, I take the opportunity to introduce Chase to Vovka.

They stare each other down like two prize fighters, sizing up the competition.

Gulp.

What's worse, I realize that I have nowhere for Chase to stay. He can't stay in my flat, and my male-friends options are dwindling fast.

Vovka. Or Caleb.

I glance at Vovka. He's got his hands in his pockets and he is slightly taller, with a supply of *GQ* muscles that accentuate his overall stun power. But Chase has this hard-bodied, simmering confidence that makes a gal gravitate toward him on a dark night. I know, because I've spent enough time on the back of his motorcycle and hiding behind him during a few "I've come to your rescue" moments outside the Howling Wolf to realize there is danger under all that easygoing charm.

I probably should separate the two men in my life before something ugly happens, despite the fact that two guys fighting over me is darkly appealing.

Except, well, I'm being rather arrogant, aren't I? *Fighting* over me? Hardly.

"Thank you, Vovka, for walking me home. I probably should find Chase a place to stay." I don't approach Vovka, and at the moment I'm praying desperately that he doesn't lean over to kiss me. I can't deal with the slobber, let alone the aftermath of the questions in Chase's eyes. Or my own.

Vovka must sense my ambiguity, for he purses his model lips, turns and stalks over to his grandmother's apartment. Then, glancing at me with a gaze that makes me feel like a wart, he lets himself into her flat.

I wouldn't be surprised if I found him camped outside my door in the morning.

But, thankfully, the move throws Chase off. "He's your neighbor?"

Hallelujah!

"Yes," is enough for now.

Caleb isn't home, which isn't a huge surprise, but offers a dilemma because you know, we missionaries shouldn't have any sign of impropriety, even if it is innocent.

Chase and I hunker down on the sofa to wait, and I don't even notice the night hours ticking away as he, like a refreshing northern Minnesota pine-laden breeze, delights my heart with stories of Gull Lake.

Wow, have I missed him. He is leaning back against the sofa, legs up on the coffee table, slouched down and eyes smiling as he tells me about Jasmine and her pregnancy, about Myrtle's attempts to fill my shoes, and about his students.

"Hey," I ask as I grab the popcorn bowl. "How did you slip away from your classes?" Among the many gifts he's brought me—a DVD of *Lost* shows (okay, I'm a groupie!), six months' worth of *People* magazine, three bags of chocolate chips—he's packed a ten-pound bag of popcorn. Oh, he knows me so well. Once, during my senior year, I popped an entire garbage can full and had a bonfire bash out on Gull Lake beach. I think they're still turning up kernels.

"Winter break," he says. "Actually, I've been planning it since New Year's Eve, but I couldn't sneak away before now."

He's been planning it since *New Year's Eve.* I feel like a salamander. "I still can't believe you're here."

He shrugs, smiles. "I figure if you can fly over the ocean, I should see what all the fuss is about."

Oh. That's so very sweet, and I'm reading between the lines—are you worth the fuss? I am! I am! But, well, wait… what does this all mean, exactly? Chase is here, but why? He can admit he misses me without admitting his love for me, right? What if this is just an innocent visit and there is nothing to read into this? I want definition!

He reaches across the table for some popcorn. Smiles at me as he chews. I can hardly believe he is here. Gull Lake in my Moscow family room. I'm trying to right my tilting reality as the lock turns in the door.

Tracey stops three steps inside and stares at Chase. I see something like interest cross her face and inside me the green monster makes awakening noises. But I shouldn't worry. Although she looks like a long-lost cave girl, she's a woman of the new millennium and not a good study subject for Mr. Anthropologist.

"Hi," she says, dropping her bag and closing the door with her foot.

"Hi," Chase says, and I see a polite smile.

"I'm Tracey, Josey's flat-mate." She sits down on the arm of the sofa and reaches over for popcorn. Since when does she eat popcorn? No wonder my supply dwindled so fast!

"Chase Anderson."

She's grinning at Chase. And there is definite interest in

her eyes. "Chase, my friend from Gull Lake?" I qualify for her. My very good friend. My, my, *my*.

She glances at me—oh, are you here?—and nods, like sure, no problem.

Yeah, right. She's had some difficulties with territory issues, like *my* bagels, *my* popcorn, *my* potential love interest.

"Where have you been?" I can smell cigarette smoke on her from across the room, but I want her to say it aloud so that Chase will know, definitely, that she's not his kind of girl.

Well, then again, I don't exactly have a squeaky clean past. But I've been saved and living like it for a few years now, and besides, he knew me when and it didn't repel him.

Which only makes me jump from the sofa and pick up the telephone to call Caleb again.

"The Gray Pony," Tracey says, answering my question. "It's jazz night."

"Jazz?" Chase says. "They have jazz here?"

"And disco and R & B, and hip-hop and even Elvis," I elaborate, listening to the telephone ring. Please, *please,* Caleb!

Tracey is peeling off her coat. Oh, joy, under it she's wearing her other skin, the lioness dress, with fur at the cuffs. It leaves oh, so little to the imagination. Yeah, Chase! He barely looks at her, and instead he pushes off the sofa, pads to the kitchen. "Can I drink the water?"

"Hello?" I hear from the telephone.

"Caleb!" My voice holds just too much relief, and I fear it'll give him the wrong impression. He pauses, and then,

"Josey. How are you?" I've had more warmth from a large mouth bass.

"Caleb, I have to ask you a huge favor."

More silence. Tracey is helping Chase open a bottle of lemonade. She probably purring, too.

"I have a friend who just arrived from the States. I didn't know he was coming and I don't have a place for him to stay. Can he bunk with you for a few days?"

Silence. Has he hung up on me? On our friendship? Not that I don't deserve it. I know I've been a toad to him.

"Yeah, I guess. You know where I live, right?"

"Thank you, thank you! Caleb, you're a lifesaver."

I get the dial tone. I'm going to pretend that the phone service cut us off. That happens sometimes.

I scoop up Chase's duffel. It's considerably lighter after Santa unloaded his gifts. "You're all set."

Chase is leaning against the counter, eyeing me. "Who's Caleb?"

"A friend from church." I see Tracey smirking at me as I pull on my boots and Dough Girl coat. Note to self: do not leave Tracey alone with Chase. Ever. "He lives a couple Metro stops from here."

"Right." Chase drains his lemonade, tugs on his jacket and shoes and we're off.

His duffel carried between us, we ride down the lift. My chest is in snarls, and I can't believe how angry I am. Across the lift, Chase is watching me with his curious blue eyes, eyes that I always find way too perceptive.

"I still can't believe you live here. And seeing your room-mate makes me only more impressed. Please don't tell me you live with Catwoman by choice?"

I want to hug him. And a huge lump blocks my air, makes my eyes wet. I'm helpless to do otherwise, so I smile at him and shrug.

Outside, the sky is black, a cloud cover obscuring the stars. The air is still. Our feet crunch on the snow as we walk in and out of pockets of dingy light. Moscow at night can be romantic. It can also be creepy, and tonight I hear the skitter of garbage, an occasional hum of a car. It's not uncommon for gangs to prowl, waiting to spring on stupid foreigners who go out past dark.

"Don't talk," I whisper, realizing suddenly that it's been weeks since I've walked home alone, and never in the dead of night. Vovka is always there to protect and serve.

"Why?" Chase whispers back. I say nothing and he frowns.

We don't talk again until we get on the Metro train. It's well lit and empty and I show him how to surf. Of course, he's a pro and gets it in a second. He was born to surf, I can see it, and I wonder for a second what it would be like to live in Moscow with Chase, to hang out at Venetsia, and wander the boulevards under the stars. He laughs as the train takes a turn and he's knocked off balance. The sound of his laughter feeds my heart. I can smell Gull Lake on him—wool and his fresh soap and cotton jeans. I'm feeling weepy again so I push him and he tumbles back into a seat, but not before he grabs me and pulls me down on his lap.

The giggles vanish, and his expression turns serious. He reaches up and touches my hair, running the strand through his thumb and forefinger. "It's different, but I like it."

I'm not sure if he's talking about my hair, or me. Because I know I have changed. I'm…bolder, maybe. And owning my life, in a way that is also a glad surrender to God's plans, and that paradox feels strangely peaceful. Despite the struggles, I feel richer, even stronger for the last six months as I've wrestled with what it means to live for God, for His glory. I hope Chase sees this in my expression. It's this richness, this strength that prompts me to run my fingers through his hair, hoping he sees invitation in my gesture. I want to kiss him, and I feel it build in my chest, and consume my thoughts. *I want to kiss him.*

No second cousin issues here. And while I do hear the beeping of a danger signal in the back of my mind, I'm tuning it out to stellar effect.

I see it in his eyes, too. He gives me a soft, lopsided Chase smile. "Are you glad I'm here?"

Is he kidding? I can barely breathe. I nod, slowly.

He runs his fingertips down my face, his beautiful eyes holding mine. "Me, too."

Then he leans forward and I close my eyes. Please.

The Metro lurches, squeals and grinds to a halt. I'm jerked against him and we bump noses. Ouch! My eyes fly open.

But he's grinning, laughing and he shakes his head. "Our timing is perpetually off, isn't it, G.I.?" He pushes me off his lap as the subway stops and the doors bang open.

I disembark, knowing that the Anthropologist has uncovered our problem and dissected it with painful precision.

Chapter Fourteen:
Stand By Your Man

There is a time and a place for H. She's my link to Gull Lake gossip, my foothold in culture, and most of all, she's the only one who truly knows what it means to have Chase here, in my kitchen, making me dinner.

Besides God, that is. And right now, although H would find the latest turn of events fodder for a lengthy IM, I'm needing solid wisdom, from Someone who can see beyond my fears to tomorrow.

So I'm locked in my bedroom, under pretense of changing my shirt after spilling pizza sauce on it, on my knees and taking this straight to the One Who Really Knows.

I figure, if God can write all that stuff in Song of Solomon about twin fawns and honeycomb lips and eyes like doves, He might know something about the leaping gazelles frolicking in my heart.

Lord, he's here, which you know, but I think just need to lay all the facts out on the table. Chase is in Russia, and I am so confused.

You alone know that I'm trying my best to live Your way, every day, whatever that means, and it's not so very easy with him dressed in my favorite black T-shirt, smelling like fresh soap and cooking for me. It is possible he's just here, like he has been over the last 20-odd years, to be my friend. Because, well, although there was that moment in the Metro when the emotions I thought I saw in his eyes matched his actions, since then, there's been nothing. Nil. Nichevo.

Which makes me wonder if I'm attaching too much importance to this week.

1. He hasn't asked me once about Vovka. What's with that? He has to be curious. Especially since Vovka has appeared twice at my door, and called three times.

2. He told me all about Panty Stealer and Holiday Girl and made it clear that they were old shoes thrown into the back of the closet. So why can't he just say it aloud…he's here for me?

3. He and Caleb have hit it off, for which I have to applaud Caleb, unless, of course, Chase told him we were Just Friends. In which case, Caleb only sees opportunity.

4. Chase has definitely had some sort of spiritual nudgings over the last six months. I saw a pocket Bible in his stuff, and he prayed with me in a café (read: in public!) before lunch yesterday. Which only ups his eligibility. And, by the way, no matter what our future brings, thank You for answering that prayer.

5. Russia is his element. I haven't missed the fact that we spend every waking minute (practically) visiting ancient buildings, going to museums and watching people. Chase has attended every English class this week and bonded with Lera and Vera and Sergei (and I don't think Sergei needed to learn words like goober *and* noogie, *complete with demonstration. I'm sorry, Lord, and would it be too much to ask if Matthew didn't find out until after I'm long gone?). All of this brings me back to the Big Question.*

Why is Chase here?

So, Lord, I'm asking, please, give me a sign. Is Chase The One? Because, You know, I'm willing to dish out chances for him, here. Or should I be leaping for Vovka, the Man Who Loves Me?

More importantly, what life do You want for me? Gull Lake or Moscow?

There are many things I love about Chase. (Wait, did I say love? Maybe really, really, really like is safer at the moment. Oh, okay! *Love*.)

1. He fills out a pair of faded jeans and a T-shirt like a Navy Seal. Where he got those muscles, I don't know, but I'm not complaining. And, as I more recently discovered, he also looks stunning in an Armani suit. (A truth I can now embrace because he's *not with Buffy*.)

2. He doesn't take me too seriously, something that I count on when I start taking soapbox positions on things like healthy eating, exercise and world politics.

3. He makes great pizza.

I am leaning over the counter, in a fresh T-shirt, snitching cheese. Tomato sauce bubbles on the stove, and the smell of oregano, basil and garlic saturates the air and is whipping my stomach into a frenzy. I have to admit, I didn't know basil really came in leaves. But Chase nearly went into a salsa dance when he found it today at the market. Actually, there are a lot of interesting things at the market, as I discovered today—fresh dill, basil, rosemary, leeks, leaf lettuce, Edamer cheese (which he informs me is German—like, how did he know that?) and roma tomatoes.

Sorta makes a girl wish she had been the one blessed with the cooking genes. *Sorta*.

Chase has perfected the art of pizza making, most likely due to his remote assignments and the lack of decent pizza delivery. He is chopping green peppers at the moment, and he looks up at me, keeps chopping. "You remember when we made pizza over the campfire?"

Oh, yeah. I would have been grounded for a half a century if I hadn't been out with Chase. We made the dough up after a football game, stoked the coals from the dying bonfire and sat on the beach for hours watching it cook. I think I pulled in around 2:00 a.m., to my father waiting in the family room. Whoops. The pizza wouldn't have won any prizes, but now, as I see the memories in Chase's eyes, I know it has its own value. I nod. "We did a lot of crazy things," I say.

"No, you did a lot of crazy things. I remember myself as the Voice of Reason."

"Ha!" I say, but I can't deny that he's been the guy I most wanted to count on, the one I hoped would roar up on his motorcycle when I disentangled myself from a particularly groping date, or when H dragged me to a party that felt scary.

In fact, before I fell to my knees in repentance and surrender, Chase was the one who felt most like my guardian angel.

My throat is thickening. "You were always there, weren't you?" That's about as vulnerable as I can get at the moment, but still, it feels like I've just wrenched my heart out of my chest for him to take a good look. Yes, Chase, I needed you. More than I ever realized.

"Yes," he says, and holds my gaze. "And I'm here, now, too."

Whoa, is he ever. I can hardly breathe. "Why?" I ask, disbelieving that the word actually makes it out of my mouth.

He holds my gaze a moment longer, then goes back to chopping. I watch the knife slice the green pepper into paper-thin slices. "I guess I missed you."

Oh.

"And, like I said, I wanted to see what all the fuss was about."

I suddenly feel like crying. "So, have you figured it out?"

He glances at me, real quick, then back to the pepper. "Not sure, still formulating my hypothesis."

I let those words settle into my constricting chest, and loosen it. I reach over and grab a pepper, and he makes teasing move to spear me with the knife. "If you eat everything tasty before it gets on the pizza, you miss the end product. Wait, G.I."

His words seem serious, however, and I wonder if they should be accompanied by a tingle or a nudge by the Holy Spirit.

"Trust me, it'll be worth the wait."

Promise?

As if seeing the rush of fear, of doubt in my eyes, he cracks a grin. "Okay, I'll give you a little morsel."

Yes, yes! I step closer to him, as he turns toward me. He's wearing his "I found you," smile and my heart fills my throat as he leans down...and reaches over to the pile of sliced pepperoni. He picks one off and hands it to me, his breath close to my ear.

"No more snitching. Okay?"

I suddenly feel terribly ashamed. And I'm not sure why, but I think it has something to do with Vovka the Trout.

"Okay," I say, pretty sure I know what I'm agreeing to.

I watch him push out the pizza dough into the pan, fill it, then put it in the oven (which he figured out how to work after a three minute perusal. What, do I have *kasha* for brains?).

I pour a couple of lemonades and we sit on the vinyl. "I told you I've been going to your church, right?" he says, picking at the label on his bottle. "And I think I've figured something out."

I tuck my legs up under me, stretch my arm out along the top of the sofa, turning my body toward him.

"In all my work among people groups, I've seen a common thread."

"What's that?"

"We all want to matter. Something you said when you wrote to me in Montana stuck with me. You wanted to do something significant. Pastor Peterson has been going through Galatians, and verse 2:20 has stuck with me. 'I have been crucified with Christ and I no longer live, but Christ lives in me. The life I live in the body I live by faith in the son of God who loves me and gave himself for me.' I'm thinking that is what all this is about, Jose. You're letting Christ live in you." He takes a drink of his lemonade, but I notice he doesn't look at me when he continues.

"I have to admit that I always looked at you with a bit of... desperate awe. You were always the one with the wild ideas, the passion. So much of the time, just being around you felt exhilarating." He glances at me, a familiar winkle in his eyes. Then it dies.

"But you scared me, too. I followed you around most of the time thinking I was going to scrape you off the highway. And that thought nearly skewered me. But when you turned to God, well, part of me didn't want to believe it." He sighs. "The other part felt cheated."

I frown at him, seeing in the back of my mind his reaction when I told him about my new faith. He had seemed more distant, even angry. Come to think of it, shortly after that, he'd accepted his first assignment studying a people group in Alaska.

"See, I was pretty sure that deep down, you couldn't live without me. And when you decided you could...I felt like you threw our friendship out in lieu of your new Savior."

He swallows, and I feel a pain deep in my chest. I want to touch his arm, to tell him no, but I have to admit, maybe I did act that way. Like some sort of spiritual giant, squashing all the little people. Josey, mounting the soapbox, again. I want to cry, because if he only knew how small I felt most of the time, he'd be right back on his motorcycle, coming to my rescue.

Only, maybe that's not so good for him. Maybe he needs to find his own road, one that doesn't have me at the end.

Ouch.

"The thing is," he continues, "after I got over the fact that you might not be slapping me across the face, and that your faith was real, I started to pay attention. And I've come to some conclusions. I want my life to matter, also. And I'm not sure, but I think that if Pastor is right and eternity is what it's all about, then I think God has some insights into how to make life significant on both sides of eternity."

"What are you saying, Chase?"

He looks at me now. The sight of my Chase at the edge of spiritual vulnerability makes me want to wrap my arms around him. "I asked Christ into my life."

"You did?" I am trying to keep my voice down, but *he did?* Thank You, God, thank You! "Chase, that is great."

But when he smiles, there is a sadness to it that doesn't match this news. I suddenly feel a swell of panic in the back of my throat.

"What would you say if I told you I might not be in Gull Lake when you return?"

What? *What?* "Where are you going?" Wow, I sound almost normal, like my heart isn't breaking into a thousand pieces. Foiled again, and this time by my own prayers!

He shrugs, and there is a sad smile. "I don't know. But my

degree in anthropology might be an asset in a mission organization, especially in, for example, Irian Jaya, where they're
discovering new tribes all the time."

Irian Jaya? Lord, this is *not* the sign I was looking for! What
about all that nonsense about waiting for the pizza? I thought
Chase meant himself, but what if he just means...*wait for the
pizza?* No wonder he said our timing was off...now that
comment makes perfect sense. He wasn't about to kiss me,
which then follows reason why he hasn't snatched any of the
other opportunities I've presented before him. He wanted to
tell me that he wouldn't be around when I returned.

"Wow," I say, because I can't think of anything else. I feel
sick. In fact I might hurl. Because as happy as I am for him,
reassessing his life and all, he *needs* to stay in Gull Lake. Especially if he doesn't know he loves me, yet. How is he going to figure that out across a couple oceans and buried in
the jungle? I probably should have outlined this in my litany
of requests to the Almighty. *Lord, when I asked You to move in
his life, this is* not *what I meant. Please, understand me here?*

"Yeah." Chase smiles at me, like he hasn't just cut me off
at the knees. "I just thought that you, as my best friend, should
know."

Best friend. Never have those words hurt so much.

"That's great, Chase," I manage, lying through my teeth.
Sorta. Because, while I am wildly ecstatic at God's activities
in his life, an existence without Chase suddenly seems like
pizza without pepperoni.

I'm not going to ask God for signs anymore. It's too
confusing.

It's country music night at the Gray Pony. And Russia's
version of down-home Alabama is women in low-cut shirts,

sequined vests and spiked boots. All black, of course. I'm looking Gull Lake in my jeans and a black pullover and my spiked boots (because you know, I want to fit in). Someone is singing "I'll Always Love You," by Dolly, and at the moment, I'm wondering what I'm doing here.

Oh, yeah, it's Chase's last night here, and it's Caleb's idea to take him out when I'd much rather be back at my place, talking Chase into making me some macaroni and cheese or something.

But I don't trust myself not to break down and sob. Or worse, drop to my knees and beg him not to leave. Because, as usual, the thought of losing Chase has overwhelmed me anew, and again I'm left wondering, are my feelings for him real, or is it the danger of not having him that produces all this angst?

He's looking painfully cowboy tonight in a corduroy shirt, rugged whiskers and his jeans. He's drinking a Diet Coke and laughing with Caleb over a pair of ladies (and I use that term loosely) bellied up to the bar, hunting trouble.

Caleb, I've decided, is an interesting Christian, and his perspective is starting to rub off on me. He's not afraid of hanging out at the Gray Pony, and doesn't compromise his principles while doing it. He has a billion friends, especially Russians and they gravitate to him like rubber bands, here, there, back again. Because he's got a smile for everyone, even me, who doesn't deserve it.

Whatever has happened this week between me and Chase, I have to thank him for making things okay between Caleb and me. I'll not take my grungy friend for granted again.

"Hey, how about a song?" Caleb says as Dolly finishes. "C'mon."

"Um, *no*," I say, but he grabs me by the elbow. I throw a

"help me" look at Chase, but he's just grinning. "Stand By Your Man!" he yells to the DJ and pushes a mike in my hands.

I ache, right in the middle of my chest, and it only halfway has to do with the terror that has vise-gripped me. What am I doing here? Mostly the pain comes from knowing that Chase is leaving, maybe forever. *Please, God, fix this?* Only, frankly, the Almighty is to blame and I don't know what to make of that. Especially after all my prayers for Chase.

The song starts, and I'm blinded, harassed by catcalls and lights. Hello? My brain is just starting to catch up to the moment and I realize I'm in the middle of Russia, about to croon a song that I, of all people, have no right to sing. I start to hand the mike back but suddenly Caleb appears. "C'mon." And then he starts singing. Stand by my man? Which one?

I'm an idiot, but standing next to Caleb, with Chase grinning somewhere outside the ring of light, I choke out the song, soon bent over in hysterics. Russians never do anything halfway, and tonight they're singing along, as if this is a Soviet oldie. Caleb and I finish off in a rousing finale, and then escape as another troubadour mounts the stage for Ronnie Milsap's "Smoky Mountain Rain." We hang on the railing and listen to the Russians decimate the song. At least they know the words. Sorry excuses for Americans, we are.

"Thanks for letting Chase stay with you," I say, watching the crowd, but peeking at Caleb.

"Sure. He's okay. And he's learning what it is to live for God, which rocks. I could see him in Moscow."

"Yeah?" I love that idea, and maybe Caleb can push him— only, I'm thinking maybe that's not the right way to go about things. Not only is there Caleb, but do I really want to stand between Chase and God telling him where to go?

Probably not. Because I'd never know if I was God's choice for Chase, and vice versa.

And, it's sorta looking like I'm not.

I blink back the sting in my eyes. Well, at least now I know.

"I have to apologize to you for something, Josey," Caleb says quietly—well, as softly as one can over the words to "Boot Scootin' Boogie."

I eye him.

"I was pretty angry with you after I saw you with Vidal Sassoon."

I tilt up my mouth, one-sided. His humor bathes the sting of those words. "Vovka."

"Right. Well, when I saw him, I wondered if maybe you'd only come to Russia for one thing—a husband."

Gulp. If he only knew. In fact, it was lack of husband that drew me here, but still, the right theme.

"But when I met Chase, I knew that you were here for bigger reasons."

Huh?

But he's not stopping for me to get to the bottom of that statement.

"In fact, I knew that God had been answering my prayers for you."

"You've been praying for me?" Which, all at once, seems a better line of questioning, so as to deter him from that husband-hunting topic.

"Yeah. Pretty much all year. I remembered our conversation about you reading Ephesians, so I prayed Paul's Ephesians' prayer."

I shake my head, realizing that Caleb is so much better at this missionary stuff than I am.

"Paul prays that the Ephesians would know God intimately, and specifically three things—that they would gain a deeper understanding of their salvation, a sense of belonging to Christ, and experience the power of God in their lives." He smiles and touches my arm. It's a brotherly touch, because there are no tingles. "After talking to Chase, and hearing about the things you are doing, the way you handed over your career and your future to God, and tackled the challenges of Russia, I know that God is working in your life." He squeezes my arms. "I'm glad to know you, Josey."

Wow. That's about the nicest thing anyone has ever said to me—well, besides Chase's "I'm proud of you" comment. I feel warm to my toes as I reach over and hug Caleb.

He smells pretty good, for a grunge guy. He's wearing mischief on his face when he steps away. "Wanna try the 'Achy Breaky Heart'?"

"Uh, no."

I glance at Chase and he's watching us, an enigmatic smile on his face. He looks kind of sad and I'm wondering if he is thinking about what isn't between us.

The Gray Pony is packed with ex-pats tonight, as well as Russians and I see Tracey sitting at a table with a few of her NGO pals. I wave, she smiles. I've done a great job of intercepting her and Chase this week. No sparks there, thank you.

I'm about to dare Caleb to Achy Break when I see trouble walk into the Pony. Vovka. And he's standing tall by the door, looking for his woman.

Yikes.

I've only seen Chase in a fight once. It was at Jerry's, after Gull Lake lost to the Miller Hill Moose. A bunch of arrogant Moosies were running their mouths and guess who was in the middle, defending the Gull Lakers without a thought to consequences. I know, big shocker, especially since I think things through so very well. I think I might have even poured a beer over someone's head.

I remember pushing, and lots of yelling and suddenly I was outside with a crowd. I shoved through sweaty bodies and to my horror found Chase squaring off with a Miller Moose the size and demeanor of said beast defending my honor.

But Chase is fast. He's smart. There were two quick punches, some blood, screaming and then Chase strode toward me, looking like he might like to have a go at me next.

He hauled me onto the back of his motorcycle and I didn't say anything as we drove through town toward Berglund Acres. I still remember him trembling, however, as I curled my arms around his waist and held on.

I never asked him where he learned to fight like that. I had a dark feeling it had to do with his father. And the resident six-pack.

That memory rushes back to me when I see Chase eye Vovka. Vovka doesn't seem happy to see my Gull Lake pal and I am suddenly visualizing International Incident. *Brawl breaks out during the Dixie Two-Step. Thirteen injured; UN troops surround building.*

Vovka ignores the Yankee, however, and stalks over to me, a proprietary look in his eye. "I've been looking for you all week." His voice holds hurt and I feel like a jerk. He doesn't deserve to be treated like yesterday's casserole. He's still so very hot. And he loves me.

Which Chase doesn't.

Or, at least in the "will you be mine forever" type of way.

I smile up at Vovka, aware that Caleb is watching me out of the corner of his discreet eye. "Hi. I'm sorry I've been avoiding you. This is Chase's last night here, so we decided to go out."

Chase is off his chair, walking over to us. He's watching Vovka, and the look he's giving him seems so high school, it makes a small ripple of half fear, half hope ripple through me. Is Chase jealous?

"I don't think we've properly met," Chase says, but I know him well enough to sense the coldness in his voice. "Chase Anderson, Josey's best friend."

Vovka smiles, and for the first time I see the lion behind the golden mane and cultured elegance. "Vovka Antrop. Her boyfriend."

Chase cuts me a look, then a frown. "Oh," he says.

Oh? That's *it*? Here it is, the moment of truth, and he says, *Oh?* Although, come to think about it, I was about as articulate when he introduced me to Buffy.

Oh.

Please, Chase, say something? Anything more than *Oh*. Some hint that if I leap toward your arms I won't land on the floor, bruised and bleeding.

I stare at him, pouring those thoughts into my eyes, and for a moment, our gaze meets. The look in his beautiful blue eyes is unidentifiable, but a shiver runs up my spine.

"Of course," he says to me. "Your boyfriend."

Then he turns and…leaves?

"Chase, wait!" I start after him, but Vovka grabs my arm.

"Let's dance, Zhozey."

No! Only, well, suddenly my future seems painfully obvious. Vovka, not Chase.

I asked for a sign, didn't I? And God seems to be all about answering prayers these days.

And me? I'm just trying to keep up with the right requests,

hoping that along the way I figure out what The Almighty is up to.

The last thing I remember clearly before dissolving into tears is Caleb stalking out after Chase, confusion on his face.

Chapter Fifteen:
The Lucky Ones

<Wildflower> He just left, just like that?

<GI> Without a goodbye or anything. I called Caleb that night and Chase had already left for the airport. By the time I got out there, he had entered the international area and I couldn't get through.

<Wildflower> I saw him at the Holiday Station a couple days ago.

<GI> That's just swell.

I've felt sick since a week ago Tuesday when I stood outside customs, painfully aware that Chase had deliberately slammed the door on us. Not that there is an *us*, really, but there is the *us* that is our history, our friendship. The fact that I haven't slept in over a week and have finished off every jar of Nutella in the flat feels painfully like a break-up. Just add shopping, a new pair of shoes and hair color and it will be a full-fledged, gain-ten-pounds end-of-a-relationship heartbreak. In fact, I don't think I've ever felt this empty. As if I'd just lost some major organs, starting with my heart and lungs.

<Wildflower> Have I ever told you that you sabotage yourself?

<GI> Thank you for that boost.

<Wildflower> No, really. Remember in ninth grade when you were dating what's his name, the lead of *South Pacific?*

<GI> Drew.

<Wildflower> Right. You were the one who introduced him to Marci. What, were you testing him? Just like you were testing Chase? How do you suppose it felt to stand there staring at Fabio? Even if Chase didn't jet over to Russia in some desperate hope to win your heart, you pretty much reminded him that he wasn't good enough.

<GI> Stop. That's not true. (I hate it when she makes sense. Someone with purple hair should not make this much sense!)

<Wildflower> It is true. Has it ever occurred to you that Chase has been CHASING you for eighteen years? I know you think your love life is a big, sad joke but if I were there I'd give you a smack upside the head. Get a hold of yourself. Do you want him, or not? Because frankly, sis, Chase has done his time. You want him, you chase him. He deserves that.

<GI> Whose side are you on, anyway? I recall SOMEONE saying that if he is the right one, he'd wait.

<Wildflower> He is waiting! But the bigger question here isn't does Chase love you, but do you love him? What more do you want from the boy?

<GI> Stop it, H. You're wrong. He doesn't love me. If he did, he would have said it.

<Wildflower> I think he has. You just have to learn to speak his language. But that wasn't my question, was it? If you love him, you just blew it.

<GI> Thanks, Dr. Phil. I feel oh so much better realizing I have no one to blame but myself. Yippee.

<Wildflower> Be in denial if you want, but you have about three months to figure it out. Maybe. You still want me to drive by his house once/day?

<GI> Maybe twice.

I log off before H can say anything else that spears me in the heart. Chase doesn't love me. He had his chance, five days of chances, in fact, and this time, no Buffy or ocean in the way. And, I don't care what she says, I am not in denial.

Not really.

Okay! Yes, I can't quite get a grip on what I feel for Chase. We've been friends for so long, all these emotions could be about finders keepers, and not the real thing. And even if it is the real thing, *he isn't reciprocating.* Which means it's a moot point, not denial. Besides, what does God want for me? Because, you know, that counts. What did Caleb say about God having a master plan? *God is for us, not against us. He is ultimately about showing Himself and His unbelievable love, to us, and through us as He takes us through life.*

Oh, I hope so!

I grab my pillow and press it to my face. Oh, great, snot on the pillow. I get up, go to the kitchen, search the cupboards. No more Nutella. And the cheese spread is gone, too. Yeah! I found some peanut butter *padushki.* I crunch it slowly as I stare out my window at the sunrise winding through Moscow.

What, exactly, are You doing here, Lord? March is tiptoeing toward spring and suddenly Moscow seems like it's been gray-scaled. The sky, slate gray and dispensing drizzle, black snow along the streets, the smell of diesel and not a lilac bud in sight. To add to the pallor of depression, Matthew has returned, and Rebecca confronted him. I found him sleeping on the sofa in his office yesterday, looking drawn. He's a lot of fun to be around.

My relationship/whatever with Vovka seems holding steady, although I've done a duck and run every time he flashes his lips near me. Keep thinking of pizza for some reason.

Most of all, I'm wondering at Chase's words. He wants to make a difference, like I am. Ha. Right. I've made a huge dent in the landscape of Russia, in fact there is a parade committee meeting tonight.

Tracey is already in bed, and I have to give her credit for not throwing herself at Rick, who has begun calling every night, asking her out. She, at least, knows what she doesn't want.

I've been praying for you. Caleb's kind words return to me like an embrace. Sweet grungy Caleb. *Praying that you would know God.*

I finish off the *padushki* and head back to my bedroom, pulling out my Bible and flipping to Ephesians, and continue on my question with Ephesians 1:15–18, and I remember Caleb's words—"Paul prays that we might know God, be *enlightened* to who He is."

And since I've been enlightened (like that word!) I'll better understand…

1. "The hope of his calling—" Meaning then that, if everything crumbles around me, I have something no one can destroy…salvation. That thought in itself should keep me in tears. But how does this hope change me? I guess it gives me an endgame. It gives my life both security and purpose. I'm not in it alone.

2. "Riches of the glory of his inheritance—" Okay, so confused. But I think it means that I belong to Jesus, I'm His inheritance, which is a pretty cool thing considering I wouldn't consider anything about me worth inheriting (even the $3,295 in my bank account). But He does. In fact, He considers me a treasure. Whoa. And that fills my chest with a strange sweetness.

But does he also think the same way about Tracey? That thought should change the way I look at her, I suppose.

3. "The exceeding greatness of his power—" Super Josey! No, sorry, that's going a bit overboard, but the verse does say God's power directed at me…in fact His *resurrection* power— the kind that takes the dead and makes them alive. Which means…well, that at the very least, I have power to not teach the class such words as "two-timing scum" instead of Mr. Winneman.

So, if I sum up verses to date—

I'm here because God likes me and wants to do something good in me. Hmm. And, as I grow closer to God, I'll get a better understanding of my salvation, my worth and God's power in me.

Which, I can probably boil down to this: it's not only about the product, but the process. Which feels pretty good as I climb into my still size-12 Gap boot-cuts, needing a refresher on my highlights and knowing that I'm starting season four here in Russia without one conversion on my notchless belt. More than that, despite the fact that my heart feels like it's been taken out, flogged and reinserted in my chest, it still beats a tune of hope that there is something bigger at work here. That God is still doing something here in Russia, in me.

I pull on a sweatshirt, then close my Bible and find myself again on my knees, something that is happening fairly often these days…in fact, something I'm starting to look forward to it, like one might look forward to a Oreo shake, or a piece of French silk pie. Yum.

"Lord," I say, "I don't know why You brought me here, but I know it is about You. About knowing You better. And if You can teach me something through this hole burning in my chest over the Chase thing, well, then please give me wisdom. I'm truly overjoyed at this change in his life, and his salvation. So, I pray that he would know You better."

I turn over H's IM, and the questions that burn in my heart. Am I a saboteur? Why don't I just throw myself into his arms?

It doesn't matter. Chase is gone. And I'm here. Still, if God does care about me, He also cares about my messes, so— "And Lord, really, I don't know if these feelings I have for Chase are love, or just…(gulp) selfishness. So, if You could help me figure that out before You send him off to Tanzania or something, I'd be grateful." I run my fingers under my eyelids, swipe away a gathering of moisture.

"Most of all, God, please use me here, for whatever Your purposes are. Help me to know You, and be changed because of it…amen."

I get up and the sun is turning my dingy lace curtains gold. And inside, the burning has begun to subside to a dull ache.

The Venetsia has three kinds of coffee. I know, I expected more from a bistro, but the fact that coffee appears on the menu along with the three pages of vodka and cognac listings, pickled herring and squid salads, makes me happy enough. I love the café *smolokom,* made with espresso and sweetened condensed milk, and I'm on my third cup when I see Matthew enter.

He's looking…pale. I know he's wearing the same clothes he wore yesterday and while that fact isn't an issue in Russia, it registers in my American brain. Ew. He orders a cup of coffee and my heart rams in my throat when he turns and walks toward my table. I'd look behind me for his true destination, but I'm seated next to the wall.

I close my book (from another care box from Jas. Who also sent a picture of her cute little basketball belly). Matthew sits down with his coffee.

"Hello?" I say, wondering if I missed the part where I'd invited him over.

"Hi," he says. Up close he looks like he's spent a week in Chechnya. Unshaven, bags under his eyes, his oxford and khakis rumpled under that fraying leather jacket. See what happens when you cheat? No I-roning!

"How are you doing?" You scumbag. No, Josey, be nice! Can't you see he's hurting? But I think of Rebecca, at home, decorating and baking and I narrow my eyes.

"I wasn't cheating on my wife, Josey."

"Please define 'not cheating' for me, Matthew. Because, well, it looked like cheating from my vantage point on the balcony." I can't believe those words come out of my mouth! Yeah, me! I probably deserve another coffee.

Matthew rests his forehead on the palm of his hands, and he sighs. I feel it in my bones. Despair. Frustration. Wow, I really relate to that. I've been sighing the same way for a couple weeks now every time I open my e-mail and don't see a listing from Chase.

It makes me soften toward Matthew, just a little.

"I'm sorry. The thing is, even if you weren't cheating, it looked...bad. And you have to know that our missionary community is small enough to talk."

He nods and suddenly appears like he might cry. I look around in panic, at the clumps of Russians in conversation. Please, Matthew, don't dissolve here. I'm not ready for that kind of crisis.

"Do you know where I went this month?"

Not a clue, Waldo. Nor do I want to know. Really.

"I was in counseling in France."

I knew it. The south of France! Somehow this doesn't improve my opinion of him. I sip my coffee.

"I went there because I'm burned out. I've been here for ten years, with hardly a break, and frankly, I just want to go home."

It really unsettles me how much I relate with Matthew the Weasel at the moment. I don't hold out my hand to him or anything, but my posture relaxes, and says, "I'm all ears."

"I've been dodging these feelings for three years, and although it seems to be getting easier physically to live in Russia each year, emotionally, I've hit the skids. Did you know that we arrived during the days when toilet paper was a luxury?"

Okay, over sharing. But I have heard stories of the lean years, right after the fall of communism when the grocery stores were empty and the black market stocked. "Rebecca loves it here. She thrives on challenge, on redoing our lives. But she's at home, and I'm out here, trying to make a difference." He sighs and the look he gives me zings me in the heart. "Yeah, right."

Don't cry! I take another sip of my coffee, pulling in the emotions that want to stand up and scream, Me, too! "That doesn't give you the right to cheat on your wife."

"I wasn't cheating. I was just—"

"Lonely?"

"Responding."

"Oh, please." Okay, my empathy has vanished. "You're not trying to tell me that Larissa came on to you?" My voice rises slightly and his eyes widen. But I don't care. "Don't go there with me, Matthew."

He swallows, and I see him redden. Then tears well in his eyes. Sheesh! I don't do well with men crying. It always makes me feel all trembly and squishy inside.

"I didn't kiss anyone. But—" He closes his eyes, wipes his finger and thumb across them. "Okay, I did consider it." He swallows, and his voice lowers. "I know what that says and I feel ashamed. But honestly, I don't love anyone but Rebecca and I know I've wronged her."

I'm getting a sick feeling. He looks up at me and I can see pleading in his eyes. No, Matthew. No. No. *No!*

"Josey, she won't even see me. Can't you talk to her? Please? Tell her how sorry I am, and that I want us to go home, to see a counselor? To put our marriage back together?"

"You call her." Please! I so don't want to be in the middle of this.

He shakes his head. "I did. I went to the flat. She won't answer the door."

And if I know Rebecca, she's probably baking a royal velvet cake or something. Maybe reglazing her living room walls...

"I don't think anything I say to her will help, even if I do talk to her."

Whoops! Wrong thing to say. He practically lights up the entire café with his smile. No person should put that much hope into anything I say.

"Really?"

I push away my cup. Sigh. "Okay. I'll tell her what you told me."

He swallows, and gives me a smile that I know I don't deserve. Then he reaches across the table and hugs me. Right there. "Thanks, Josey. I knew you'd be a blessing."

And, as I scramble for response, I see Vovka swing through the doors. Wow, he has uncanny timing, and an amzing ability to track me down in a city of ten million people. Matthew pulls away and doesn't see Fabio stride toward him.

What is that look on Vovka's face? I stand, a strange fear pushing me to my feet. But I'm a millisecond too late.

Vovka pulls a psycho, grabs Matthew by the arm, turns him around and lands a fist right in the chops.

Ouch. But on the other hand, Yeah!

Except now Vovka is staring at me, breathing hard. "I've been looking all over for you."

I'm thinking that might not be a good thing. Despite the fact that I've dreamed of a man coming up to me in a bistro and saying those very words to me, Vovka is not the man in that dream, and it doesn't feel at all like I had hoped.

A shiver runs down my spine.

"Don't you know that I love you?"

"Love me? This is how you act when you love me?" I'm not going to help Matthew off the floor or anything, but still, the fact that Vovka defines his love for me by decking someone has sirens sounding. "Hitting is not okay." I sound like a kindergarten teacher.

Vovka looks stunned. As if this might be news to him. He glances down at Matthew, back to me. "I'm your boyfriend."

If he says that word again, there might be more hitting. I shake my head. "Vovka, I don't—"

"I'm sorry, I really am. I just thought he was—"

"Hugging me in public?" Although, considering the fact that Matthew has a reputation at MBC now, well, maybe Vovka isn't over-reacting. In fact, he reaches out his hand and apologizes to Matthew, with sincerity on his beautiful face.

Matthew eyes him warily, rubbing his chin.

Well, at least one of us got to hit him.

Tracey is standing at the door looking like she's been in a fight. At Baby Joe's House of Mud. She's also sobbing and her runny mascara only adds to the jungle-girl aura.

"What happened to you?" I come out of the bedroom where I'm successfully fitting into my skinny Gap jeans. I help her peel off her muddy zebra skin/jacket. "You look horrible."

"I...I stopped by the Gray Pony on the way home and... Rick was there. With Stacey." She leaves the muddy coat in a heap on the floor and heads straight for the bathroom. I stand outside the closed the door while she shouts out the details. Stacey? Who's Stacey? "I'd heard he was dating her, but until tonight I wasn't sure."

"So you what—mud-wrestled her?" I knew Tracey had it in her, but I didn't expect her to do it with her furs on.

"No," she snaps. "I was mugged. About a block from the subway."

"Near that bank of metal garages?" I always knew that was prime ambush territory.

"Yeah," she says, and I hear water running.

Just call me Lara Croft. This is why I cross the street when I pass that place.

"Did they get your purse?"

"I carry that inside my coat. They got my laptop." She comes out, wiping her face. I can see she put up a fight, the cat woman she is, and she's shaking, probably the rush of adrenaline.

"Are you okay?" I reach out, and to my surprise, she lets me hug her.

Okay, this was an encounter I never expected. I pull away and we don't look at each other for a moment. Yeah, weird.

"I'll live. I just thought—well, Rick's been calling me, right? And then tonight I see him draped around that twit of a secretary." She heads for the kitchen, pulls out a pot and pours in oil and popcorn. My popcorn. Oh well. "I'm pitiful. I can't believe I actually fell for him, or that I ever considered taking him back."

There's a big "Me, either" forming on my lips, but I'm not giving in. She needs me to be above that right now.

"Do you suppose I could borrow yours?" she asks as she shakes the pan. Kernels bang against the lid, the smell fills the flat.

"My...?" What? Popcorn. Supply of bagels? My Solomon wisdom?

"Your computer."

Oh. "Sure. I'll set up an identity for you."

She gives me a half smile, and for the first time, really, I see past the jungle veneer to a girl, just like me, who is just trying to cope, one day at a time. To find her place here, in the Moscow jungle. So she's a size four and has amazing hair, she knows what it feels like to be afraid. To hurt. To be jilted for another woman.

I smile at her, and she smiles back. It's a nice moment.

"Hey, have you heard from your friend Chase yet?" She pours the popcorn into a bowl, adds salt.

My appetite has vanished. "No. He's probably busy with school." Liar, liar, leather pants on fire. Oh, but I'd like to believe that.

"Oh," she says and hands me a bowl. I decline, because I've just managed to squeeze into my skinniest Gap jeans, and I'm feeling thin and powerful.

She takes the popcorn into the next room, sits down. "You're so lucky, Josey. This kind of stuff never happens to you."

What kind of stuff? Having life slip out of your hands like a walleye? Maybe now isn't the time to tell her that I started this adventure stuffed in a poppy-colored bridesmaid dress. I sit down next to her. "Are you going to be okay?"

"Yeah." She dips into the popcorn. "Thanks for letting me have some of your stash."

That was really nice of me, wasn't it? I mean, I didn't go for her jugular, and I count that as one of those "for the praise of His glory things." Besides, she's had a rough day. "You're welcome."

A tear squeezes out of her eye, runs down her cheek and—
Josey, I'm so glad I met you.

What? Oh, no, she didn't say that, but she wants to. Because I'm here for her, her roomie who shares popcorn. Who lets her use my laptop, who tells her the truth about Rick.

Good works, which God hath before ordained... That thought zings me, right in the heart and suddenly I see past my own petty sacrifices to the truth.

Tracey has seen her pseudo-beloved in the arms of another. And, well, I know exactly the cut-me-off-at-the-throat feeling that generates. And the life beyond that. In a hallelujah moment that should be accompanied by angels trumpets, I'm seeing a little glimpse of heavenly perspective, and while I never, ever imagined that God could be at the helm of the Dark Moments, like Milton and Jas, and even Chase doing an one-eighty in my life, God is all about surprises. And turning the bad into good.

"Tracey, I'm not lucky at all in this life...God has just given me a perspective that gets me past the dark moments. A perspective that says I'm not only special to God, but part of some grand plan that makes all this is okay. I'm trusting Him for that, one day at a time."

She looks at me like I've spoken Taiwanese and tilts her head as if to clean out her ears. My heart has climbed up to my throat and it is presently enlarging, choking me. Any second now I'm going to faint, so I clutch the back of the sofa and paste on my smile. Still, I shoved the words out there, and I'm hoping she sees a hint of God's love for her in them.

"Then I think you're doubly lucky," she says quietly.

I blink at her. Yeah, okay, I see her point. *Please God, if You're trying to say something through me, help me not to blow it!* "But you can have that perspective, too," I say, on the barest remnant of breath. "He loves you and wants to show you that, if you can trust Him."

She holds my gaze. "Are you going out?"

What? Crud! Evangelistic moment lost. "Maybe. Vovka called."

"He's such a nice guy."

Yeah. Overly protective, maybe. Slobbery. The unrealistic cover of a romance novel. But nice.

"Yeah." I stand up, disappointment burning in my chest. I didn't really expect her to drop to her knees in ecstatic conversion, but I was running over 1 John 1:9 and the Romans 6:23 evangelism diagram in my head and for the first time since coming to Moscow felt as if maybe I might earn my keep.

She pulls on her headphones as I close my bedroom door.

Maybe I should stay home tonight. I stand there, staring at my clothing choices, longing to tug on my sweatpants and dive into the new romance novel Jas sent. What if Tracey has a relapse and needs me?

I see myself reach for the new leather pants I bought at the market, a Vovka-approved selection. Mr. Sassoon has turned rather…committed…on me lately, calling in the morning, meeting me after class to walk me home. I've even seen him lurking outside my flat, as if making sure I'm safe. Only, it doesn't feel protective.

It feels leechy.

Which makes me wonder why I never got that feeling when I turned around and found Chase on my tail. It's not like he hasn't decked a few overly friendly gropers for me. I feel acid pool in the back of my throat. But Chase doesn't love me.

And Vovka…okay, the kind of love he's offering feels a little like a line drive to the throat, but on a good night he also makes me feel stunning and exotic. When I'm with him, heads turn. Only they're probably thinking, what is she doing with him?

Is that how I want to go through life…a question mark?

More than that, in general, the leather is starting to chafe and I think I might be a sweatpants girl. Maybe.

I rehang the pants, and tug on a Gull Lake sweatshirt and a pair of jeans. We're only going to the Gray Pony for jazz, so there's no need to wear my new leather skirt, or the Italian boots. In fact, I grab my Morrell hikers, feeling suddenly nostalgic for a place with peanuts on the floor and greasy burgers.

The doorbell rings and Vovka is standing in the hall, looking his stunning self in a ribbed green sweater and black jeans. "Hello," he says in his rumble-under-my-skin voice. His gaze scans my attire and his smile dims. "How about wearing those leather pants I bought you?"

How about not?

"I'm tired, Vovka. I think I'll stay home." And maybe pray for Tracey. Because, at the moment, that thought is nearly eclipsing every other. Why, I don't know, except that I think she needs it.

And I oh, so greatly, feel her pain.

Vovka leans against the doorjamb, a small smile on his lips. He does the little smile thing well (not as well as Chase, but still). It chips a dent in my stay-home demeanor. "You promised."

I did? Don't remember that, but well, it's either that or stay home and…what?

Sit and wait for an e-mail from Chase?

Pray that he doesn't go to Mozambique?

Maybe, in fact, that's a pretty good idea.

"Please," Vovka says, sweetly, his smile so perfect. Too perfect for a down-home gal like me.

"I'm sorry, Vovka," I say as I close the door.

It could have been the shadows, but I was almost positive his eyes turned glittery cold.

Chapter Sixteen:
Chocolate Chip Cookies

Matthew owes me big because I've sacrificed a Saturday shopping on Arbat Street to make chocolate-chip cookies with Rebecca. Venetsia has even moved their tables back out onto the sidewalks, and lilac buds grace the few trees I've spotted in unlittered Moscow corners. The smell of spring tinges the air and Moscow has shed the we-will-survive demeanor that makes people closed and testy. Instead, there's frolic in the air, and I've even spotted a gold-toothed smile from Igora the KGB Metro Guard.

And, although spring beckons from the open window, I'm wearing a dishtowel/apron, and trying to focus on Rebecca's words. "I usually use one cup of sugar, one of brown sugar," she's saying as she pours the mix into the bowl. Her children, dressed in pressed khakis and aprons, peer over the Tupperware bowl, eyes on the dough. Yeah, me, too. I have a take-no-prisoners attitude when it comes to cookie dough. And, since I'm bigger, I'm going to win.

She pours in the sugar. "I'm out of brown sugar, however, so we'll just have to skip it."

I should interject here that while Jasmine inherited the full complement of baking genes, I did manage to slide in on her laurels and learn to make a pretty decent cookie. Well, the dough addiction helped. But a gal doesn't sit at the table watching her mother and sister bake around her without picking up a few hints.

"Why don't you use molasses?" I say. "Or honey?"

"What?" Rebecca frowns slightly. "Why?"

"Because brown sugar is just white sugar with molasses. Dark honey is even better. My sister uses it all the time." I stand up and search through her cupboards. Of course, they're alphabetized. I don't find molasses, but surface with a bottle of honey. I unscrew the top and before Rebecca can sputter, I pour in about three tablespoons.

She makes a grab for the honey, but I'm so Lara Croft I dodge her and cap it myself. I put it back and then, notice a spice container. Nutmeg. Yum. Jas uses it religiously in her cookies and cakes.

I turn, uncap it and sift in a couple dashes.

"What. Are. You. Doing?"

I glance at her. "Rebecca, trust me, it'll taste good."

"You've ruined them!"

Whoa, take a chill pill, honey, a big one. "No, I didn't. We use nutmeg all the time in Gull Lake."

"You're not in Gull Lake."

Oh, really? Because I could easily get confused by the sound of snarled traffic and the smells of rotting garbage. "I know. But these will taste just as yummy."

But June Cleaver is near tears and the kids and I are staring at her as she unravels. "You ruined the cookies!

Don't you know that the secret to good recipes is following instructions?"

Can anyone say overreacting? "I'm…ah, sorry Rebecca. I didn't mean to wreck your dough."

"No, you wouldn't mean to, would you? You just barge in and do what you what want."

What? "I'm sorry, Rebecca. I just wanted to help."

"Well, you haven't! Haven't you learned anything this year?" She takes her apron and pulls it up over her head while her children stare at her, white faced. Her shoulders are shaking and I hear gulping sobs.

Ooops. Time to practice my auntie skills. "C'mon, kids, let's watch Winnie the Pooh."

They slide off their stools and I situate them in front of the television, crank it up a little as Tigger bounces on his tail. I'd like to bounce on my tail, all the way home.

To Gull Lake.

Because, deep in my heart, I wonder if going back to the beginning and starting over might help me figure out where this year derailed. Chase hasn't written, although it's been over a month, and Vovka has moved in with his grandmother in order to watch me and appear instantly the moment I leave my flat.

What kind of person tracks another's every move?

Don't answer that.

Actually, I feel just the slightest guilt about Vovka. I've deflected his requests to go out, hoping he'll catch onto the "I'm sliding out of your life" routine. Sorta like how I'm catching onto Chase's own version of it in my life.

That thought doesn't make me feel any better.

I go back to the kitchen. Rebecca is stirring the dough,

having added the flour, the baking powder, the eggs and vanilla. Tears cruise down her face.

I take the wooden spoon and bowl from her and stir. (No
need to put the dough in jeopardy.) "Sit down."

Miraculously, she obeys me, blows her nose on a napkin.
"I'm sorry. It's just that everything comes easy for you. Everyone likes you, you have a purpose here that is important and
even Matthew respects you."

I look around to pinpoint the person to whom she is
referring.

"I know I shouldn't be angry with you about seeing Matthew with Larissa, but sometimes I wish I hadn't found out."

I frown at that. Hadn't found out her husband crept toward adultery? But in a sad, June Cleaver type of way, I can
understand. Life is easier when it fits into the box. And Rebecca is all about keeping all her corners tucked in, about
living life according to the recipe.

I pour in the chocolate chips, stir them in and set the bowl
between us. "Dig in."

"What?" She asks and her eyes widen in horror when I
lick the wooden spoon. "You could get worms, you know."

I guess now I really can relate to the need to not know
about a few things. "It's really good, I promise." I reach over
and take out another wooden spoon from the crock pot on
the counter, the one with "The Winneman's" painted on the
front. "Dig in."

She scoops out a tablespoon, and tastes it. "Not bad."

"Don't tell me this is the first time you've ever tasted
cookie dough?"

She shrugs, goes in for seconds.

"Not even as a child?" How can this be? I honed my Lara
Croft "sneak and grab" while watching my mother make

chocolate-chip cookies. "Maybe you need to learn to live outside the box. It's okay to break the rules once in a while."

She licks her finger. "Not if you're a missionary."

Oh, yeah? What about Caleb? I smile as he cascades into my mind. He's got the essentials down, and still manages to live life outside the lines. "Even if you're a missionary." I set down my spoon. "I have to confess something. I come on a peace mission. Matthew wants to throw himself at your feet and repent. He didn't kiss another woman, but he knows he betrayed you in his heart and is sick about it."

I can't believe I actually went through with my plot, and I feel like I somehow betrayed all of womankind. I mean, isn't this just what Milton did to me? Don't I have, by way of victimization, a mandate to protect womankind from near-adulterers like Matthew? Unfortunately, before I can qualify my words by saying something like "it would be understandable if you just kicked him in the teeth…" Rebecca actually lights up, and I see the barest hint of a smile.

"Really?"

"Yeah. He says he wants to go to counseling, if you're game." Oddly, my stomach doesn't writhe as I say this, a sign that maybe this is really a good deed, one that is God-sanctioned.

She takes another bite of cookie dough. "This is really good, isn't it?"

"It's my sister's recipe. Nutmeg and honey. A little bit of spice to the basics."

"Perfect."

Did you know that World War Two was this morning, right here in Moscow? I know because I saw the tanks, the

Katusha rocket launchers, the parades, the soldiers and felt the testosterone in the air.

By the way, Russia won, and saved the world from Nazi fascists. As I stood on my tiptoes, trying to peak over the wool *shopka* of a stout babushka (hello, can anyone say May? As in lilacs scenting the air, short sleeve shirts, the occasional bared—and hairy! Yikes!—leg?), I wanted to raise my hand and say, "Um, correct me if I'm wrong, but weren't America, and oh, a few other countries (read: Allied Forces) involved in that whole *World War* thing? I decided against my own personal march, however, when I saw a group of teenage patriots hanging in effigy an ugly rendition of our current president. Guess they didn't like the toys in their Happy Meals.

Still, all the singing, marching, saluting and gunpowder swelled my own arsenal of patriotic emotions. I strolled by the embassy, twice, just for a glimpse of the Marine guarding the door.

Love those guys. (And, of course the uniform!)

I'm sitting in the Venetsia, trying to still the thundering in my ears, watching foot traffic and trying to decide if it's too soon to pull out my summer sandals (and thus, schedule the mandatory pedicure). My feet are propped on another chair, and I'm sipping my café *smolokom,* when I see him pull up, on a motorcycle, no less. He's looking sun-buffed and a little bit chagrined. I'm going to cut him slack because although he hasn't written for nearly six weeks, and left without a word, he's looking oh, so very desperate, with his hair askew and his blue eyes searching for me.

Chase.

I don't signal for him. It's good to let him look for me. Chase-Me. I can't deny the nickname feels like warm honey in my chest. He's wearing his Gull Lake sweatshirt, cut off at the sleeves, and as he strides up the sidewalk my heart does a tumble.

He arrows right for me. I smile up at him. "Hi."

"*Zdrastvootya.*"

Huh? I blink and my daydream clears and there's Vovka. He's looking Russian in a black mesh shirt, a pair of black driving gloves and black leather pants. Man-in-black.

"I thought I'd find you here." He sits down, and his cologne washes over me, something spicy, exotic.

And with that whiff, my heart cracks open and I see *The Truth. I don't want exotic.*

What? Since when? But that thought feels right, even peaceful, like some sort of long-quested Holy Grail. *I don't want exotic.*

Yes, I like cafés and bistros, but in the deepest corners of my heart I long for a breakfast blend at Java Cup, for the sound of the lake lapping the shore under a golden moon. For the feel of a cool breeze in my hair as I prop my chin on Chase's shoulder, the smell of cotton and the feel of his whiskers against my cheek.

Chase is chocolate-chip cookies with nutmeg and honey. A little bit of spice to the basics. Vovka is just spice. He belongs with Zhozey, but I'm not her, not really. In the crevasses of my heart, I'm G.I. Chase's girl. And while I know I can't have Chase, I can't be with Vovka, either.

I probably should tell him that rather than just trying to dodge him for the rest of my time in Russia.

And, as long as I'm being forthright, I should admit it has nothing to do with him having Trout Lips. With training, he might be able to suck in all that slobber. It has to do with the fact that all my life, I've been looking for adventure, not realizing that it was *right there,* living next door.

Oh, no, I *am* a saboteur! I am remembering back to the beach when I told Chase that I'd come home for him if I didn't find anyone else…not realizing that I wasn't even going to go looking. Chase knows me better than anyone. He rescued and enjoyed the scandalous Josey, is proud of the new, reformed Josey. His words at the wedding drift back to me and right now they sound like prophecy from heaven, "You didn't want him anyway." Oh boy, the thought of being with Milton makes me turn slightly green. No, I didn't want Milton. And I'm suddenly thanking God for all that heart-break and angst. Just think, right now I could be cleaning Berglund cabins.

Oh, thank You, thank You, God!

Chase even liked my new hair.

And I let him go.

I want to bang my head on the table, but it would probably topple over.

Sadly, I've probably known I loved Chase since I was five years old and hiked over to his place to build my castles in his sandbox. Definitely since I took that head-over-heels crash on Bloomquist Mountain and opened my eyes to see him shadowing the sun. And it has *nothing* to do with his being unavailable…expect to jolt me to my senses, perhaps.

What am I doing in Russia?

Please let this be part of God working out His Great Plan, because He loves me. Because how would I have known I didn't want exotic, if I hadn't had a taste?

"Vovka, I'm sorry, but it's not working for me."

He frowns, and I'm thinking we might have some sort of

cultural gap here. How do I break up with someone in Russian?

Nichevo?

Sadly, I see that he is getting it. His face darkens, then twitches. Oh, no, I've really hurt him. "I'm sorry," I repeat.

"Why?"

I shake my head and tell him the truth. "You're just too incredible for me."

Dear Chase,
I know that I haven't written in a while but—

Dear Chase,
How are you? I know that we haven't talk—

Dear Chase,
You left so quickly I didn't have a chance to tell you—

Chase,
Why haven't you written, you big jerk!

Chase-Me,
Your job isn't done yet. I'm not releasing you.

Dear Chase,
I know you said you wanted to move to Irian Jaya, but I hear they eat people over there and I'm thinking that's a waste of good—

Dear Chase,
Please forgive me for being so stupid. I should have never let you go.

One of the reasons I like H is that she's always online when I need her.

<Wildflower> You broke up with Romance Man?

<GI> Yes. Because I've figured it out. I love Chase.

<Wildflower> Well, duh.

<GI> No, really. I love him. I finally figured it out. And it has nothing to do with Buffy. Or Holiday Girl or even him being my second cousin.

<Wildflower> He's your cousin?

<GI> No! Not really. Just forget it. But have you seen him around? What's the latest?

It hasn't been easy to break up with Vovka, but in the three days since our chat, I've only spotted him once outside my building. And Auntie Milla has stopped dropping off gifts. Which bums me out in a way because those liver *peroshke* have a great aftertaste.

<GI> H?

<Wildflower> Yeah, okay. I saw him.

<GI> And?

I e-mailed him a letter four days ago, although he hasn't written back. (I'm hoping that he hasn't moved to Joppa already or anything.) I didn't go into too much detail, mostly apologized for the fiasco with Vovka and told Chase I hope we can restart things when I get home. I think that's enough commitment for now, when I can't read his face, but still, it's something for him to hold on to, right? (More than he gave me, don't you think? Oh, don't answer that!) In the meantime, I'm flexing my auntie muscles and have babysat twice for the Winnemans. Matthew is still camping on the sofa at the college, but he's smiling more. And Tracey has a new boyfriend, someone she met online. I figure that's fairly safe, for her. No overnight guests that way. And maybe he'll turn out to be a keeper.

<Wildflower> Well, and I feel just a little sick telling you this, but I saw him at the Java Cup last night.

<GI> What? Just tell me.

<Wildflower> He told me that he met someone. And that he's going to ask her to marry him.

What? It's only been six weeks since he was here? Is he crazy? Or rather, am I that easy to forget?

<GI> Oh.

Is this fair, Lord? C'mon, please. Because You know, I'm feeling drop kicked.
I go into the next room, pull my blanket over my head and rue my life.

Tracey is online as I walk into the flat after class. I'm starving and picked up a bag of new potatoes and fresh dill on my way home. Yes, I'm going to attempt to cook. No comments necessary.

"Hi!" she says, not looking up from her/my laptop.

"Chatting with your new online pal?" I dump the potatoes into the sink. Russia is on the cutting edge of the farmer's market craze—they don't even wash the veggies when they pull them out of the ground.

"Yeah. He's so sweet. He says he can't wait for me to come home this summer."

"You're going to the States?" I scrub down the potatoes and dump them into a pot.

"Yeah. I already planned a vacation, but this will be fun. I ordered my ticket today."

"Where does he live?"

"Uh…the Midwest."

I glance at her. "Wow, small world. Gull Lake is in Minnesota."

She gives me a quick glance. "Oh." I put the potatoes on, light the stove (all by myself, thanks!).

"He says that he thinks of me in Moscow, and wishes he were here."

I come out, sit on the sofa and put my feet up. This is the same place Chase sat when he was here, and that memory hits me square in the soft tissue of my heart. The fact he still hasn't written to comment on my declarations and contradict the news H gave me is slowly shredding my insides. But I am not going to let it deter me from giving my last six weeks my best go.

"He sounds like he's really taken with you," I say with a forced cheer.

"Yeah. We really clicked." She's smiling as she disconnects and closes her computer. I feel something warm inside at the look of happiness on her face. While she isn't my first pick at friends, she deserves to find a nice guy, someone who will love her, treat her like Sheena, Queen of the Jungle.

My potatoes have come to a boil; I hear the water bubbling against the cover.

"What are you making?"

"Auntie Milla's potatoes."

Tracey stretches her legs out, and leans back into the sofa, closes her eyes, joy on her catlike face.

The telephone rings and since she's making no move, I jump up for it. I'm hoping it's Caleb—I haven't seen him for weeks, even in church, and have a sneaking suspicion he's been sent out east again.

"Hello?"

"I couldn't catch you," says a voice, and although it is coming from under the ocean and through a few billion fiber-optic cables, it still has to the power to yank my heart out through my ribs.

"Chase?"

"I'm sorry, G.I. I didn't know how to tell you, and then you disappeared."

I'm frowning because according to my recollection, he's the one who disappeared. "What are you talking about?"

"I just wanted to tell you how sorry I am."

I swallow, disbelieving this moment. I hear the angst in his voice, and tears rush to the surface. He's sorry! For not writing? Or not declaring his love, not sweeping me in his arms on the Metro or the billion other opportunities he's had? Oh, it doesn't matter! He's sorry! "Me, too."

"I know. It's just horrible and I wish you could be here now."

Slightly overreacting, but isn't that sweet? It's *horrible* to be without me! "I'll be home in about a month. We can talk about it then." In my mind I see him standing in his kitchen, barefoot, wearing that cutoff Gull Lake sweatshirt, golden-tanned, hair damp and curly, smelling like soap. Oh yeah, we'll talk about it then.

"Okay. But I think Jasmine needs you to call her. She's really grieving."

What? My stomach falls first. Then I reach out for something, miss and crumple to the floor. "What are you talking about?" My voice pitches just a little high and I can hear my own panic.

I hear him pause, then in a voice that sounds as confused as mine, "G.I., don't you think you'd be grieving if you lost your first baby?"

Chapter Seventeen: Dear Josey

Me: I'm going home. My sister had a miscarriage and lost her baby.
Matthew: I'm sorry to hear that, Josey. Is she married?
Me: Of course she's married! (Jerk!)
Matthew: Well, then her husband is there to comfort her, right?

Really, I *am* Lara Croft and Matthew is about to get hurt. My other alter-ego, Mother Teresa, bought it about six months ago under the red line Metro.

Me: She needs me. I'm her only sister.
Matthew: Your students need you. You made a commitment to them and you can't leave them now. Besides, Rebecca and I are flying to France for some counseling and I need you until the end of the year.
Me: (Who vows to make sure all my students can say

Weasel—Veezel!—by the next lesson) I'm leaving and you can't stop me. Sorry, Bub.

Matthew: That will be twenty-seven thousand dollars, please.

Me: What?

Matthew: The amount MBC paid for your time here.

Me: You're a jerk, did you know that?

Matthew: (Shrugging.) I'm just trying to get you to see reason. Your sister needs you, but we need you more. You'll be home in a month. She'll still be grieving.

Me: (Lord, I'm going to need a little more of that resurrection power, please! Or maybe, Matthew will...) This isn't fair.

Matthew: We leave Tuesday.

Note to self: Next time two-timing veezel comes groveling, kick him in the nostrils.

Two things about my conversation with Chase on the telephone, however short, have drilled into my brain and kept me awake.

1. He acted as if we'd just talked. As if he hadn't left me in a cloud of pain and confusion nearly two months ago.

2. He told me I'd done the disappearing. (Okay, three things!)

3. He assumed I already knew about Jasmine.

These thoughts nag me as I walk home from class nearly a week later. Yes, I see you Vovka, about a half block away, a tall and painfully gorgeous shadow. But to turn around would only encourage him and while I appreciate the protective hovering, I also know that like a puppy, it would only take the slightest encouragement and he'd be rolling over on his back, begging me to rub his tummy.

Ew.

I'm not sure why Vovka is so smitten, except that maybe he sees me like I saw him...a taste of something exotic. He needs his own chocolate-chip cookie, or rather, strawberry-filled *peroshke*.

I haven't managed to catch Chase online since the "call." Although I have him listed in my IM, he's never lit up and I haven't screwed up the courage to e-mail him. I'm secretly hoping that he'll call me again.

I could use a refreshing dose of his sweet voice to balm my broken heart.

Poor Jas.

She does have Milton, and I know this. In fact, she told me that I could stay, but the ache of knowing she's going through all this without me has chewed me raw. Or maybe it's just the fact that everything I want is in Gull Lake, a reality that still has the power to broadside me when I'm not looking.

Imagine, longing for Gull Lake.

I am walking down Leningradskaya street, and the smell of jasmine sweetens the air. I stop at an ice-cream vendor and buy a drumstick. Russians are funny—during the winter, ice-cream is a booming business. But in the summer, suspicion dwindles the supply to a meager few. Evidently, the sudden rush of cream and ice in the heat causes instant death. Or at least a head cold.

I'm living recklessly.

Tracey is gone when I arrive home. My/our laptop is on the coffee table. I finish my cone, then change into my jammies and a T-shirt. This far north, the sun stays aloft until 9:00 p.m., and it gives me surreal energy, like a chocolate carbo bar, or an entire bag of semisweet chips.

I log on, and to my glee discover H online.

<GI> Hi. Something weird happened. Chase called. And acted as if we'd talked yesterday. Do you find this weird?

<Wildflower> I find everything that happens to you weird. Here's weirder. When I asked him a couple weeks ago if he'd talked you, he gave me a frown and said, "Of course."
<GI> (Feeling my stomach clench.) No, he hasn't talked to me.
<Wildflower> Then why is he smiling like he might have discovered the lost tribe of Israel?

I log off and sit there for a long time, debating my options.
1. Call Chase and ask him what's going on.
2. E-mail Chase and ask him what's going on.
3. Sleuth through Tracey's files and see if she knows anything about Chase's weirdness.

I change identities and am stopped by a password. Phooey! What is in here that Catwoman doesn't want me to see? Feeling guilt claw at me I enter a few ideas. Our address. Our telephone number. Her birthday.

Rick?

Nada. *Nichevo*. It was just a guess, for crying out loud!

I lean back, feeling like a thief. What am I thinking? Tracey is my friend, my compadre in pain. She wouldn't...

I'm remembering, suddenly the predatory look she gave Chase when she prowled her way into our relationship.

I click open the start menu, open up Explore and after a second of computer savvy, I'm fishing around in Tracey's directory.

My heart stops at a file called, IMs.

Hmm.

I click. They're labeled by date. The first of which is a week after Chase left. The night Tracey's computer was stolen.

Hmm.

I open it. And something inside me lets out a wail.

<NomadC> Hi. This is me. I'm having problems with my system, so I'm switching user names. How are you?

<GI> I'm good. How are you? (So far, she sounds like me, if not a little cryptic.)

<NomadC> Getting over my jet lag. I'm sorry I left so fast. Did Caleb give you my note?

Caleb? What?

<GI> No. (So, so far, truthful, in a shady sort of way.)

<NomadC> Good. I told him that I would let you know if I wanted you to read it. I wrote it in a hurry, but I think, well, it's accurate. I'm sorry, by the way, I left without saying goodbye. Your boyfriend took me off-guard.

<GI> We're not dating anymore. (Yeah! He knows! Except, well, this isn't really me, is it? Great.)

<NomadC> You're not? Why?

<GI> He was just a fling. (Okay, I would never say this. I don't

fling, and certainly not with Vovka. See through this, please, Chase!)

<NomadC> Really? Because he looked like he wasn't giving you up easily. Not that I would blame him.

Oh, my heart be still!

<GI> Really, it's over. I'm a free agent. (Again, not something I would say!)

<NomadC> Well then, maybe don't read my mail from Caleb. Because, I miss you.

I sit there, watching the cursor blink, feeling nauseous. How could she do this? Did she do it from my identity? She must have, then deleted his name from my user list.

I'm going to kill her. Take her furs and wrap them around her skinny neck and dangle her from the balcony.

I open the next file. More correspondence, more lies. More Chase saying how he misses me. Chitchat about his day. Fairly innocuous stuff, if you've known someone for a lifetime and are just enjoying friendship. If you're not spearing your roomie who's shared her popcorn with you through the heart.

I hear her key, then the door opens. I exit quickly and close the computer. But my heartbeat is in my ears, cutting off all thought. Tracey walks in, smiling, and all I can think is, two steps and a lunge and she's on her back while I pummel her.

Missionary Kills Roommate Over False IM Identity.

Maybe that's not the etching I want to make on the landscape of Russia. I swallow, rise, grab my computer and go to my room, manufacturing a smile that, with the right outfit, would confuse me with a Siberian Tiger.

"She used your identity?"

I am so thankful to hear the disbelief in Caleb's voice. It's been nearly a week since discovering Tracey's double-cross, and while I haven't yet dangled her from the balcony, I have spent a lot of time asking forgiveness for the litany of names that rise from the depths of my mind like flotsam.

"I can't believe it. And, when I fished through the deleted files, I found two letters from Chase and one from Milton, telling me about Jasmine. Not only that, she deleted my outgoing letter to Chase, the one where I told him…that I, umm…well, I am going to kill her."

Caleb and I are sitting in McDonald's, the scene of our first non-date, and like the true friend he is, he's treated me to a shake and fries. He's looking Hawaiian today in a floral shirt, cargo shorts and Birks. And I was right about the business trip.

"Don't kill her, Jose." He reaches out and touches my arm. He still has kind eyes, and he uses them now with humbling effect.

"I am kidding, Caleb."

"I know, but your heart isn't. You want to hate her. And that's normal. But the fact is, you have a chance here to be someone more than what you want to be."

I narrow my eyes at him. "What?"

"Ephesians 2:4. 'But, because of His great love for us, God, Who is rich in mercy, made us alive with Christ even when we were dead in transgressions—it is by grace you've been saved.'"

I deliberately suck my shake loudly, hoping he sees I'm not buying. I pull out my straw and run my tongue along the end. "Nope."

"Josey, c'mon. All year you've been praying for Tracey. This is your chance to show her a taste of that mercy and grace God gave you. It could be the very reason why God sent you here this year."

And here I thought it was because we shared a similar heartbreak, not because she was going to pull a Jasmine in my life.

I stare at him, however, and with a *cha-ching* in my heart, I understand.

To the Praise of His Glory. That's what it means. To do the hard thing not because I can, but because God can. Because He is trustworthy to work it all out, and because He loves me. And by forgiving Tracey in the face of betrayal reveals the very essence of Christ.

Wow. Not sure I'm up for that task. Again, maybe that's the point.

Still, I cringe, shove the straw into the cup and bury my face in my hands. "No. I'm not forgiving her. N. O. T."

I feel Caleb's hand on my arm. Again, no tingles, but it's warm and strong and in it I feel his very displaced hope. "Jose, what have you learned this year?"

I swallow, breathe deep. "I don't know, Caleb. Maybe that I'm an utter failure at this missionary stuff?"

Caleb laughs and it brings my gaze to his. His eyes are sweet, full of humor. Excuse me, what part of my roomie homing in on my non-boyfriend is funny?

"For one, if I know Chase, you have nothing to fear. And two, I don't know a perfect missionary, Jose. The fact that you're not is a good thing. If we had it all together, then we wouldn't need God, would we?"

I frown at him, because, as usual, he's so much deeper than I ever hope to be.

"'For it is by grace that you have been saved, through faith—and this not from yourselves, it is the gift of God—not by works so that no one can boast.' It means that we'll never get it right, but that God saves us anyway. He knows you can't forgive Tracey on your own. But He'll give you the power you need."

The power I need. The power to pack up my life in two suitcases and move to Moscow, the power to surf the subway, eat liver *peroshke,* wear leather, hug a muddy Tracey, and grit my teeth and speak the truth to Rebecca.

The power to trust the process, even when it seems like I'm at a standstill. Or headed south.

I take Caleb's hand. "Okay, fine. I'll forgive her, if you pray for me."

"Done." He grins and it feeds the wounded places in my chest. "And, by the way, here is the letter Chase left you."

Dear Josey,
I miss you. I should have said that when I was standing there looking at you and your Russian boyfriend, but I was so shocked, well, words couldn't form in my brain fast enough. I felt like I'd been skewered.

And then I realized it was my fault.

Because, up until this point, I felt like you needed to wake up and realize that you loved me. But maybe that's the problem. You never will, because you don't.

I was just kidding, sorta, about going to Irian Jaya. Because I wanted to see your reaction. I wanted to see if you'd be heartbroken, if you truly loved me, or not.

Now I know the truth. You were right when you told me before I went away to UND that we'd only be friends. And, I tried to accept that. Even dated other girls, including Elizabeth. But the thing is, although that might be true for you, it will never be enough for me.

Because I love you. You're in my every thought, in my breath, in my heartbeat. I think about you all the time, and have since I asked you to marry me while we were making our tree fort.

I put too much stock in your "of course" answer. It's taken me years to realize that you don't even remember that.

I came to Russia to see if you missed me half as much as I missed you. And, I got my answer. As painful as it was to see you with your friend, I don't want to stand in your way. I want you to be that girl God wants you to be even if it is a million miles from me.

I am still so very proud of you. And, even if you can't see it, I see God working in your life. I know that following Him, you'll be okay. And so, I resign as your protector, your Chase-Me. (You didn't think I knew about that, did you?)

But I will always love you.

Chase

I hear nothing but the scribbling of pencils and I feel like my English professor on the last day of class, peering out upon her subjects. Evgeny glances up now and again, gives me a smile. All those extra hours in private tutoring have cemented his place in my heart, and if he doesn't pass this exam, it's going to cut a chunk out of me. Vera and Lera are sitting across the room from each other—my move. Not that I think they'd cheat...okay, yes, it crossed my mind. Because although I believe Lera a billion times more than Matthew, the fact is that she probably did have some part to play in the Matthew fiasco. Matthew and Rebecca and family are in France, and I received an e-mail yesterday filled with smiley face icons from Rebecca. I think that's a good sign.

I'm not sure yet how I feel about that.

The evening air carries with it the essence of summer. Freshly cut grass, the chirp of sparrows, the sun still high and pushing into the room. After the test, we're all going out to the American Grill, where Matthew is going to treat us to Oreo malts. (Okay, no, he doesn't know it yet, but that's what happens when you leave me with the petty ruble envelope!)

I fold my hands on the desk, still mulling over my conversation with Caleb, and the ensuing one with Tracey.

Alas, it wasn't pretty, despite my prayers.

Tracey: Are you accusing me of stealing your boyfriend? Excuse me, but I didn't think you and Chase were an item.
Me: Then why did you say you, alias me, had broken up with Vovka?
Tracey: Because you didn't see what you had, and I knew, in time, he'd come to love me. In fact, he already does, he just doesn't know it.
Me: (Trying not to choke) Tracey, listen, it doesn't matter why you did it. Or that Chase thought he was talking to me. There are only two important things here. 1. You can't write to Chase on my computer anymore. (Which then leaves her free to write to him on her new one, right? Gulp.) 2. I forgive you.
Tracey: (Frowning. Swallowing. Turning red.) Whatever.

See, all that angst, the bruises on my knees, for naught! I hate it when I'm right.

Only, I'm not right. Because forgiving her has not only stretched me, it's made me realize that maybe God is doing something good in me. It makes me feel at peace. Whole. Happy.

Sadly, now I don't know what to do about Chase. I look down at that desk and again, I'm doodling his name. That's about as far as I get. Because, what, exactly, do I say to him?

Hi, Chase, Just a note to let you know you were hornswaggled, and the woman you were talking to was my roomie, but that's okay, because I really love you....

Yeah, and then he deletes my e-mail and packs for Indonesia.

Probably I'm overreacting, but still, I'm wondering if this conversation might be better eyeball-to-eyeball. Or lip to lip. Yes, I have been thinking about that scenario more than that is healthy.

Only, what if he really is in love with Tracey? Her humor, her wit, her words?

Yeah, but I have home-court advantage.

Still, the fear haunts me, and has paralyzed all action.

I will always love you.

I feel a smile creep up my face as I hear Sergei rise and thump to the front of the room. He hands in his paper with a grin. *"Maladyets,"* I say to him in congratulations.

He gives me a "hang loose." Thanks again, Chase, for that sign language lesson.

I "peace" him back, and watch him clomp out of the room. He works on a construction crew by day, and I'll miss the smell of sawdust as well as his smile.

In fact, I'll miss them all. Evgeny's melted-chocolate eyes, Lera and Vera's giggles, Sergei's I-ron. I'll miss the way they look at me like I might have answers, even wisdom. I'll miss their chuckles when I try and use my own pitiful, Tonto Russian.

In fact, I think that, without knowing it, I've given them a rather large chunk of my heart. The thought sweeps my breath away and my eyes burn.

Lord, I pray that You would give them a spirit of wisdom and revelation so that they might know You better. Know their salvation, the richness of being Your children and the resurrection power that You give.

Yeah, that feels right.

Evgeny rises, brings his exam to the front. *"Spaceeba,"* I say.

"You're welcome," he answers with a grin. I could easily enjoy his smile for the next decade.

There is one consolation in my leaving—every member of my class is saved. They're all headed to Bible college, or ministry.

But, you know, I'll be leaving Tracey and Vovka and even Auntie Milla for eternity.

I put a hand to my chest, push against the sudden rush of pain. I can't help but feel that if I were taking the exam, it wouldn't take long for God to grade.

One by one, they finish and an hour later I'm locking Matthew's office. Evgeny is waiting for me, as are a handful of other students. "Let's party," says Evgeny. Another Chase phrase.

I can't escape him.

It's nearly midnight and about a thousand calories later when Evgeny walks me home. I leave him at the lift (which I ride up, just for a change of pace) and my heart stops dead in my throat when I see a figure hunched over at my door.

Chase?

No, Vovka.

I try not to cringe as I draw closer, but really, didn't we talk about this? Except, he's wearing a crumpled expression, one that streaks ice through my veins. He stands and for a second I think he's going to cry.

"Vovka, what's the matter?"

He does cry. And you know how that makes me feel. I can already feel my inside start to cook.

"It's my babushka. She's had a stroke."

What? No! I brace my hand against the wall, feeling the corridor sway. "Is she okay?"

He nods. "But she wants to see you before you leave."

I know it is probably a bad idea, but I reach out and give him a hug. He wraps those gorgeous, muscular arms around me and holds tight. I can hear his heartbeat against his mesh shirt, feel him tremble. But there are no tingles, and any lingering doubts I had about dumping him are scuttled.

"How about we visit her in the morning?" I still have a couple days until my flight leaves, and about a billion people to shop for, but I can certainly sacrifice a morning for the woman who taught me how to use my stove, among other things.

"Thank you, Zhozey."

Not sure why he's thanking me, especially since my breaking up with him is probably the thing that drove her over the edge.

Ouch. *Missionary Causes Death of Neighbor.*

Not quite what I meant when I said I wanted to add a soul to the eternal attendance ledger.

Chapter Eighteen:
The Gold Ring

I am up early, due to the summer sun and the noises in the kitchen. Even for Tracey this is early....

She's packed. And hauling her bags out the door with the help of a taxi driver. While I feel like an idiot standing in my Taz T-shirt, I'm even more stunned at the cold look she gives me.

"Where are you going?"

She smiles, and yes, I feel a shiver. She's wearing a pair of black-and-orange stretch pants and a nearly mesh black top. "Gull Lake, Minnesota."

I want to lunge for her throat, but I'm paralyzed. Frozen. My mouth opens, but no words emerge. What?

"I told you. Chase loves me, not you, and I just have to tell him who he's been writing to and he'll get it. Besides, when I add in the fact that you're still dating Vovka, what can he say?"

I blink, racing to keep up. "You're going to Gull Lake?"

She laughs, hands her bag out to the driver.

"But I'm not dating Vovka."

"That's not what it looked like last night in the hallway."

Huh? Oh, no, the hug!

"Tracey, you can't do this—"

She rounds on me and I freeze, because she is taller, and wears all those animal skins. Still, if she thinks she's stealing Chase...

"I'm sick of you having all the right answers, and your happy attitude all the time. You didn't even get angry when you saw I stole your computer ID—you don't deserve Chase. You dumped him and he's free game. He loves me now."

If she wants to see me angry... "Oh, please. He doesn't even know you."

"He will. He'll see that I'm the one who can make him happy." She has tears in her eyes, and I'm not sure if that is an edge of desperation in her voice, or challenge. "Besides... you don't need Chase like I do."

She turns and before I can protest, slams the door behind her.

Need Chase? I've always needed Chase. But more importantly, she's going to Gull Lake? I should have tossed her over the balcony when I had the chance.

I'm still standing there, feeling like someone scraped me over a glacier when I hear another knock. Excuse me, it's only 6:00 a.m.

It's Vovka. "You should change."

Really? Because I thought I'd run out in my jammies. "I'll be out in a bit."

"I'll be next door."

Right. I shut the door, lean against it. I've sent my neighbor to the hospital and my roommate is going to sabotage the last chance I have with the man I love. Not that I have great fears that Tracey will snag him, but certainly the Vovka thing is the last thing Chase needs to hear.

I get out my laptop, turn it on, log on. Chase's ID is blank. That's right, he changed it! I open explore only to discover that Tracey has deleted her entire identity. What did he call himself?

Oh, no! I disconnect, grab the telephone. In Moscow, I have to order an international call from the operator, but my Russian is so garbled, I can barely get out, "America" before I slam down the telephone. Foiled again.

Another knock at the door. Vovka. "Are you ready?"

Do I look like I'm ready?

I smile, shut the door.

Breathe, Josey, just breathe.

Have I learned nothing this year? God is here, even in the moments when panic and jealousy reaches up and grabs me around the throat. And He'll work this out, to the praise of his glory.

Right, *right?* I so want to believe it, as I fling open my closet and search for something clean.

But, what if? What if Jungle Jane does woo him with her...pheromones, or something, and he runs off to the Congo with her? Or, and more likely, he slams the door on Tracey, but also on Josey, because she is *still dating Vovka.* And then leaves for...wherever, with no forwarding address?

This is going to get ugly. I'm seeing that time I jumped KC Johnson outside The Howling Wolf and tore my Guess jeans. Worst-case scenario has me returning to Gull Lake, right behind Tracey, waving my hands and calling her a liar. What if he decides that he likes the psychological, almost anthropological mystery that is Tracey and dumps me like one of Auntie Milla's potatoes?

Calm down.

I climb into my size ten Gap jeans and pull on a T-shirt, a feeling of foreboding clamping my chest. Because, no matter how much God loves me, I can't see how He's going to work this out to His glory.

Another knock at the door.

Vovka! No, no, it can not be happening that God should call on me right in the middle of my crisis! Can't He wait until I'm having a deep moment, maybe after I've freshly memorized a verse or just etymologized a cool Greek work?

I take a deep breath, and force my priorities into submission. I have to see Auntie Milla, and the fact that she is lying in the hospital should sober me to focus on eternity.

Lord, I say as I shove my feet into my oh-so-dependable mules. *Please just…stop Tracey at customs or something…maybe give her a fine for all those skins?*

That's the best I can do at the moment. What did you expect, more surrender? Remember, I'm Lara Croft. I don't do surrender well.

Russian hospitals have the smell and texture of a quick death and lots of formaldehyde. I can't escape the experience without thinking…Chechnya. Patients lie in stretchers along hallways, or even stretched out on the cement floor. Roaches crawl the walls, a few cats prowl. I stifle a shudder as I follow Vovka up the stairs and to the third floor.

I hold in a gasp as we enter a room of fifteen beds filled with frail elderly gasping their last breaths. There are no oxygen machines, no IV lines, no EKG machines. Just death, hovering, waiting for its next victim.

Auntie Milla has aged about a thousand years and lies swallowed up in a skinny bed. A stained cotton blanket covers her and she stares at the ceiling.

My throat thickens as I crouch beside her. How can this be the same woman who sliced and diced a salmon and toasted her birthday with prune cognac?

I take her hand. Her skin is soft and paper thin. "Auntie Milla?"

She cuts her eyes my direction, but doesn't move. My eyes burn, glaze, and a tear escapes. "I'm sorry," I whisper.

Her lips move and Vovka leans down, his ear next to her mouth.

He sits on the bed, takes her hand. "She asks, why?"

Why? Why do our bodies give out? Why must she suffer? These questions are over my head and I just take her other hand. "I don't know."

"Why did you come here?"

I look up at him, and he too has questions in his pretty eyes. "Why, Zozhey?"

"Because, well…" Why? I scroll back to that moment after the wedding, H and I in the car. The gold ring. Eternal significance that makes this life worthwhile. A calling. "I came because God loves you and wants you to know it. He has a plan for us and that plan doesn't end with this life. And all He wants from us is our heart." I smile, run my hand over Auntie Milla's cheek. "I guess that's what I'm supposed to tell you."

Vovka smiles at me, and translates. Auntie Milla's lips move and Vovka leans over again.

"What did she say?"

He runs his fingers through her hair. "She said thank-you."

"Pazalusta," I say quietly.

★ ★ ★

The Cathedral of Saint Basil the Blessed in Moscow has a story. It's said that when it was finished, the Czar asked the two architects if they could ever create another building so beautiful. They deliberated their answer, and decided that they would please the Czar by answering no.

He had their eyes plucked out as a guarantee.

I think of this as I stand in Red Square and stare at the church. It is beautiful. Breathtaking. Glorious. Unequalled.

But its glory doesn't compare in the least to one heart surrendered. I am raw and empty leaving Auntie Milla at the hospital. I have explained to her the particulars of salvation—the depth of our sin, Christ's overwhelming sacrifice, God's abundant grace and the hope of eternity. And, while Vovka translated, she cried.

Maybe, Lord, maybe?

I had planned to shop at the Arbat today. Instead I find myself back where I started, Red Square, pondering nine months in Russia, losing Chase, finding him, and losing him again. Most of all, finding, finally, the Josey I am. A Josey that might end up in a poppy dress once in a while, and other times in leather. A Josey that might not make an etching on the map in Moscow, but one who is just discovering God in her life, one step at a time. I'm so keenly aware that I'm saved by grace, by God's love and not my own abilities and maybe it's this discovery that is most precious. This intimacy with the Almighty is the gold, er...*brass* ring. God in me, working out His perfect plan, one day at a time. A God who chooses to makes my life significant by revealing Himself in me. To the praise of His glory.

I'm painfully aware that I might lose Chase to Tracey's schemes. But frankly, Auntie Milla's salvation is worth it.

I scatter a grouping of pigeons and head toward the Venetsia. Tracey won't get to American until tomorrow, but frankly, now that I'm past the panic, I'm going to let God be in charge of that, too.

In fact, I wouldn't have it any other way.

Still, if when I get home on Friday I find Tracey eating *kringle* at Berglund Acres, well, she better run. Because while I'm not going to panic, I do have righteousness on my side. And this time, I'm not going to let my false expectations and fears keep me from telling Chase exactly how I feel. That my hero has been right here, chasing me all my life.

Besides, all this walking has dropped me down three sizes. And I am a lean, mean, fight-for-your-man machine. I can take Sheena.

The Venetsia is packed, and I wait for a table.

I sit and put my feet on a chair. The waiter brings me a lemon slushy with an umbrella. I lean back in the seat, and am pushing my straw through the ice when I see him pull up, on a motorcycle, no less. He's looking sun-buffed and a little bit chagrined. I'm going to cut him slack because although he did court the affections of another woman, he thought she was me, and that counts. And, he's looking oh, so very desperate, with his hair askew and his blue eyes searching for me.

I don't signal for him. It's good to let him look for me. Chase-Me. I can't deny the nickname feels like warm honey in my chest. He's wearing his Gull Lake sweatshirt, cut off at the sleeves, and as he strides up the sidewalk my heart does a tumble.

He's pushing through the crowd, and his eyes are on me. Blue, beautiful and full of concern. I sit up, enjoying my daydream. I do them so well, don't I? I can even smell him as he comes my direction, clean, soapy, with a touch of sweat because he's been in a hurry to get to me. His hair is touched by the sun. And he's wearing my favorite jeans and a pair of Nike running shoes.

He's so cute, isn't he?

"Hi," I say.

About now he'll dissolve, but it's been a nice fantasy, and my heart is pounding.

Only, he doesn't dissolve. In fact…

"Josey, I found you."

Uh, *yeah*. Because I'm in charge of this dream.

"Caleb told me where you were. I didn't think I'd remember how to get here."

Remember? Caleb? I sit up and frown. Chase?

The waiter arrives. "Something for your friend?" he asks in Russian.

He can see Chase?

"Da," I say. "A slushy."

The waiter nods, but my gaze is on Chase, a *flesh-and-blood* Chase who is sitting across from me, grinning. Oh, wow, his grin does me in. Really, I can't breathe.

"Chase," I say and it sounds like my voice has left me for Africa.

"Hi," he repeats and scoots his chair over to the table, takes my hand. "You're freaking me out, Josey. What's gotten into you? First you act like you don't want me, then you start e-mailing me every day—and what's with the bar scene? And all these embassy shindigs you're hanging out at? That's not you anymore…I thought you'd changed. As if you were trying to make me jealous…" He shakes his head as I try to keep up. "And the tickets to Tahiti? We've been planning for me to come over and get you for nearly a month and suddenly you send me tickets for a vacation in Tahiti? And then, when I IM you about them, you get all snippy and you tell me not to come to Russia?" He actually looks angry and I feel a little knot of panic in my chest. Tahiti? I wonder if he still has those tickets....

"I thought I knew you...but now..." He frowns and something in his look makes me want to cry. "I'm worried about you."

So he came to Russia?

"Wait, Chase, there is something I have to tell you." Wait, whoops. Do I? Now that I have him here?

For the praise of His Glory. If God is really going to be in charge of this moment, and *us,* then He'll have to start now.

"Tracey assumed my identity and pretended she was me."

He would have startled less if I'd clobbered him with a brick. He stares at me, goes pale... "You know, I wondered if...I mean, you were so...I'd never heard you talk that way before, but the things you said about us..." He swallows and I see the question in his eyes.

"But everything she wrote was true," I rush on. "I broke up with Vovka. And I...am a free agent." I want to wince. But it's true. Sorta. Wait, No! It's not true. I'm *not* free at all. I'm so in love with Chase it hurts, right through to the center of my chest. And this is what I have to say to him.

"Chase, do you remember when we were sitting on the beach before we went to college. And I said that if I got desperate I could come home and marry you?"

I know him well enough that he can't mask his hurt from me. Again, I freshly hate that moment, and my words. He nods.

"Well, what I should have said is, 'Please, can I come home and marry you?'"

He takes my hand, runs his thumb over it and I feel sparks

and firecrackers ripple up my arm. "Yeah, you should have said that."

I swallow, blow out a breath. *Okay, God…* "Can I come home and marry you?"

He is smiling now, that lopsided sweet Chase smile that turns me to honey. "I think I asked you first."

"Oh, yeah," I say softly, as he scoots his chair closer to mine. I let him see the emotion in my eyes. "Chase, I love you. I'm sorry that it's taken me twenty or so years to say it. But you're the only man I've ever loved. I need you in my life. You're my best friend, the only man for me."

"I know." He pushes my hair behind my ear, his beautiful eyes sweet and shining. Then he leans close and finally, *finally,* kisses me. It is so gentle, so achingly perfect that my heart stops. *Chase.* My eyes are closed long after he pulls away.

When I open them, he's still smiling at me. "Was it worth the wait?"

"I think I need another taste." I reach out and pull him close, kiss him with everything I've ever felt. His arms go around me and pulls me onto his lap. He's kissing me like I've always dreamed, always hoped, with tenderness, with hope and expectations. He tastes of coffee and toothpaste and twenty years of waiting. The answer is yes. And Yes!

"So, now do you believe me?" he asks as he pulls away. I feel him tremble, and he's breathing just a little harder than when he arrived. I'm vaguely aware that we're attracting attention, but who cares? *Missionary Finds True Love In Bistro.* Yeah, I like that headline.

"Believe you?" I ask running my hand down his handsome, whiskered face.

"That you didn't want Milton."

I laugh. "Oh, that. Yeah, Chase. You were right."

He cups his hand behind my neck and kisses me again. I'm pretty sure we're going to get clapping soon.

But he pulls away just as my blood pressure threatens to take the top of my head off. "Our return tickets are for tonight, G.I. It's time for you to come home." He smiles, sweet, sly and I could melt on the spot at the gleam in his beautiful eyes. "So, how are you at packing?"

An hour? He's here for an hour? To *get* me. My Chase-Me. "Everything I want is in Gull Lake," I say.

He laughs, runs his strong hands over my arms. He smells so delicious, so home, I just want to hold on tight, forever.

Slowly, his smile dims. "And what if God wants us to go somewhere else?"

I see in his eyes that he's serious. And I feel a tingle to my toes. "Anywhere, Chase. Anywhere. As long as God says Go, and gives the green light."

"Good," he says as he holds my gaze. Then he fishes in his shirt pocket and pulls out a box. A box holding…a little gold ring.

Oh, see? There you have it.

God wasn't joking after all.

★ ★ ★ ★ ★

Discussion Questions

1. Josey is confronted with her worst nightmare on the day of her sister's wedding. What is it, and why does it rattle her? How has a childhood friend played a significant role in your life?

2. God uses Josey's friend, H, to define her restlessness. What is it? What does H suggest as the cure?

3. Josey leaps on the idea of going to Russia—why? How does she think it will change her?

4. Josey is confronted with a question at training—a question about "calling." What is a calling? What callings have you had in your life?

5. What is Josey's mental description of a missionary? How does it match up to yours?

6. When Josey first arrives in Russia, she's confronted with a number of challenges. What are some of them? How would you have reacted in the same situation?

7. How does Caleb change Josey's idea of what a Christian should be like?

8. Josey isn't sure of her feelings for both Vovka and Chase. What different sides of Josey do they represent?

9. Tracey betrays Josey in a big way—how? Do you feel Josey handled the situation properly? How would you have handled a similar situation?

10. Josey realizes that God has been at work in her life, even when she couldn't see it. How? What realization, based on Ephesians 2:8-10, does Josey come to ? How do her interpretations apply to your own life?

Kringle Recipe, courtesy of John and Mary Hay

Crust:
¼ lb butter, softened
1 cup flour
2 tbsp cold water

Cut butter into flour, mix and add water until it makes a soft dough. Divide dough into two parts. Hand roll into two long strips, as long as a cookie sheet and about 4-5 inches wide. Put dough on ungreased cookie sheet. Pat it until it is flat.

Topping:
1 cup water
¼ lb butter
1 cup flour
3 eggs
½ tsp almond extract

Heat water, melt butter in water, remove from stove and add flour. Mix until moist. Add eggs one at a time, stirring the mixture until it is smooth. Add almond extract. Spread on crust while still warm. Bake at 350°F for 50 minutes. Spread frosting (below) on Kringle while still warm.

Frosting:
1 cup powdered sugar
1 tbsp milk
1 tbsp melted butter
½ tsp almond extract

Cream together. Spread on Kringle while still warm.

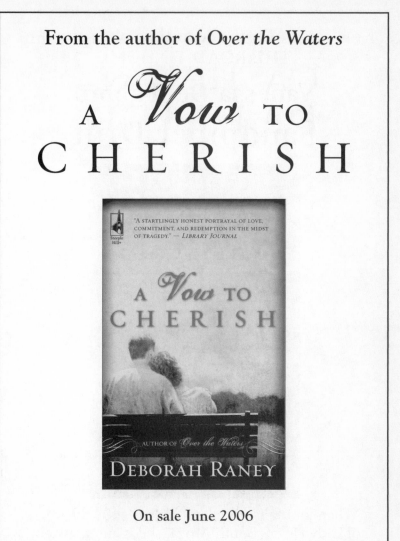

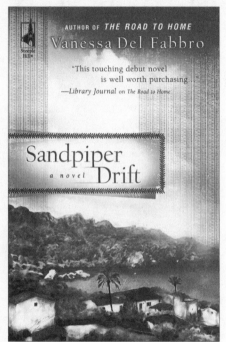